GRAND CENTRAL
PUBLISHING

LARGE
PRINT

"PATTERSON BOILS A SCENE DOWN TO A SINGLE, TELLING DETAIL, THE ELEMENT THAT DEFINES A CHARACTER OR MOVES A PLOT ALONG. IT'S WHAT FIRES OFF THE MOVIE PROJECTOR IN THE READER'S MIND."   —Michael Connelly

"JAMES PATTERSON IS THE BOSS. END OF."   —Ian Rankin, *New York Times* bestselling author of the Inspector Rebus series

"JAMES PATTERSON IS THE GOLD STANDARD BY WHICH ALL OTHERS ARE JUDGED."   —Steve Berry, #1 bestselling author of the Colton Malone series

"The prolific Patterson seems unstoppable."   —*USA Today*

"Patterson is in a class by himself."   —*Vanity Fair*

THE SHADOW

For a complete list of books,
visit JamesPatterson.com.

THE SHADOW

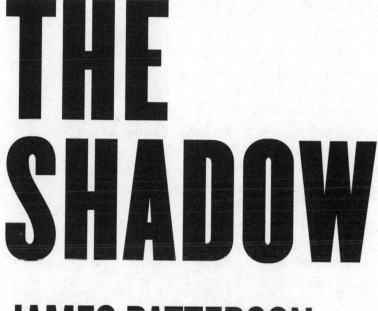

JAMES PATTERSON
AND BRIAN SITTS

GRAND CENTRAL
PUBLISHING

LARGE PRINT

Grand Central Publishing
Hachette Book Group
1290 Avenue of the Americas, New York, NY 10104
grandcentralpublishing.com
twitter.com/grandcentralpub

First Edition: July 2021

Grand Central Publishing is a division of Hachette Book Group, Inc. The Grand Central Publishing name and logo is a trademark of Hachette Book Group, Inc.

The publisher is not responsible for websites (or their content) that are not owned by the publisher.

The Hachette Speakers Bureau provides a wide range of authors for speaking events. To find out more, go to hachettespeakersbureau.com or call (866) 376-6591.

ISBN 978-1-5387-0395-3 / 978-1-5387-0631-2 (large print)
Library of Congress Control Number: 2021936026

Printed in the United States of America

LSC-C

Printing 1, 2021

NEW YORK CITY / 1937

ONE

IN THE BAR room of Jack & Charlie's 21 Club, toys dangled from the ceiling. Airplanes, ships, and trucks—whimsical gifts from rich and famous patrons. First-time visitors were usually distracted by the playful clutter overhead, but Lamont Cranston was a regular, and had been since the place opened. Besides, his focus tonight was totally on his dazzling companion.

The venue had been Margo's choice. She knew this place was Lamont's favorite, and tonight was a very special occasion. She had hinted on the car ride that she had something special to tell him. Usually that meant a lead on an intriguing new case, but with

Margo Lane, you never knew. She was full of surprises, both naughty and nice, which was one of the many, *many* reasons Lamont adored her. As his partner in the crime-fighting business, Margo was the only person in the world who knew all his secrets.

Except one.

Tonight, Lamont had planned a little surprise of his own. Out of all the women he had known—and there were many—no one else had impressed, challenged, and excited him like Margo. From the day he met her, he knew they were meant to be together, and the ring he was hiding in his pocket would seal it. Assuming she said yes.

As for Margo's little secret, Lamont was very curious. But clearly she was going to make him wait just a little bit longer.

"Remember this place during Prohibition?" she asked, looking around the room. Lamont stretched his tuxedoed arm to signal a waiter for refills. His first drink had given him a pleasant buzz, and he didn't want to lose it.

"I remember the liquor shelves would tip

back whenever Jack and Charlie got wind of a raid," he said.

"And then," said Margo, "all the pretty bottles would slide right down into the sewer." With her long, slender arms, she made a swooping gesture, goofy and elegant at the same time. "Such a *waste!*"

Margo was wearing a white Schiaparelli evening dress, with black velvet flares over her bare shoulders and a matching bow in front. In the room's amber glow, she could not have looked more beautiful. Lamont noticed that even the bartender, no stranger to stunning women, had angled himself for a better view. A waiter appeared with two fresh drinks on a silver tray. An old-fashioned for the gentleman. Champagne for the lady.

Lamont and Margo plucked their glasses off the tray before the waiter had a chance to place them on the table. As the young man started to turn back toward the bar, Lamont put a hand up to stop him in his tracks.

"Shall we order?" he asked Margo.

"Why not?" she said, running a manicured fingernail around the rim of her glass.

"But please, Lamont—nothing heavy." She passed her other hand lightly over her belly, with its barely perceptible bump, so slight Lamont hadn't yet noticed.

"Two lobster salads," said Lamont, without even glancing at the menu. It was September. A good month for lobster. He put his glass to his lips and sipped, feeling the sweetness of the sugar on his tongue and the warm burn of whiskey in the back of his throat.

"Well?" he said, leaning forward. "You had something you wanted to tell me?"

Margo just smiled, her thin eyebrows slightly arched.

"Is that the *Titanic*?" she asked, pointing toward a corner of the ceiling, where a model of a large steamship hung between two pairs of brass opera glasses.

"I think that would be in poor taste, considering," said Lamont, squinting into the collection overhead. "It's probably the *Queen Mary*."

"You're probably right," said Margo.

She looked like she was about to say something else. But before she could speak, two plates were already being set on the table. The service in this place was impeccable. On each plate, gobs of snowy-white lobster meat nestled in a tangle of chopped greens, topped with a lace of cream sauce and flecked with small croutons. Lamont and Margo each speared a morsel of lobster. They lifted their forks and tapped them together in a playful toast.

"To us," said Lamont.

"To *secrets*," whispered Margo, her eyes on his. She slid a chunk of lobster into her mouth as Lamont took his first small bite.

"You can't hold out forever, you know," he said, "I have my methods."

"Maybe I'm just holding out for dessert," said Margo. Her eyes widened. She dropped her fork. "Lamont!" Her voice was suddenly pinched and pained. At the same moment, Lamont felt a hot rush in his skull, like somebody had just set his frontal lobes on fire. His throat tightened in a sharp spasm and his hands flew up reflexively to his neck. Margo's head rolled back as a small stream of white foam oozed from between her rose-tinted lips. Her slender body went limp.

Lamont knew instantly what had happened. But his vocal cords were tightening. He could barely squeeze out the word.

"Poison!"

TWO

LAMONT LURCHED TO his feet with so much force that the small round table crashed to one side, dumping a clatter of glasses and plates onto the floor. Guests at other tables sat frozen in place. A busboy backed up against the wall, his metal tray trembling against his chest. Margo was already past standing, almost past breathing. White foam now cascaded in a bubbly froth across the bow on her dress.

Lamont spun his chair aside and reached for her. He slid one arm under Margo's knees, the other behind her shoulders. Her head was loose and hanging back, her eyes half shut.

As Lamont staggered toward the door with Margo in his arms, a few waiters jumped to push chairs and serving carts aside. Lamont couldn't think. He could hardly see! Through the small window in the front door, he could barely make out the vertical lines of the iron gate outside. Just a few more steps until they were outside.

Near the door, a maître d' loomed. Not moving to help. Just staring, arms folded across his chest. In a flash, for just a split second, Lamont saw the man's elegant evening suit replaced by a golden robe. Or did he? Was he delirious? Was this really happening? Margo! Margo was all that mattered. He barely noticed the foam spilling from his own mouth, running down the front of his tux, dripping onto the tips of the maître d's expensive shoes. As Lamont kicked the door open, he felt the maître d' lean toward him.

"Was everything to your liking, Mr. Cranston?" he asked with a cruel smile.

In that moment, Lamont knew the truth. Now he realized there was only one chance. One way to possibly save Margo and himself. And he knew it was the longest of long shots.

The sidewalk was a few steps up from the restaurant's sunken entrance. Lamont stumbled on the lowest step, hard enough to scrape a hole in his trousers. He adjusted his grip as he struggled to hold Margo up. Her high-heeled shoes hung from her small feet by thin, glittery straps. Then, through the fog and fever clouding his brain, Lamont heard a maniacal, deep-throated laugh.

He knew that laugh.

THREE

"MY CAR!" LAMONT shouted.

The young valet always kept Lamont's roadster close. For a crisp five-dollar bill, he would sit in the sleek black Mercedes-Benz SSK for the whole evening, keeping it warmed up and ready. When the valet heard Lamont call out, he put the powerful car in gear and pulled up to the entrance. Lamont freed one hand enough to wrench the passenger door open. As gently as he could, he slid Margo onto the soft leather seat. He pushed her long legs into the narrow passenger compartment and slammed the door.

The valet was trembling as he held the driver's-side door open. Just twenty minutes earlier, Lamont had tossed him the keys with his usual blind over-the-shoulder flip. And, as always, he had tried not to stare too long at Mrs. Cranston. And now there she was, crumpled and soiled, her beautiful makeup smeared on Lamont's jacket sleeve. The valet had seen plenty of passed-out drinkers being dragged from the 21 Club. This, he could tell immediately, was not that.

"Mr. Cranston," said the valet. "What can I . . . ?" But Lamont was already sliding behind the wheel. "Move!" he croaked.

The car was pointing east on Fifty-Second Street. Lamont jammed his foot down on the clutch, shifted into first gear, and pressed on the gas pedal. Lamont knew Manhattan as well as any cabbie, but the pain in his head and the haze in his eyes were already making driving a challenge. His destination was 6.2 miles south. He had measured and timed it from midtown twice, just in case. But he had always assumed that he would be riding in an ambulance, not driving himself under the influence of a potent neurotoxin.

He blasted through the Fifth Avenue inter-section, dodging well-dressed couples and a beefy beat cop. A yellow Ford cab swerved onto a sidewalk to avoid a T-bone collision with the speeding Mercedes.

Lamont took the turn south onto Second Avenue hard, mounting the curb momen-tarily and nearly crushing a pair of leashed poodles walking a couple of yards ahead of their master. Margo's head rolled left and right on the headrest and banged against the side window. But Lamont knew she couldn't feel it. She couldn't feel anything. He looked over and forced a few words through his constricted throat.

"Do not die!" he said hoarsely. "Do not die!"

Margo stirred slightly. Her lips moved and her eyelids flickered. Then she slumped back again, silent and still.

"Do not die!" Lamont ordered again. Had she even heard him?

He swerved to avoid a woman with a baby carriage and almost sideswiped a city bus heading in the opposite direction. Still, he kept the pedal down, his hand on the horn, blasting a warning to anyone within earshot. As he accelerated, the roar of the supercharged Mercedes engine made its own statement.

At Houston Street, Lamont careened into a screaming right turn, then headed south on Bowery and hooked onto St. James. As St. James turned into Pearl, a path of light stretched overhead, out to his left. The Brooklyn Bridge. Not far now!

Suddenly the darkness beneath the bridge was blasted into fiery brightness. A lightning bolt struck the pavement just in front of Lamont's car.

Pulverized roadway spidered his windshield as he swerved through curls of white smoke. One headlight was shattered, the other cracked. Lamont was half blind, and so was his car.

Seconds later, another bolt struck just behind, showering Lamont and Margo with pellets of asphalt. Lamont grimaced and gripped the wheel even tighter. Along with the echo of the blasts, a single name reverberated in his brain.

"Khan! Khan did this!"

Lamont sped down Water Street. To his

left, he could make out the shapes of docks and barges crowding the edge of the East River. Ahead, a row of darkened warehouses loomed as thick black profiles against the night sky.

Lamont pulled off Water Street into a narrow alley, where the surface turned into rough gravel. He eased the Mercedes between brick walls and battered loading platforms. At the last warehouse in the row, he stopped abruptly and killed the engine. He didn't bother to open his door. He just threw himself over it, then clung to the hot hood of the car as he moved around toward Margo's side. When he opened the passenger door, she toppled into his arms like a sack of bones.

He flung one of her limp arms over his shoulder and dragged her toward the warehouse's heavy metal door. Her elegant high heels scraped on the pavement. The first, then the second dropped off. Lamont was wheezing, his chest now burning as fiercely as his head. He wiped a fresh stream of foam from his mouth.

Supporting Margo with one arm, Lamont

pounded on the warehouse door. There was no special code. Or if there was, he had forgotten it. All he knew was that he needed to get inside. Right now! He pounded again, scraping his knuckles on the rough, rusted metal. He felt his knees buckling and struggled to keep Margo upright. As he raised his fist again, the door opened. A blast of hot light shot out into the night. It was almost too much for his eyes to take. A figure in a white coat stood in the doorway. Lamont gasped. He didn't have much breath left in him. Just enough for three short sentences.

NEW YORK CITY / 2087

CHAPTER 1

I HEAR THEY used to call it "lockdown." Back then it was mostly a drill, a just-in-case thing. At my high school, it's pretty much a permanent condition. Same for every school in the world at this point. Bars on every door and window. Armed guards in every hallway. Except now they're not so worried about shooters getting *in*. They just don't want the students to get *out*.

"Gomes, Maddy!"

It's my teacher, Ms. Baynes, the one with the really annoying voice. She's reading out the class roster like a prison roll call. One after the other, every kid stands up and delivers the correct response, which is "Present, ma'am!" Me, I just raise my hand and move it slightly from side to side, like an olden-times princess waving to a crowd. Baynes decides not to nail me for it, at least not this time. The roll ends with "Zale, Renny," who practically *shouts* her "Present, ma'am!" then adds, "Pleasure to be in your class, ma'am!"

"Suck-up."

It's Lisa Crane, sitting two seats away from me. She says it under her breath, but Renny hears it. In a split second, Renny jumps out of her chair and goes after Lisa. She wrestles her out of her seat and they both land hard on the tile floor.

"Learn your place, ferret!" shouts Renny. Her hair is hanging in Lisa's face.

Lisa can't shout back because Renny has her hand pressed hard over her mouth. All that's coming out of Lisa are grunts and squeals. Half the kids are out of their chairs now. The other half are pretending that nothing is happening. I'm in the first half. Baynes moves toward the fight, but not too close.

I've seen these two go at it before. Renny's dad works for the government, and it makes her crazy to be mixed in with the daughter of an irrigation worker.

Class warfare at its finest. Their last fight turned into a full-scale riot, and the whole class got work duty all morning.

That can't happen today. Not to me. I have plans.

I reach out and grab Renny's shirt and yank it hard. She's bigger than I am, but I catch her off-balance. When she falls backward, we're nose to nose.

"Enough, Renny!" I say. "Leave it!" In a few seconds, it's all over.

Renny gets to her feet, breathing hard, and slumps back into her chair.

Lisa is still on the floor, her face red and splotchy.

"Ass polisher!" she mutters to Renny's back. One last shot.

"Seats! Now!" shouts Baynes. She has her hand on her red pendant button, ready to call the guards. But I know she'd rather let things calm down on their own. Another disturbance report wouldn't look so good on her *record,* seeing as class control is her main job.

Everybody settles. Baynes shuffles her notes on the lectern and starts to drone away. But I'm not listening to her. I'm not looking at her.

I can't keep my eyes off the clock.

CHAPTER 2

THE NEXT TWENTY minutes feel like twenty hours.

Sometimes I wish was born in the age of smart boards and tablets.

I bet they made classes go faster. But that was before the Confiscation, ten years back. Now teachers are stuck with notes and lectures, like in the Dark Ages. I'm old enough to remember cell phones. I had one until I was eight. Then one day they just shut down the com grid and that was that. We were all supposed to turn in our devices and most people did. I still keep mine hidden at home, like a fossil.

I feel my foot tapping against the bolted

steel base of my desk and I try to control it. No use. The clock says 9:22. Almost time to bust out of here. I've got a meeting in midtown that I *cannot* miss. It's a once-in-a-lifetime thing, and I'm *really* pumped about it. I don't have all the facts yet, but it's a meeting that could completely change my life. And my life definitely needs changing.

The only challenge is getting out. Leaving class without an armed escort, even to go to the bathroom, is not in the picture. This is the routine: When you feel the need, you raise your hand and say "Permission for lavatory?" The teacher presses the blue button on her pendant and a guard shows up to walk you there and back. It can be really embarrassing on days when you have stomach issues, or your period. But I've got things scoped out, and I think I can make it work.

9:25. Time to move. I shoot my hand up like I'm launching a rocket. Baynes looks up from her notes. "Gomes?"

"Permission for lavatory?" I ask. I wince a little to look desperate. Otherwise she might make me hold out to the end of the lesson.

She can be a real hard-ass that way. But waiting for the class switch is not an option. I need the halls to be empty. Or nearly empty. That's the only way this is going to happen. Baynes presses the button and goes back to her lecture. I fidget in my seat. But not for long.

About ten seconds later, the door unlatches and the guard steps in, rifle across her chest. She's in tac gear, head to toe. Her eyes are hidden behind a one-way lens panel. Bullet-proof, no doubt. It's a bit extreme for keeping a bunch of schoolkids in line, but I guess they're not taking any chances.

She doesn't speak. They never do. Not to us, anyway. I get up from my seat and walk to the front of the room. She holds the door open as I pass through. She follows me down the hall toward the bathroom. More guards are pacing the corridor in teams of two or four. Like I said, they're everywhere.

I push open the bathroom door and head for stall number three. This part is not a total scam, because I actually do have to pee, and toilet three is the only one that actually flushes. When I'm done, I wash my hands and splash some water onto my face.

"Piece of cake," I mumble to my reflection in the mirror.

When I open the bathroom door, my personal armed escort is waiting outside. But instead of following her back toward the classroom, I walk the other way—toward a door that leads to a locked corridor. I see the guard tense up. She knows this is a restricted zone, and she knows I know it too.

"Open the door," I say softly.

The guard starts to move toward me. I see her finger twitching over the rifle safety. I look her straight in the helmet and say it again, a little louder.

"I said, open the door."

This time, she reaches for the keycard chained to her belt and swipes it over the lockpad. I yank the door open and look down the empty corridor.

"Stay right here," I say. And she does.

Don't ask me why it works. To tell you the truth, I'm still kind of surprised that I can control people this way, one on one. It's been part of me since I was a little kid. Maybe someday I'll figure it out. But I can't really think about it now. After the door closes behind me, I take a couple of short steps to make sure the guard isn't raising her rifle. She doesn't move. All good.

At the end of the corridor is a metal ladder leading to a hatch in the ceiling. I noticed it through the window on the door my very first day. And since it's in a hallway with no classrooms, it only gets patrolled once every five minutes. I counted.

The bottom of the ladder is about seven feet off the floor, which means I can just reach it when I stand on tiptoes. I stretch up and grab the bottom rung, then kick-swing my feet up to a small ledge in the tile wall. My arms aren't strong enough to do a legit pull-up, but my legs are pretty fit, and once I get some traction on the ledge, I muscle myself up to the second rung. The metal of the ladder makes a hollow banging sound, and it echoes against the walls. Shit!

The next sound I hear is footsteps in the outer corridor. Not running. But definitely coming this way. *Move your butt, Gomes!* I swing one knee up to the bottom rung. From there, it's a one-two-three climb to the hatch.

By the time the guards pass through, the hall is empty and I'm on the roof. Just one rusty fire escape from freedom.

CHAPTER 3

MY SCOOTER IS stashed in the usual spot. It's covered with a tarp so filthy nobody would ever want to touch it, and locked underneath with the thickest chain I could steal. I pull the scooter out and head downtown. I *love* my scooter. It's a real relic, but I've tuned it to the max. Fresh brake. New wheels. Dense foam grips. I've seen pictures of kids from fifty years ago wearing helmets to ride, but that's not for me. I love feeling the wind in my hair—the way it tickles my neck and whips back over my ears. It feels like flying.

I timed my breakout pretty close to the end of class, so they might not wise up until third period. Of course, sooner or later, they'll realize I'm missing. For sure, I'll get another write-up and another mark on my record. But at this point, does one more really matter? I already made it to the last semester of my senior year without getting totally expelled.

Besides, this meeting today might be my way out. The lawyer's letter said that something had been "bequeathed" to me. The mystery is: from who? As far as I know, my family is just me and Grandma. I barely remember my parents, and they sure as hell didn't have anything to leave me. So it looks like I have a mysterious benefactor. Who knows? Maybe I'm the long-lost heir to a Caribbean island or a big juicy yacht. If so, I'm *definitely* getting out—assuming I can escape the city, that is. Dropping out in the last half of my last year of high school would make me a legend!

The city police are on almost every corner, as usual. They're a notch up from the school guard variety. Better trained and a lot more dangerous. They wear all black and their helmets have some kind of weird crosshatch pattern at the bottom. Whoever designed it was probably going for "evil skull." But it ended up looking more like braces. TinGrins. That's what everybody calls them. Just not to their faces. They eye me as I roll by, more curious than anything else. I'm not worth a stop—or a bullet.

Being locked up in school all day is a pain for sure. But being out on the street reminds me how bad things are everywhere. The only businesses still left for us are little shops selling basic foods and stuff like batteries, soap, and candles.

The rich people and government types get everything they need in their neat daily deliveries. They don't even need to step outside of their mansions. And mostly, they don't. The only books I ever see are in the library, and they've whittled the approved list down to almost nothing. Basically, history before the Alignment doesn't exist. Kids in kindergarten now will grow up thinking this is all normal. But I know it's not.

"Have a beautiful day!" A man's voice.

It's a guy on the corner selling bootleg magazines from a cardboard box.

I've seen him before. The expected response to "Have a beautiful day" is "And you as well." It's just what people say. Not a law exactly. More like a strong suggestion passed down from on high, which I almost always ignore. I decide to do the vendor a favor though.

"Patrol squad. Two blocks up," I tell him. He nods, then folds up his stuff in about two seconds and starts to move out. He doesn't want to get caught with historical material. People get disappeared for that. I kick hard against the pavement and I'm off again toward midtown. Like flying.

The avenue is a crazy patchwork of the haves and have-nots. On one block, gated estates with irrigated lawns. On the next block, people in tents and plywood shacks. Some of the slum-dwellers wear masks to throw off the facial recognition cameras. Cartoon bunnies, frogs, foxes, stuff like that. It's a small way of protesting, I guess. Or "acting out," as the school shrink would say. I've been known to wear a mask myself when I'm out and about, but never when I'm riding. Messes with my peripheral vision.

Most of the old skyscrapers in this part of town are empty now or just used for government offices or surveillance towers, so I'm curious about the address in my pocket. But mostly, I can't wait to collect my inheritance. It better be something great!

CHAPTER 4

CREIGHTON POOLE, ATTORNEY at Law, plucked a plump cigar from the humidor on his desk. He had been looking forward to this morning's meeting for a long time. The truth was, he didn't have much else to do.

His practice had dwindled to a single client, passed down from the firm he had inherited from his father—and he from his—going back generations, all the way to the 1920s.

For Poole's first few years out of law school, the world still dealt in torts and motions, arguments and settlements, guilt or innocence. But that was all gone now. At this point, having a legal practice was about as useful as running a shoeshine stand.

Poole's office, a glass-walled corner in a Fifth Avenue high-rise, was paid for through the next decade. No worries there. But he had no staff, no associates, and no assistant. His last admin was taken last year to work for a manager in bridge maintenance. So Poole was by himself, preparing for his one and only meeting of the day.

The phone on his desk buzzed. It was the intercom from the front door, street level, thirty flights down. At least he still had a phone, even if it didn't always work. He picked up the handset.

"Creighton Poole," he said.

"Hey!" said a female voice. "It's me. I'm here. Maddy. Maddy Gomes."

Poole was thrilled that she actually showed up. But he didn't reveal any of that in his voice.

"I'll buzz you in," he said. "I'm on thirty."

"*Thirty*?" came the voice from the speaker box. "As in three *zero*? Please tell me there's an elevator."

"Sorry," said Poole. The elevators in the building only worked for an hour in the morning and an hour at night. Otherwise, the electricity was diverted elsewhere for more essential functions. "Enjoy the hike."

Thirty flights would take her at least ten minutes. Poole lit his cigar and stared out over midtown. Below, small cooking and trash fires burned on street corners and empty lots, clouding the sky with sooty smoke. The ashy haze blew across the lawns of the pillared mansions nearby. There was no escaping it, even for the rich.

This was a delicate matter he had to handle today. Ostensibly, he was there to provide a girl with information about her inheritance. But first, he planned to get information on *her*—information that he might be able to use for his own benefit. He had wanted to meet this girl for a long time. But the agreement, written in 1937, was quite specific about the age at which she was entitled to the inheritance. Eighteen. So Creighton Poole had waited patiently. For eighteen years.

He heard pounding on the outer door of his office. *Already?* Athletic.

He walked past the desk of his nonexistent

assistant. He held his cigar between two fingers and undid the locks. One latch. Three bolts. He opened the door.

"Mr. Poole?"

"Miss Gomes?"

"You should really think about moving to a lower floor."

CHAPTER 5

POOLE EVALUATED HIS guest. She wasn't as sweaty as he expected for somebody who had just walked up thirty flights, but she was no prize in the appearance department. Her hair was blond, and it was a tangled mess. Her clothes were definitely second-hand. Over her shoulder, she held an antique metal scooter.

"You carried that thing up thirty floors?" asked Poole.

"Versus leaving it downstairs and having it sold for scrap?" said Maddy. "I sure did." She stepped past Poole into the outer office. Then she caught a glimpse of the view outside. She set her scooter down on the carpet and walked to the window, pressing her hands and nose against the tinted glass.

"Whoa!" she said. "You've got a crazy view from up here!" She looked to her left. "And a *balcony*?" Sure enough, Poole's office wall had a sliding glass door leading onto a small cement platform edged with a thick iron railing. Maddy reached for the door handle.

"Don't open that!" said Poole sharply. "You'll let the smoke in."

"As opposed to the smoke that's already here?" said Maddy, waving her hand in front of her nose to clear the cigar fumes. She turned and flopped herself down in a chair. Poole made a show of walking behind his desk and taking a power position, back straight, head up, arms folded. He tapped his cigar ash into an antique ceramic bowl.

"Maddy Gomes," he said, like an official pronouncement. Then, more casually, "Is Maddy short for Madelyn? Or maybe Madison?"

"Just Maddy, as far as I know."

"I see."

Maddy considered herself an expert judge

of character, and she instinctively distrusted Creighton Poole. Her eyes darted to the exit, planning her getaway in case the need arose. She was pretty sure she could get the jump on this dumpy lawyer. If he even *was* a lawyer. But for now, she decided to play along. Just in case he was for real. It would be a shame if she'd climbed Mount Everest for nothing.

"Somebody left me something, right? That's what you said in the letter."

"That's what we're here to discuss," Poole confirmed. Maddy scooted forward until she was literally on the edge of her seat.

"Okay, I'm hooked. What *is* it?"

"Miss Gomes," he began. Then, with a smile, "Maddy." A little trick. Implied intimacy. *I'm on your side. You can trust me.*

Maddy didn't. Not for one second.

"Maddy, your inheritance is somewhat unusual, to say the least, and I want to be certain that you fully comprehend the implications and responsibilities it may entail. After all—forgive me—you are still a teenager."

She'd thought about this angle, and she was ready for it.

"The age of majority in New York is still eighteen," she said. "General Obligations, Section One, Domestic Relations, Section Two, Public Health Law, Section Two-Five-Zero-Four. I'm legally an adult. So let's get on with it."

Poole studied his guest with new interest. He tapped another ash into the bowl. "Indeed," he said. "You seem like a very self-possessed young lady."

And a bit more knowledgable about the law than he had anticipated.

"I can take care of myself," said Maddy, "and whatever it is you still haven't told me about."

Poole decided to plunge ahead. He needed to find out how much Maddy knew about her past. He was gambling that she didn't know as much as he did.

And knowledge, as always, was power. He was hoping to use his position to gain some advantage. But for now, he knew the object of the game was to just keep talking. And he was a world-class talker. "Let's start with some background so I can fill in some details on you. I know where you go to school, obviously. That's where I sent the letter. Let's review a bit about your family history." He picked up an expensive-looking pen and pulled a sheet of paper in front of his belly. "Then we can get into the specifics about your inheritance."

He settled in his chair as if he expected this to be a lengthy and cordial discussion, mostly one way, guided by him.

Maddy felt a flicker in her gut. One thing she knew for certain is that when people started writing things down about your family, it never led anywhere good. Enough. She stood up and leaned forward, her hands pressed hard against the front edge of Poole's massive desk. It was her turn to talk. She looked through Poole's bloodshot eyes and directly into his mind.

"I want my inheritance now," said Maddy. "Where is it?"

Maddy thought Poole might produce a check or document from a drawer, or write down the number of a safe-deposit box. Instead, he looked back at her, blinking slowly.

"Water Street," he said. "Last warehouse on the left. East River side."

"Good," said Maddy. She walked out of the office, scooping up her scooter on the way. She turned back to Poole, sitting numbly at his desk.

"You stay right there," she said, opening the outer door. "Have a beautiful day."

"And you as well," replied Poole. For once in his life, for reasons he did not understand, he had absolutely nothing else to say.

CHAPTER 6

AT THE SAME time, miles north, Councilwoman Maria Fernandez and Councilwoman Aida Almasi approached the World President's Residence, in what was once called Manhattan's Museum Mile. They paused for a moment to look up at the elaborate stonework that crowned the building. Openmouthed granite gargoyles stared back.

"It's like a fairyland castle," said Maria.

"Right," said Aida, "or Dracula's tomb."

Maria and Aida were good friends. They were also both relatively green as public officials. Maybe, they thought, that's why they got the invitation from President Nal

Gismonde. Maybe he thought it would be easy to manipulate them, or get them to ease up on their very public complaints.

Maria and Aida were both in their late twenties and had both been named to the city council in last year's cycle. They knew their positions were largely ceremonial, but both firmly believed in the squeaky wheels getting the grease. And so, against all odds, they kept squeaking. Even if it sometimes meant confronting people who wished that they would simply shut up and disappear.

That's why, when the invitation arrived, they decided to make the most of it. In her journal that morning, Maria had scrawled the words of a twentieth-century diplomat: "You negotiate peace with your enemies, not with your friends."

So here they were, prepared for a polite audience with a man who repulsed them in every possible way.

"Remember, hang tight," said Maria as they passed through the outer perimeter.

"But don't take any crap," replied Aida.

They both laughed—nervously. Dark humor was one of the many things they had in common. And although they openly pooh-poohed the trappings of power, their pulses were starting to pound. This meeting was a very big deal.

"Ready for teatime in hell?" asked Maria.

"Pass the sugar," said Aida.

The front of the Residence was patrolled by armed guards, augmented by a fleet of surveillance drones weaving overhead like buzzards. Maria and Aida presented their passes and papers and were waved through to an entry corridor. There, in harsh contrast with the Beaux-Arts design of the building itself, sat a massive military-grade full-body screener. Passing through the machine's imposing arc one at a time, the two women and everything they wore and carried were quickly analyzed.

Then, as if the electronic clearance were not enough, they were required to stand on low platforms under bright lamps. Guards tapped their knees apart and poked their arms into outstretched positions and then—more slowly than necessary—ran gloved hands up and down their entire bodies.

"Have a beautiful day," said the guards as they completed their pat-downs.

Neither Maria nor Aida responded. A few steps away, they paused to straighten their clothes.

"I think they picked my pockets," whispered Maria with a tight smile.

"I think I just re-lost my virginity," Aida whispered back.

They composed themselves and walked forward into a small portico, where a stylish assistant, a woman about their age, was waiting.

"Good morning, councilwomen," said their escort. "My name is Kitani. Please, follow me."

As if to wash away the indignity of the screening, Kitani smiled and ushered them gracefully through a door and into a long hallway with a checked tile floor. In here, Maria and Aida could almost imagine that they had been invited to a society function in the middle of the last millennium.

"Is this your first visit to the Residence?" Kitani asked, looking back over her shoulder.

"It is," said Maria.

"I can't believe people still live like this," said Aida. Her comment edged more toward disapproval than envy, which Kitani politely ignored.

"The Residence is an absolute treasure," said Kitani. "Made even brighter by your presence, of course."

Kitani had a comforting warmth about her, as if she were truly interested in her guests. But it was lost on Maria and Aida. They were just taking in the spectacle, mentally measuring the opulence around them against the makeshift apartments and squalid group residences where most city-dwellers now lived.

"You're probably wondering how many rooms the Residence has," said Kitani.

"Not really," Maria mumbled under her breath.

"Thirty-two," Kitani continued, "with eight full baths. The floors are Italian marble, the moldings solid oak, and each of these balusters," she said as they passed a curved staircase, "was carved from a single piece of ivory."

Maria leaned close to whisper into Aida's ear, "Nice. An elephant graveyard." If Kitani heard, she was trained to pretend that she hadn't.

The councilwomen were shown into a first-floor dining room, with high ceilings and gilded central skylights. At the far end was a dining alcove, sheltered under an arch of elaborately carved wood. A table for three was centered in the intimate space.

"Please," said Kitani, sweeping her open hand toward the alcove. Maria and Aida slid into the cozy nook and onto perfectly formed antique dining chairs.

"The world president will be here soon," said Kitani. "Have a beautiful day."

At this point, if being gracious was part of the game, Maria was willing to play along.

"And you as well," she said, though mostly to herself. Aida just nodded and put on her best fake smile. She hated this charade with her entire being.

Kitani seemed to evaporate behind a panel they had not noticed. As she left, the women heard the soft sound of classical music floating through the space, mixed with the sound of chirping birds.

When they heard the latch of the main door turn, they looked at each other and nodded.

He was here.

"Showtime," whispered Maria.

CHAPTER 7

IN MARIA'S EXPERIENCE, famous people were usually less imposing in person than in their images. But Nal Gismonde seemed larger in real life. He stood over six feet tall, with a straight-backed bearing that stretched the impression even higher. His features were delicate, his skin agelessly smooth, his long hair black and silky.

Goddamn. He's prettier than I am was Aida's immediate thought.

"Councilwomen!" Gismonde said with a grand sweep of one arm. "I'm honored." Against every instinct in their bodies, Maria and Aida both rose to their feet and dipped their heads.

"No, no, please sit," said Gismonde, waving

off the protocol. To Maria's surprise, he was more charming than pompous, and he appeared to meet her eyes with genuine interest. Maybe they would get somewhere with this tyrant after all.

As the women settled back into their chairs, Gismonde took the seat at the head of the table. They had expected him to arrive with an entourage—a security detail, at least—but it was just the three of them. Gismonde leaned forward, his forehead furrowed with serious intent.

"I understand that we have some issues to discuss," said Gismonde. He looked earnestly from Maria to Aida, and then opened his arms in a gesture that seemed to embrace them both, his expression suddenly bright. "But who can negotiate on an empty stomach?" On cue, a door at the far end of the room swung open, and a server appeared with a silver tray holding three small plates and three glasses of champagne.

"I never eat a big meal while conducting business," Gismonde said. "Small servings are better, don't you agree? Less blood to the belly. We all need our brains working at full capacity, do we not?"

Maria and Aida stepped on each other's replies, a mumbled mangle of "Definitely" and "Of course." Gismonde smiled as the server set the plates down. Each plate held several small toasted bread slices surrounding a tiny glass bowl. The bowls were filled with what looked like tiny white pearls. In spite of themselves, the councilwomen leaned in, curious.

"Almas caviar," said Gismonde. "Harvested only from sturgeons over one hundred years old. The finest in the world—and so hard to come by." He plucked a single tiny egg from his bowl and held it between his thumb and forefinger.

"We taste like this," he said. He placed the egg in the middle of his tongue. His guests reached into their bowls and followed suit. "Now," said Gismonde, "crush it and let the flavor pop."

Maria went first. The texture of the tiny orb was like a large grain of couscous, but when she crushed it, her mouth flooded with a briny, creamy flavor. Unbelievably rich.

Aida went next. An involuntary "Wow"

escaped her lips. She mentally scolded herself. The last thing she wanted was to be enjoying any part of this.

The servant had disappeared. Gismonde lifted his glass and held it up to the light, appreciating the slow rise of the bubbles. "Twenty seventy-seven," he said with a confidential whisper. "Exquisite year."

Maria couldn't remember when she'd last tasted alcohol, let alone a glass of vintage champagne. She took a modest sip and felt the cool bubbles in her mouth. She looked across at Aida, who had already emptied her glass. She imagined Aida's Muslim father revolving in his grave.

Aida nodded to Gismonde as if to confirm his opinion of the vintage. Suddenly, bubbles started to ooze from her mouth, as if the champagne were spilling back out. But Maria, a former physician, knew that this foam was something else. A shock of adrenaline shot through her gut.

"Oh my God—what's wrong?" asked Maria. She turned frantically to Gismonde, who was sipping slowly from his own glass.

"Mr. President!" said Maria. "We need help!" Aida's eyes were starting to roll back, showing only white. Agitated and scared, Maria craned her neck toward the door, expecting a rush of assistants or medics. *Anybody!*

"Please," said Gismonde, placing his cool hand on Maria's arm. "At this point, the key is to avoid panic." At that very moment, Maria felt a bitter warmth rise in her own throat, accompanied by a sudden hot stab in her skull.

Oh my God, no! thought Maria. It was the final thought of her short life. Aida, mercifully, had not even had time to think.

The two women sprawled back in their chairs, heads rolled to the side, white foam trickling from their mouths. Gismonde leaned forward, his hand wrapped in a silk napkin. Slowly and carefully, he wiped the ooze from Maria's face, then from Aida's.

"So unappetizing," he mumbled to himself.

He settled back, placed another delicate fish egg into his mouth, and felt its tiny, delightful explosion.

CHAPTER 8

MY SCOOTER IS good for most of the ride downtown, but off the main streets, it's pretty useless. I sling it over my shoulder and start walking. Down here near the harbor, the air is even smokier. There's a little breeze coming off the river, but it's not exactly refreshing. More like a mixture of dead fish and wet garbage.

Maybe it's just a coincidence that the sky is clouding over. There aren't many people around, and the ones I *can* see are the type I keep my distance from. Definitely no eye contact. This whole place feels weird and spooky.

The kind of neighborhood you should *never* come to all alone. But here I am.

The first two warehouses I see are abandoned, doors torn off, windows broken, I'm sure people sleep here at nights when there's no place else to go, but they're taking a chance. Those brick walls look like they might cave in at any minute.

When I get to the last warehouse, I realize I've got nothing else to go on. No key. No secret password. I wonder if Poole has warned somebody that I was coming. I'm not sure whoever's here will even let me in.

There's only one door, smack in the middle of the side facing the river. It's big and metal and covered with rust. There's no intercom or bell. So I step up and knock—hard. I wait. Nothing. I knock harder.

This time, I hear a creaky sound from inside. The door starts to swing open. There's a man behind it. I can see his frizzy hair silhouetted by the light from inside.

"Hey there," I say. "I'm Maddy Gomes."

For a few seconds, the guy doesn't say anything. He just stares.

"Hello?" I say, waving my hands in front of his face, waiting for some response.

"I'll be damned," he says finally. "You actually exist."

CHAPTER 9

"PLEASE," HE SAYS, opening the door just a little wider to invite me inside. I notice that he checks behind me to see if there's anybody else. He's kind of pudgy, with a pasty white face. He looks like he's been trying to grow a beard for a while but still hasn't produced much foliage. Age? I'd guess about forty. But an *old* forty. Thick glasses. Spongy gut. If it turns out I inherited a yacht, I doubt this guy is the captain.

I step inside and right away, I realize that this is a grade-A textbook setting for a pedophile lair. This wasn't a very bright move on my part. I do a quick look-around. There's nothing obviously evil in sight, but I pull my scooter off my shoulder and hold it in front of me, just in case.

"Okay, what's going on?" I ask. "What this place about? Who are *you*?"

"I'm Dr. Fletcher," he says. "*Julian* Fletcher." He holds out his hand. I shake it. It's slick with perspiration. I can tell he's more nervous than I am, and that shifts the power dynamic a bit. I put down my scooter.

He looks me up and down, but not in a creepy way. Then he focuses in on my face, like he feels he should know me. "It's incredible," he says.

"*What's* incredible?"

"That you're actually here. That this is actually happening."

"You mean you've been waiting for me?"

He lets his breath out in a slow stream.

"You have no idea."

I decide to give Fletcher a quick recap. I'm not sure that I totally trust him, but I've got to start somewhere. I need to get this process off the dime!

"Here's all I know," I say. "I got a letter saying that I was the beneficiary of some mysterious will. The letter sent me to a lawyer. The lawyer started to give me the runaround."

"Poole," said Fletcher. "He's an associate of mine. I'm surprised he let you come down here without him."

"Not his choice," I say.

I step deeper into this huge musty room, which looks like an old-time science lab. The windows are covered with some kind of black-out paint, but there must be a solid electrical feed, because the lights are steady and some of the electronic boxes are humming. There's a big metal table covered in wires and dials and old electronic parts. Real collector's items. Not a single IC board or LED strip in the pile. It's like I'm stuck in an alternate time zone, and it's getting weirder by the minute.

I see a hallway leading from one side of the room. There could be *anything* back there. But so far the only sound in the place is the beeping from the machines on the table.

Fletcher scratches his head. He rubs his palms on his shirt. He clears his throat. Finally, he looks around the room and pulls up a metal stool.

"Here," he says, patting the seat like he's training a puppy. "Sit."

I slide onto the stool and hook my feet around it. Fletcher pulls up a worn and slouchy office chair. He's obviously spent so much time in it that it's molded to his shape. I'm perched above him on the stool, looking down on the bald patches on his blotchy scalp. I can imagine him plucking out strands of his own hair in his spare time. Nail-biter too, I'll bet.

"I've practiced this a million times in my head," says Fletcher. "But I can't believe I'm saying it for real."

Now I'm starting to get a tingle. Not fear, exactly—just that feeling you get when all your senses are on high alert because you're not sure which way things are going to go. Fight or flight, right? I lean down.

"So *say* it."

He nods his head slowly, like he's working up his nerve. Then he rolls his chair closer and looks straight up at me.

"What you've inherited, Miss Gomes...is a body."

CHAPTER 10

"A *BODY*? LIKE what? An Egyptian mummy?" Maybe somebody left me a valuable museum relic.

Fletcher takes a deep breath. "Bear with me," he says. "I know that this will make me sound crazy." He runs his hand through his hair again. "But I'm not." He looks about to launch into some big monologue, then stops himself.

"Nope," he says. "Enough talking. You need to see this."

He walks toward a huge metal door on the other side of the room. In the center of the door is an enormous wheel, like the kind they use to turn off water ducts. He cranks the metal wheel and I hear the door give way with a little suction sound. The hinges are wider than my whole hand. The metal is about two feet thick.

The wispy little hairs on the back of my neck are tingling. My pulse is racing. The air from behind the door stings my nose, like vinegar or cleaning solution. Fletcher steps over the lower metal rim of the doorway.

"Let's go," he says.

I follow him into a small room with metal walls and a hatch on one side. Fletcher yanks a long lever and the hatch door drops down. He reaches in with both hands and pulls on a horizontal bar. He leans back for leverage. The bar is attached to a narrow table, with tubes and wires running in from one side.

I feel kind of sick and scared and excited at the same time. Because things have just officially gone from weird to *insane*. The table is all the way out now.

And lying in the middle of it is a dead guy in a tux.

"Holy mother of *crap*!" My heart feels like it's going to explode through my clothes. I take a quick step back and feel the cold metal wall against my spine.

"What the hell is this?" I say. "Is that guy really dead?"

"Not exactly," says Fletcher. "His bodily processes have just been massively decelerated."

"Decelerated?"

"Slowed way down. Heartbeat. Circulation. Tissue growth. Everything has been happening in slow motion."

I take a step closer to the almost-but-not-quite-corpse. There's a thick IV tube running under a bandage sticking out above his sock, and there's a low hum from some kind of coil under the table.

"Who the hell *is* this? And why is he dressed for a party?"

"It's just what he happened to be wearing in 1937."

"Nineteen thirty-seven?" I run the numbers in my head. You're telling me that he's been lying here for a hundred and fifty years?"

"That's correct," says Fletcher. "I know it's hard to . . ."

"And what are *you*, some kind of zombie assistant?" I wasn't trying to be funny. I was just trying to tie this situation to *any-thing* that made sense, and I wasn't having much luck.

"I inherited his care," says Fletcher. He's nervous and excited. "This facility has been in my family for generations. I've been wait-ing for the right time to move him to the next stage."

"What stage is *that*?"

"Revivification. Bringing him back. That's what I'm here for."

I take a deep breath. No way this is hap-pening.

"You're going to bring him back to *life*?"

"That's the plan."

"So why have you been waiting all this time?"

"Like I said—I've been waiting for *you*."

I've got all kinds of questions running through my head. Big questions. Starting with *Why me?* But sometimes when the ques-tions are too big, it helps to focus on details. At least that's the way my brain works. So

I focus on the guy on the table. Handsome. Maybe early forties. His face looks perfect, but there's some kind of yellowish-whitish crust on the front of his tux and shirt, like he threw up at a wedding.

"What's that mess all over him?"

"Poison residue," says Fletcher. "He probably vomited after ingestion. A reflex reaction."

"What the *hell*...!"

"Relax. We're fine," says Fletcher. "The compounds are inert. The potency dissipated with the deceleration process, which was the whole theory in the first place. That part worked. The poison didn't kill him. Whether it damaged him internally, who knows? Whether I can actually bring his organs and consciousness back to anything close to full function, that's the real challenge."

I've never been the kind to get queasy at the sight of dead bodies.

But something about this situation is too bizarre. Too creepy. I'm done.

I start backing toward the door.

"No way I'm part of this!" I say. "This is *nuts*!"

Fletcher grabs my arm. "Stop. Wait," he says. "Think about it. It's not just *me* who's been waiting for you." He points to the guy on the table. "*He's* been waiting for you! *Him!* He's been waiting since before you were *born*!"

Fletcher is holding my upper arm like a vise. When I tug at him, he relaxes his grip.

"What makes me so special?" I ask. "Why not some superscientist or brain surgeon? Why not some big shot from the government?"

"I don't know," says Fletcher. "Maybe *he* can tell you. But he can't tell you while he's like this."

I step back toward the table and look at the guy's face again. In some ways, it looks like he just went to sleep, like the guy in that old story. Rip Van Whatever.

"So, who *is* he?" I ask. "Does he have a name?"

"He does," says Fletcher. "His name is Lamont Cranston."

"What did you say?"

Fletcher repeats it, pronouncing each syllable: "Lamont Cranston."

Okay. Good joke. That's obviously a fake name. Because I'm an expert on Lamont Cranston, aka the Shadow.

And there's no way that's a real person.

CHAPTER 11

FLETCHER'S NOT IN the mood to debate names. "Mr. Lamont Cranston" is what it said on the intake sheet. That's all he knows. So I decide not to push it. All Fletcher cares about right now is bringing this guy back into the land of the living. In fact, he looks a little obsessed.

"Okay. How do we do it?" I ask.

"'We'?" says Fletcher. "Do you have a medical degree?"

"I get straight-As in science," I say. "How many bodies have *you* brought back to life?"

"Actually," he says, "this would be my first."

"All right then, let's call us even. What's the process?"

Fletcher steps out into the main room and comes back with a stack of old binders and notebooks. *Really* old. Torn and falling-apart old.

"It's all in here," he says. "Theoretically." He points to his head. "And in here."

"And the theory is . . . ?" I ask.

I think Fletcher has probably spent so much time alone in this temple of doom that he likes having somebody he can lecture to. He starts flipping through the binders and notebooks, looking back and forth. As he flips, he talks—like he's been waiting forever to spill it out.

"When Mr. Cranston arrived in 1937, he was dying from ingestion of an erabutoxin, possibly derived from sea snake venom. Incredibly destructive. So before he was clinically dead, his body was cryogenically cooled."

"He was *frozen*?"

"Supercooled," says Fletcher. "Human cells can't survive actual freezing. Ice crystal formation ruptures the cell membranes. There's no way you could thaw a fully frozen organism and expect a positive result."

He points to the IV tube running into the guy's ankle, right above his rolled-down sock. "He's been suffused with a vitrification solution to keep his cells viable at low temperature."

"Like antifreeze?" I ask.

"A bit more complex than that, but yes, similar notion. Under cryogenic deceleration, his heart has been pumping. His blood has been flowing. His cells have been regenerating. But barely. In a hundred and fifty years, he's probably aged ten." He taps one of the old notebooks. "If the solution reacts with an electrical charge in the right way, it should restore function."

"You're going to *electrocute* him?"

"Yes," says Fletcher. "Very gently."

CHAPTER 12

GENTLY, MY ASS!

The first jolt makes the body jump an inch off the table. Fletcher adjusts the settings on his little hand controller. It's connected to the coil under the table by a couple of wires. The body settles back down again. Fletcher flinches. This doesn't look good.

"Well, if he wasn't dead before," I say, "he's probably dead now."

"Quiet!" said Fletcher. He thumbs through his notebooks again.

I can tell he's trying to come up with another idea. And he does.

"All right," he says. "I'm going to try a saline flush." He points to a metal chest on the other side of the room. "There! Get two bags for me!"

I open the chest. It's an aluminum cooler filled with sacks of clear fluid. I hand a couple to Fletcher. They feel like thick water balloons. He hooks them to a rack at the side of the table and attaches tubes so that the fluid runs into the IV line, which runs directly into a vein above the guy's ankle. Then he attaches a syringe to a rubber connector.

"What's this for?" I ask.

"The concentration of the preservative solution might be too high. I'm trying to dilute it. Plus, the saline is conductive."

"So they covered all this stuff in med school?" I ask. When I'm nervous, I just try to make conversation. Fletcher's nose is buried in the binders again, turning pages back and forth.

"I'm not a medical doctor," he says. "I'm a PhD in organic chemistry." He looks up. "Big disappointment to my family."

"Great. So what if this guy wakes up and has a heart attack?"

"I'm really hoping that doesn't happen," says Fletcher.

The IV line is wide open. I can actually see the solution flowing through the tube as Fletcher presses the plunger on the syringe.

"Okay," says Fletcher. "I'm ready to re-apply voltage. Stay clear." He picks up his little box again, like a kid with an old-time game controller. He turns the dial slowly. The coil begins to whine again. I see the body start to pulse and vibrate, shaking the whole table. Fletcher is sweating. "C'mon! C'mon," he mumbles. Suddenly, the IV line bursts from under the bandage and whips out, spraying solution all over the place. The body goes into a spasm, then settles back down. Fletcher turns pale and shuts the power off.

"Dammit!" he yells.

At this point, I'm past being grossed out by anything. I grab the end of the IV tube and hold it up. Sticky liquid drips all over my fingers, but I don't care.

"Fix it!" I say. "Reattach it! Let's go!"

"It's not working," says Fletcher. "I have to

modify the protocol." He shoves the pile of notebooks aside.

At this point, I have no idea if the guy on the table has any life left in him, but it still hurts to see him like this. I put the IV tube down on the side of the table. The back of my hand accidentally brushes the bare skin of the ankle where his sock is rolled down. The skin feels cool, but not ice cold, like I expected. Then, something else—a little shudder. A flicker of movement, right under the skin.

"Wait! Look!" I shout.

Fletcher leans over the table next to me. The ankle twitches again.

"Just a fasciculation—an involuntary muscle movement," says Fletcher. "A little aftershock."

But now the spasm gets bigger. It runs up his side until his whole leg is trembling. I move to the head of the table. I see a slight movement in his chin. Maybe I'm just imagining it. Or maybe there's still a chance.

"There has to be something else we can still do!" I say.

I hate to fail at anything. Always have. Now my face is just a few inches from his. There! Another twitch of the chin. And now a little jerk in his neck.

What happens next is a blur. Don't ask me to describe my thinking, because I can't. I'm operating on pure adrenaline. Why else would I lean over and plant my mouth over the mouth of a guy who's been in a musty vault for more than a century? But that's what I'm doing. My lips are locked over his. I'm blowing air into him. Yuck. Maybe this is my punishment for cutting class.

I push in a couple of quick breaths. Nothing. Fletcher is frozen like a statue.

He can't believe this. I can't either. I adjust my angle. I press my fingers over his nose so air won't escape. This is nothing like kissing. It's the *opposite* of kissing. I feel like a human air pump. I give him two more breaths— harder this time. I feel Fletcher's hands on my shoulders, pulling me back. "Stop it!" he says. "Are you crazy?"

Suddenly, the guy arches on the table. I hear a deep scratchy rattle in his throat. Then his eyes pop wide open. His head flexes up for a second and then drops back onto the table. His head turns. His eyes look straight at me. His lips move. He gasps. Then he starts talking—slow and hesitant.

"What time is it?" he asks.

I check the clock on the wall.

"Twelve o'clock," I tell him. "On the dot."

"And what day is this?"

"July first, 2087," I say. "Twelve o'clock."

CHAPTER 13

AT THE WORLD President's Residence, two levels below the dining room, Sonor Breece, chief of staff, carefully examined the two dead councilwomen. They were now lying naked on stone slabs in what he liked to call his study. "Laboratory" sounded too clinical, although he certainly used the space for experiments.

Unlike the grabby guards outside, Breece had no prurient interest in female bodies. He was interested only in efficiency and effectiveness, and in what the bodies could teach him. He was a scientist and a scholar. The room was filled not just with instruments, but also with beautiful things—leather-bound books, some of the last in existence, graceful furniture, and ancient pottery.

The walls, already two feet thick and made of granite, had been augmented by sound-proofing panels, because some of Breece's procedures could get a bit noisy. But now the silence was broken only by the chirp of a pair of rainbow finches, fluttering from perch to perch in a cage suspended in a corner of the room.

"Pretty birds," said Breece, in a soft, affectionate voice as he pulled a pair of syringes from a plastic case.

From each woman's cephalic vein he drew a small sample of blood and deposited it in a petri dish. He used a thin titration tube to add a few drops of test solution. He watched as the mixture bubbled and turned powder pink. Breece frowned. Acceptable potency, but not optimal. For mass quantities, the formula would need to be perfected. He pulled a small notebook from his pocket and jotted down some figures.

Back in his years as a university professor, he would have had a team of assistants to work on the project, but now he would have to do it all himself. No matter. It was a passion for him—researching the very best way to kill the maximum number of people. Breece was fond of the old-fashioned saying "Find a job you love and you'll never work a day in your life."

Right now, of course, he had a task that most people would find highly distasteful. For Breece, it was just a matter of selecting the proper tool. He ran his eyes over the two bodies in front of him and made some quick mental calculations.

Yes.

The nine-inch reciprocating saw would work perfectly.

CHAPTER 14

I CAN'T BELIEVE what I'm seeing.

An hour ago, this guy was lying on a metal table. Now he's sitting in a chair out in the lab, trying to make conversation. Incredible. I can't even imagine what he must be feeling. At first, his sentences were kind of choppy, as if his brain were broken into a bunch of puzzle pieces. But gradually he's getting the hang of it. He shrugs off the blanket Fletcher gave him, like he's in a rush to get back to normal. Does he even remember what normal was? Does he remember anything?

"My name . . . is Lamont Cranston." That's what he keeps saying. I know he's *not* Lamont Cranston. Lamont Cranston was a radio detective from the 1930s. Totally fictional. But I decide not to make a thing of it. I'll call him Lamont for now, just to humor him. We can get his true identity straightened out later. I'm sure he has bigger stuff on his mind. Assuming his mind still works. I think that's up for grabs. He looks around the room. He looks at Fletcher. He looks at me. His eyes flicker.

"Where is this?" he asks.

Fletcher rolls his saggy old chair up close to him. "Hey," he says. "Let's take one thing at a time. Baby steps. Okay? I'm Dr. Fletcher."

Lamont's face brightens a little.

"*Fenton?* Fenton Fletcher?"

Fletcher leans closer.

"Fenton Fletcher was an ancestor of mine," he says. "Way back. My name is Julian. *Julian* Fletcher."

Lamont tries to absorb the connection, but gives up. He turns to me. "And you?"

"I'm Maddy. Maddy Gomes."

"Why am I here?" asks Lamont.

I look back at Fletcher. He clears his throat. His PhD classes probably didn't prepare him for *this* conversation—the one where you tell a guy that he's been almost dead since the last century.

"Mr. Cranston," Fletcher says. "You were poisoned. A fatal dose. Back in 1937."

Lamont blinks. I can almost see his brain starting to make connections. Thinking back. Somewhere in there, neurons must be firing. He rubs his face, starts to talk. Hesitates. Then starts again. His voice is still cracking.

"I died?" he says. "But now I'm alive?"

"Something like that, yes," says Fletcher.

Lamont exhales slowly.

"Can I get you anything?" I ask. "What do you need?"

Lamont looks at me in a way nobody's ever looked at me before—like he's actually trying to reach into my mind. Suddenly, he stands up. But he has no sense of balance. He starts to fall forward. I reach out to catch him, but Fletcher gets to him first. Lamont twists away and starts back toward the vault.

"There's nothing there," says Fletcher. He's

trying to sound soothing, but Lamont is getting more and more determined. He starts down the dim hallway that leads off the main room. Fletcher moves to block the way.

"Stop," he says. "You'll get hurt."

Fletcher wraps Lamont up in a bear hug and practically carries him back to the chair. Lamont doesn't have the strength to fight back. Just standing up and moving across the room has taken a lot out of him.

"Margo!" he says. "Margo Lane! Where *is* she?"

Margo Lane? Wait. I'm totally confused. Margo Lane was Lamont Cranston's friend and companion. On the radio. There's no way she's a real person either.

"Air!" Lamont starts shouting. "I need air!"

CHAPTER 15

ON THE WIDE cement step outside the warehouse, Lamont took his first outdoor breath in a very, very long time. It was a big disappointment. In fact, it reeked. There was someone at his side. The girl. Maddy? Was that her name? Lamont was still trying to figure out who she was. A secretary? A nurse? She was standing close—as if she expected him to tip over.

His brain felt like cotton and his eyes were slightly out of focus. Everything in his view was cloudy. It was just one of the thousand ways in which his body didn't quite feel like his. He tried to orient himself to his surroundings.

"Is that . . . the East River?" he asked.

"It is," said Maddy.

"Why is it so high?" asked Lamont. The brackish water lapped across the bare lot in front of the warehouse, only a few yards from where they stood.

Maddy shrugged. "The water's been rising for years," she said. "For as long as I've been alive."

"And what's that in the air?" Lamont asked. "Is something on fire?" The air near the river was filled with smoke.

"Just cooking fires," said Maddy. "People need to eat."

Lamont shook his head. It was like the damned Depression had never ended. As his vision started to clear, he saw small groups of people shuffling nearby. They all had matted hair and wore shapeless clothes. He saw a line of them passing close by the warehouse, heading for the river. A young woman was in the lead, trailed by a string of small children, following like silent lemmings.

"Where are they going?" asked Lamont. Then something flashed in his memory. He'd seen this before. More than a century ago. Drowning was one way to end the pain, and sometimes the poorest of the poor took that way out. This was a suicide walk!

Lamont stepped off the cement step and walked toward the woman. In seconds, he was in water up to his calves. Maddy tried to support him but he shook her off.

"Stop!" he called out to the woman. His voice was still weak. It didn't reach. He heard Maddy shout too. She was right behind him. The woman heard Maddy. She paused as the children crowded around her, just inches from the edge of the water.

Lamont was close now, close enough to reach for her. The woman turned her face toward him. Lamont looked at her intently, deeply, deliberately.

"Do not jump," he said. "Back away."

The woman was hollow-eyed and pale. She said nothing.

"Do not die," said Lamont. "Do not die."

Slowly, the woman turned away from the river. The others followed. The woman placed her hands on the shoulders of the children as

they shuffled back toward the smoky camp-
sites beyond the warehouse. Lamont looked
down. Maddy was staring at him.

"What did you just do?" she asked.

Lamont looked out over the river, where a
few abandoned barges floated aimlessly, then
back at the woman and children, disappearing into the haze.

"Maybe," he said, "I gave them hope."

CHAPTER 16

AS WE WALK back toward the warehouse, I can see Lamont getting more energetic, a little more sure on his feet. He stops to look at me.

"Maddy," he says. "That's a good name."

"Thanks," I say. At least he has some short-term memory left.

I wonder if I should tell him that it was my little mouth mambo that that finally brought him back. But I decide not to say anything. Let him believe that advanced science revived him. That's what he paid for, right?

"Maddy," he says, "I need to go home. Maybe Margo will be there."

"Where's home?" I ask. I realize that I have no idea where he's from, where he lived, how he got here.

"My townhouse," he says. He turns to face north. "That way!"

After a hundred and fifty years, any place he used to live has probably been torn down or boarded up. But I decide to play along.

"No problem," I say. "We'll find a way there. *Slowly.*"

But Lamont is already gathering steam, heading for the alley between the warehouses. He's shaking his arms like he's trying to get the feeling back.

"Hold on!" I yell. "Wait up!"

I duck back inside the warehouse to grab my scooter. Fletcher is still sitting in his saggy seat, scribbling in a notebook.

"Lamont's on a mission," I tell him. "He wants to go uptown."

Fletcher closes his notebook and leans forward in his chair.

"Are you crazy?" he says.

"What?" I say. "You want to put him back in the vault?"

"You know he could drop dead at any minute, right?" says Fletcher. "We kick-started him, but nobody knows the effects of long-term deceleration."

"Look," I say. "I know he's your little science experiment. But he's my inheritance. I'll watch him."

"I'm telling you, he needs to be monitored!" says Fletcher. "He's not ready for a goddamned tour of the city!"

I realize that what Fletcher is saying makes sense. Things are moving a little too fast. What if Lamont needs another jolt?

"You're right," I say. "I'll get him."

I head back outside. It's been less than twenty seconds. But now I realize that it was a mistake to let Lamont out of my sight. Because when I look down the alley, he's gone.

CHAPTER 17

CHIRP-CHIRP!

It's the sound of an electronic alert from a parked car just up the street. A luxury L20 electric coupe, the latest Chinese import. I spot Lamont looking baffled in the driver's seat as I run up alongside the car and tap on the half-open window.

"Hey!" I say. "You've been alive for two hours and now you're stealing cars?"

"We'll just borrow it," says Lamont. "Just show me how to work..." I can see him struggling for the right words "...the god-damned thing!"

He looks over the dashboard and shakes his head.

"Where's the tach?" he asks. "The fuel gauge? The speedometer?"

He's staring at the black plastic control screen and I realize that he has no idea what it's for. I open the driver's-side door.

"Lamont," I say. "Maybe we should do this tomorrow."

"No!" he shouts. *"Now!"*

I decide not to argue with him. Truth is, I can't wait to get out of this neighborhood myself.

I nudge him on the shoulder. "Shove over."

I toss my scooter into the rear compartment. Lamont slides over to the passenger's side. I've seen cars like this, but I've never touched one. Never sat in one. Never driven one. Never driven at all, in fact. Cars are for rich people, not for poor kids like me.

But how hard can it be?

I press the red power button on the console and the car starts to hum. The screen lights up. The icons *kind* of make sense.

"Where to?" I ask.

"North," says Lamont. "Fifth Avenue. Number…" He pauses and rubs his head, trying to remember.

"Never mind the number," I say. "The addresses have all changed anyway."

"Just *go!*" says Lamont. "Please!"

I tap the icon for forward. As I move away from the curb, I sideswipe a traffic-control stanchion. The car's side panel crunches like popcorn.

"Sorry about that," I mumble. "Not too familiar with this model…" I quickly re-tap the touch screen and switch to auto run. The ride smooths out when the car locks into the lane sensors.

I look over at Lamont. "Don't worry," I tell him. "If your house is still there, we'll find it."

Within ten seconds, the car is up to fifty on First Avenue. I see Lamont bracing his feet against the floor panel and pressing himself into the seat back. I look down at the screen and barely miss a guy carrying a stack of salvage wood.

At the Fourteenth Street intersection, I see

a crew of pavers ahead. I think they expect me to slow down. When I don't, they jump out of the way, dropping their tools in the middle of the street. I run over the tip of a shovel and the handle flips up. *Crash!* So much for the driver's-side headlight.

"Good lord!" shouts Lamont. "Where did you learn to drive?"

"Self-taught," I say. I lean out my window and let the wind whip my hair away from my face.

This beats the hell out of a scooter any day.

CHAPTER 18

NORTH OF TWENTY-THIRD Street, the underground suppressors automatically slow the car down to thirty. I take it off auto and make some quick doglegs to avoid police checkpoints, just in case somebody's already reported a stolen vehicle. After a few maneuvers, I head up Third Avenue.

The slower speed gives Lamont a good look at the city, and I can see that he's disgusted. In this part of town there's no mix of rich and poor. It's all poor. Everybody with money has moved closer to Fifth Avenue. On this block, just about every building is shuttered and boarded up. The few shops that are still open have long lines outside. When I pause at a stoplight, a squad of grubby kids scurries up to knock on the window.

"Get away!" Lamont yells. "Leave!" He pounds back from his side of the window.

"They just want candy," I tell him, then press the horn to startle the kids so they move on. I'm not worried about the candy kids. I used to be one myself. I'm more worried about the teen gangs, like the one I see lurking on the next corner. That bunch would think nothing of slashing a tire or throwing a waste bin through a windshield.

"Who's in charge here?" asks Lamont, his voice rising. "Where's the mayor?"

"There's no mayor," I tell him. "Gismonde runs everything."

"Who?"

"Nal Gismonde," I reply. "The world president."

"What happened to Roosevelt?"

"Never mind."

I don't think Lamont's up for a history lesson right now. Like Fletcher said, baby steps. I doubt he'd believe it anyway.

As we approach a little bodega at the corner of Fifty-Third Street, I hear shouts from inside. Through the shop's dirty window, I can see figures scuffling. Suddenly, two young guys burst out of the front, carrying bags. The shop owner runs after them. He grabs one guy by the arm. Not a good idea. The young guy swings his elbow back like a hammer, catching the store man hard in the face. He falls onto the pavement.

"Did you see that?" Lamont says, pounding on the smooth dash panel. "Where in God's name are the *police*?"

"The police don't bother with street crime," I say, "unless the victim is rich, or connected. Otherwise you're on your own."

"That's *insane!*" says Lamont.

"That's life," I tell him.

I can see that Lamont is starting to boil inside. I'm sure he's wondering what kind of world he came back to. I see him looking back at the shop owner in the street.

"Who knows what evil lurks in the hearts of men?" Lamont says.

I have to laugh. Just a little. I can't help it.

Whoever this guy is, I have to admit he does a pretty decent Shadow impression.

CHAPTER 19

"WHAT'S FUNNY?" LAMONT asks.

"Nothing," I say, keeping my eyes locked on the road. "It's just..." I lower my voice and imitate his imitation. *"Who knows what evil lurks in the hearts of men?"*

"What about it?" says Lamont. "It's not funny—it's true. There's no telling how deep evil can go. I mean, look around! I'm seeing nothing *but* evil!"

I can't tell if Lamont's putting me on. He seems sincere, really troubled about the state of the city. On the other hand, he's had a weird brew of drugs circulating through his body for a long time. Who knows what that might've done to his brain?

"So, are you a fan of the Shadow?" I ask. "I mean, from the radio show? That was on during the 1930s, right?"

Lamont is staring out the window. Nobody I know has the slightest interest in an obscure comic book hero from the past century. But there's something about the Shadow that always appealed to me—especially his power of invisibility. I mean, how cool would *that* be?

"Wait!" I have another thought. "Are you an *actor*?" That might explain the fancy tux and the handsome face. "Were you *on* the radio? Did you *play* the Shadow? Were *you* the Shadow?"

"An *actor*?" Lamont says. "You think I'm some kind of *fake*?"

"I just figured...maybe that's why you picked the name."

"My name is my *name*!" he says. And then,"Watch *out*!"

A car is veering toward us. I make a hard left onto Fifty-Seventh Street, missing the other guy by inches.

"Sorry!" I say. "I'll pay attention."

But it's just a good thing I turned west

when I did. Any higher and we'd be getting close to Central Park, which is one place on the island I did *not* want to be.

We're coming up to Fifth Avenue. One block away. As we pass Madison, Lamont starts looking anxious. He whips his head from side to side, checking out various buildings, back and forth. Suddenly he sits right up in his seat, so fast that his head almost hits the roof panel of the sedan. He points straight ahead.

"That's it! Right there! That's my house!"

I slow down and pull the car over to the curb. I look up the street to where he's pointing.

"You're kidding, right?"

"Of course not!" says Lamont. "That's it! I live right there! I should know—I designed every inch of it!"

I recognize the building. Who wouldn't. But there's no way we're getting anywhere near it.

Because it's the official residence of the world president.

CHAPTER 20

LAMONT DOESN'T UNDERSTAND.

"The world president?" he says. "Who are you talking about?"

"Lamont, listen to me," I say, turning to look him straight in the eye. "There is no mayor. There is no Roosevelt. No kings. No queens. No prime ministers. They're all gone. One single, solitary man holds all the power. *One man.* He runs everything. If you question him, you're gone. And he lives..." I jab my finger toward the mansion. "Right *there!*"

We're stopped about twenty yards short of the main gate. Already, I've attracted the attention of a few perimeter drones and a squad of sector police. The police roll up in two patrol vehicles with armor plating and huge black bumpers.

"TinGrins," I say. "Right behind us."

"Who?" says Lamont.

"Police. Coppers. The Fuzz. Whatever the hell you used to call them."

Four men hop off the running boards and form a human barrier in front of our car. The drivers pull their vehicles into a V to block my way.

"We're screwed," I say. "Do not move."

Lamont opens his door.

"Stop!" I shout. "They'll *kill* you! What are you *doing*?"

Lamont slams the door behind him and walks right up to the two officers on his side. They raise their rifles. When they see Lamont's tux, they think it's some kind of crazy costume. One of the officers actually laughs. This gets Lamont more fired up. His sentences are almost normal now. Even though he's talking crazy.

"Hey!" he says. "That's *my* house. Right there! *Mine!*"

The officers aren't overreacting. They probably don't want a scene that would attract the presidential guards. That would be a mess.

"This is as far as you go," says one of the TinGrins. I can hear his voice amplified through his chest speaker.

"I don't think you heard me," Lamont says. The barrels of the rifles are an inch from his belly. Suddenly the squad converges on him from all sides.

I sit frozen in the car, terrified of making a wrong move. A *fatal* move. I have one chance. If I can isolate the squad leader, one on one, maybe I can get him to back off. But as I try to open my door, one of the other TinGrins leans his solid hip against it. I'm trapped—and now Lamont is locked inside a pack of officers.

I see the side door of one of the police vehicles slide open. It's like a dark box inside. Lamont is now totally surrounded by black uniforms. Only his head is visible. He turns my way and jerks his chin upward. I know what he means. He means "Go!"

I hesitate for a second, but there's nothing I

can do to stop what's happening to Lamont. And there's no sense in getting locked up with him. As long as I'm free, I still have options. Maybe.

I tap the screen to put the car into reverse. I swerve backward, spinning the TinGrin on my side to his knees. I back up until the front of the car is clear of the police vehicles, then whip around and head back in the other direction. In two seconds, I'm speeding down the block. I know I'm an easy target, but gunshots would stir the presidential detail. And that's the last thing they want. They don't care about me, anyway. They know they've got the real troublemaker.

I'm so mad at myself that I can hardly see. I promised to watch out for Lamont. Great job.

CHAPTER 21

LAMONT FELT HIMSELF being half dragged, half shoved toward the open door of the police vehicle. He was close enough now to see a metal bench running the width of the interior. One of the officers went in first. The two men holding Lamont's arms shoved him forward. He shook off their grip and stepped into the vehicle on his own. He slid onto the cold metal seat.

Lamont was no stranger to police. He'd dealt with them all the time. Sure, some of them were crooks, some were thugs, but most of them were okay—men you could work with, drink with, share tips with. But that was then. This was now. And these guys weren't the talkative type. Lamont was in trouble and he knew it. Had he come back to life just to end up with a bullet in his head? There was only one way out. And he figured he had only about three seconds to make his move. He wasn't sure that he could do it. It had been a long time.

As the officer to Lamont's left slid further in to make room, another officer stepped into the box to bracket Lamont on the seat. Lamont closed his eyes. It was now or never. Then it happened. Just like he remembered.

The feeling was like the rise over the top of a roller coaster. A burst of energy shot through him and seemed to cause his organs to vibrate. There was a moment of near blackout and then a fluid sensation. He saw the officers panic and spin around, looking in every direction. They brought their rifles up. But there was nothing to shoot at. Lamont stepped outside the vehicle feeling a power that he hadn't felt in more than a hundred years.

He was back.

He was alive.

He was invisible.

CHAPTER 22

MY HANDS ARE sweating. My heart is pounding. I turn in to an abandoned parking garage and pull into a dark corner. I watch the garage opening for TinGrins. Are they chasing me? Did I lose them? Are they taking positions outside and waiting for a clean shot?

A few hours ago, my biggest problem in life was getting marked up for skipping class. Seems like pretty small potatoes at the moment. Now I've got a choice to make. I can abandon the car, sneak out the back, and act perfectly normal. In a half-hour, I'll be back home with my grandmother. That would be the reasonable choice. What can I do for Lamont at this point anyway? Why is he my problem?

Who am I kidding? Of *course* he's my problem. He's my goddamn inheritance! I hear a loud bang behind me. I duck! But it's only some old guy dropping the lid on a dumpster.

After a few minutes, I peek over the hood and ease the car out of the garage. I turn north. About a block from the World President's Residence a huge black SUV moves up behind me, right on my bumper. Shit! But the next second, it pulls around me and speeds ahead down the street. I slow to a crawl to create some space. Then I hear my passenger door opening. Am I getting carjacked? I pop my door latch and get ready to roll out and ditch the car.

"Maddy, stop!"

Lamont's voice?

When I turn back, it's him! He's sitting in the passenger's seat like nothing happened.

"What are you waiting for?" he says. "Drive!"

"What happened?" I say. "They let you go?"

"Not really," says Lamont. "I just ... left."

I move the car forward. Slow this time. Let's not attract attention.

"I don't understand."

I'm running out of patience now. I took it easy on Lamont at first. Didn't want to send him into a mental tailspin. I did what he said, took him where he wanted to go. Which almost got him killed. Now I need some answers.

"Okay," I say. "That's it. I'm tired of the mysteries. Tell me the truth. Who the hell *are* you?"

"I thought I made it perfectly clear," he said. "I'm Lamont Cranston."

I pound the door panel and shout. "Lamont Cranston is a character from the radio! He's totally made up! Maybe somebody gave you a false identity before you...you know...went under! Maybe all those chemicals turned your brain to mush!"

"Lamont Cranston is very real," says Lamont, calm and smooth. "And so is the Shadow. Same coin, two sides."

"I don't get it," I say. "What's your *story*?"

"It's a very long story."

"Try me. *How* long?"

"Ten thousand years."

"*Ten thousand years?* Lamont, you're not making any s—"

The windshield shatters into a million tiny pellets. The air cushion hits me like a hard punch in the chest. I hear the crunch of metal and fiberglass. When I look up, I see the front end of the L20 wedged under the back end of a dump truck. In the few seconds it takes me to realize what happened, the driver of the truck is already at my door, his fists clenched. He's huge and red in the face.

"Hey!" he shouts, leaning in to my window.

I shove the door open, forcing him backward. When I stand up outside the car, I come up to about his chest. I'm pretty sure he's not going to punch a girl half his size, but he's really pissed.

"You rich bitch!" he says.

Of course. He thinks I actually *own* this thing. And now he thinks he can wring some cash out of me to pay for the minor scrapes on the underside of his ten-ton truck.

"It's all fine," I tell him. "Go back to your rig and just drive away."

And that's exactly what he does. Lamont opens his door and gets out. I reach into the back of the car and retrieve my scooter as the truck drives off.

"Impressive," says Lamont. Or is it the Shadow? Or is it just a crazy man who has no idea who he really is? At this point, I don't really give a crap. We just need to get out of here. New plan.

The front of the L20 is a crumbled mess. The scrappers will show up soon. An hour from now, there won't be anything left. Which is good. Because that means there won't be anything to trace.

"We're going home," I say. "*My* home this time." I head through an alley, moving south. Lamont is right on my heels. I still haven't gotten any real answers to my questions. But that can wait.

For right now, I just need to keep us both alive.

CHAPTER 23

THE CITY STREETS were crowded at this time of day. Now that his vision had cleared, Lamont realized how conspicuous he looked in his dinner jacket. Just about every person they passed was wearing worn-out clothes, stained and sooty from smoke. He was getting a lot of stares. Here in midtown, the congestion and filth were even thicker than by the docks. More misery per square block. A lot of people wore goofy masks, the kind Lamont remembered from Halloween parties. But this didn't look like a party.

"What *happened* to these people?" asked Lamont. "Why is everybody so poor and dirty?"

"That's the way it is," said Maddy. "The people at the top get everything. The rest of us just get by."

On light poles across the street, Lamont saw glass panels hanging at eye level. Like movie screens. But so much smaller. Amazing! On every screen, a man was talking. Lamont wasn't close enough to see his face, and his words were lost in the rumble and rush of midday truck traffic.

"Who's that?" Lamont asked, pointing at one of the screens.

"Are you kidding?" Maddy asked. "That's him. Gismonde. The world president. The guy whose home you just tried to break in to."

"What's he saying?" asked Lamont. He saw small groups of people gathered at the base of the poles, faces tilted up, listening intently.

"It's his daily message. New rules. New warnings. Words of inspiration," said Maddy. "Depends on his mood. I never pay much attention."

At Forty-Third Street, they saw a transport stopped at the corner. It was a converted city bus filled with families, mostly mothers and kids. An armed guard stood on a wide platform near the front door. Most of the children inside were crying, some scratching or banging on the thick plastic windows. The mothers, stone-faced, were trying to calm them.

"Who are those people?" Lamont asked. "What's happening?"

"Suspects. Strays. Violators," Maddy replied. "Just part of the daily roundup."

"Where are they going?" asked Lamont. "Where are they taking them?"

"Quiet," said Maddy, tucking her head down. "Stop asking questions."

Lamont felt his insides stirring. An old feeling. Anger rising up. He pulled Maddy to a halt.

"We have to *do* something!" he said. "We can't just let this happen."

Lamont was determined. Some primal instinct was kicking in, and he was aching for action. Maddy nudged him forward.

"Are you *insane*?" she said.

"You distract the guard," said Lamont, "and

I'll get everybody off the bus. I can do it, I *promise!*"

"You do that," said Maddy, "and ten minutes later, the TinGrins will round them up on another corner and beat the crap out of them for escaping. Keep moving. We can't be hanging around like this."

Already, Lamont's furious gesturing had caught the bus guard's attention. The guard's prime responsibility was to keep the prisoners in line. It was boring duty and it didn't require much effort, so he was always watching for random deviations in his vicinity. Those two across the street definitely stood out.

Maddy glanced up in time to see the guard looking their way. A passing truck blocked him for a few seconds. In the interval, Maddy spun Lamont around and grabbed the sleeve of his jacket.

"Follow me," she said. *"Now!"*

Maddy tucked her scooter under one arm and tugged Lamont hard. They broke into a run. The entrance to the abandoned subway station was a half-block away. When they reached the crumbling station entrance,

Maddy took the steps down two at a time. Lamont did his best to keep up, but his coordination was still not quite back to normal. A couple of times, he almost fell headfirst onto the cement.

When they reached the bottom of the stairs, Maddy led the way across the deserted platform and down to the far end, where a rusted metal ladder reached down to track level. She looked back at the entrance and saw the guard profiled by the light from outside. Maddy scrambled down the ladder. Lamont followed. She pulled him down into a crouch at the base of the ladder and put a finger to her lips. They heard the sound of footsteps and the cold jangle of metal equipment. Lamont leaned back into the darkness, trying to find his footing in the uneven gravel. The footsteps on the platform stopped. A green laser dot danced across the wall at the end of the platform.

"Let's go!" Maddy mouthed. She tugged Lamont's sleeve and led him past the edge of the platform into the dark tunnel beyond. When she looked back, she spotted the silhouette of the guard moving down the platform slowly, rifle in firing position.

"Move!" she whispered to Lamont. He stumbled over a rotted railroad tie. When he recovered his balance, his foot sank into something mushy.

"Good God!" he whispered. "It smells like a *crapper* down here!"

"Welcome to the underground," whispered Maddy. She led the way by feel, a few yards at a time, keeping one hand against the damp cement wall.

The guard reached the end of the platform and spotted the ladder. He slung his rifle over his shoulder and started down. As his right boot landed heavy on the bottom rung, the ladder pulled free of its rusted mounts, opening a jagged hole in the cement wall. Suddenly the gravel bed and tracks were alive with scurrying shapes. The guard heaved himself back up onto the platform, flat on his belly, eyes wide. He looked down into a solid sea of wriggling, greasy rats.

Suddenly, bus duty didn't look so bad.

CHAPTER 24

FIFTY BLOCKS SOUTH, Maddy's grand-mother, Jessica, reached into the refrigerator and tossed a cube of cheese to her scrappy Scottish terrier, Bando. As always, he caught it on the fly.

"Good boy!" said Jessica. The brown-haired mutt chomped twice and swallowed hard. Then he scooched forward on the floor—head angled, tail wagging. Jessica held her hands up and spread her fingers wide. "Sorry, kiddo, no more where that came from."

Actual dog food, like everything else, was hard to come by. But Jessica always said she'd rather starve herself than deprive her crazy pup. He was one of the two loves of her life—the other being her granddaughter, who was not nearly as obedient.

"I might be late, Grandma," Maddy had said as she left for school that morning. "Something *big* is happening today!" No hint about what it was. But Jessica knew that an eighteen-year-old girl couldn't be expected to share everything with her grandmother. God knows Jessica had kept a few secrets from her.

The lights in the apartment flickered and dimmed. The bulbs buzzed from the lower voltage. They were rerouting the power again, and this part of the city was always the last priority. Jessica was lucky to have electricity at all, along with four walls and a few actual rooms. A lot of her friends were not so fortunate. She knew families who were crowded into a single open space, and others who moved every few nights, just one step ahead of the housing police and the street gangs.

Jessica heard footsteps on the stairs. Boot thuds. *Maddy.* That girl stomped like a construction worker. Bando ran to the door, tail wagging, body shaking with excitement. For Bando, Maddy coming home never got old.

The door opened a crack.

"Grandma?" Maddy called out. Bando was already poking the front half of his body through the door opening, pawing at Maddy's lower leg. She reached down to scratch his head. Then Bando suddenly backed up and growled.

"Shhhh!" said Maddy. "It's okay, Bando. He's a friend."

Lamont tucked himself behind Maddy in the dark stairwell.

"Get back here, you little brute!" called Jessica. "Maddy? Is there someone with you?"

Jessica saw Maddy step through the door into the tiny apartment, pulling in a man behind her. The sight of him brought Jessica up short. He was dressed like an old-time lounge singer. Good-looking, but in his early forties—*way* too old to be hanging around a teenage girl like Maddy.

"Well," Jessica said cautiously. "Hello." Maddy never brought anybody home. Scooter parts, yes—people, no.

"Grandma," said Maddy. "This is Lamont. Lamont, this is my grandma—and that's Bando." Bando yipped, still suspicious.

Jessica reached out to shake Lamont's hand. *Smooth. Certainly doesn't work for a living,* she thought. *And what's that mess on his shirt?*

"Welcome," she said. "Call me Jessica."

Maddy had been thinking about this little meeting for the whole nasty trek home. Grandma was pretty sharp, and this would not be easy to explain.

"'Lamont,'" Jessica repeated. "Is that French—'from the mountain'?"

"Ancient Norse, actually," said Lamont. "'Man of law.'"

"Interesting," said Jessica.

At the moment, the only man of law on Maddy's mind was Poole. The reason she hadn't told her grandmother about the lawyer's letter was that she hadn't wanted to get her hopes up.

Maddy, of course, had been thinking that she might inherit money, preferably cash. What a treat that would have been! For starters, she would have bought her grandmother some clothes that actually fit and a heater that actually worked. Instead, she was bringing home a strange guy covered in dried vomit.

"Do you teach at Maddy's school?" Jessica asked. A shot in the dark for sure, but she had to start somewhere.

Lamont looked at Maddy.

"Grandma," said Maddy, "we need to talk."

First things first, thought Jessica. In a world lacking comforts or even basic sanitation, she remained a stickler for hygiene. She leaned toward her guest.

"Lamont, let me clean that shirt for you."

CHAPTER 25

SONOR BREECE REVIEWED the surveillance clip for the third time. The resolution was excellent, but the angle from the drone was not ideal. He ran one finger down the curve of his prominent nose and tapped his lips. On one side of his office, right in front of the window, a trio of king parrots squawked incessantly.

At first, he considered whether this was something the world president even needed to see. Most surveillance videos were routine, showing the endless procession of curiosity-seekers trying to get a glimpse of the Residence, or of Gismonde himself. There was the occasional protestor, quickly disposed of. At times, groups of small children would walk up to peek through the gates.

Depending on their mood, the guards might toss them candy or knock them away with the butts of their rifles. It was the responsibility of the local police to keep disturbances away from the Residence gates, and the officers had done their job.

But something in the frantic reactions at the end of this incident had caught Breece's attention. This was not a neat cleanup. At the very least, it would be a point of discussion, and besides, it would give Breece some valuable face time with his mentor.

He took the vid-card and walked down the short hallway from his office to Gismonde's reception area. Several ministers waited nervously in straight-backed chairs. A menacing guard, the largest in the residential detail, stood squarely in front of Gismonde's double doors. But at the sight of Breece, he immediately lowered his head and stepped aside. Breece brushed past him and pushed the doors open.

"Mr. World President," he said. "I have something you may find interesting."

Gismonde did not look up. He was busy reviewing a sheaf of plans and figures on his ornate desk. He gestured toward a conversation area, where a computer sat on a low wooden table between a pair of leather-covered sofas. Breece walked over and tapped the vid-card against the screen. The computer blinked to life, with the video already in motion. Breece let it run, then froze it just at the point where a man in a vintage tuxedo stepped out of a luxury sedan. The man's wardrobe had caught his attention instantly. Nobody dressed like that. Not in this century.

Breece hadn't heard Gismonde get up from his desk, but now he was looming over him, inches from his neck.

"What's this?" asked the world president.

"A disturbance near the perimeter earlier today," said Breece. "Probably nothing. But it's a bit out of the usual."

Gismonde watched intently as the video played.

"Field in," he ordered.

Breece magnified the image. The man in the tux seemed to be defying the guards. Brave? Stupid? A decoy?

"Freeze it," said Gismonde.

Breece tapped again. The man's face filled the screen.

Gismonde exhaled slowly and folded his arms across his chest.

"Lamont Cranston," he said. There was a touch of admiration in his voice.

"Is he on the list?" asked Breece. All known agitators were.

"No, he wouldn't be," said Gismonde. "He hasn't been in the city for a very long time."

Gismonde was silent for a few moments. Breece, as always, was eager for orders.

"Shall we..."

"Find him," said Gismonde finally. "*Eliminate* him."

"Of course," said Breece. It was exactly the kind of order he lived for. He slipped the vid-card into his pocket and turned toward the door.

"Mr. Breece." Gismonde called out to stop him.

"Sir?"

"Be thorough," Gismonde said. "Mr. Cranston has a way of not staying dead."

CHAPTER 26

I'M SITTING ON the sofa with Bando in my lap, Grandma right next to me. Lamont is in an armchair facing us. We're all sipping tea, like this is a completely normal get-together. But it's not. Not at all.

It's a good thing Grandma collects cast-off clothes in her spare time. She managed to find a pair of sweatpants and a T-shirt for Lamont that almost fit. His fancy tux jacket and pants are hanging from a hook in the bathroom. His shirt is soaking in the sink. I'm hoping that soap is really strong.

"So, how *do* you two know each other?" asks Grandma.

There's no easy way to answer that question. I decide to start at the beginning.

"Okay, Grandma, a lot of this is going to sound strange." I take a deep breath and then release it. "Right. Here we go. About a week ago, I got a letter at school. From a lawyer." Grandma's head tilts and her eyebrows lift.

"Don't worry," I say. "I didn't murder anyone."

Lamont just sits there sipping his tea.

"I went to the lawyer's office today and he told me that somebody had left me some kind of inheritance from somebody's will."

"An inheritance." Grandma repeats the word carefully. She looks at Lamont.

"Don't look at me," he says. "I never even made out a will."

Now I launch into the whole story, talking fast. The warehouse. Fletcher. The lab. Lamont waking up. Him asking about Margo. The fact that Lamont has basically been in a coma since 1937. I leave out the stuff about the Shadow for now. I mean, enough is enough.

Grandma listens to everything. Very polite. At the end, I expect her to flip out, or say she doesn't understand, or that she's confused, or that she thinks it's all a big joke. Instead, she just nods.

As if this weren't strange to her at all.

"We should eat," she says.

CHAPTER 27

SUPPER WAS PEAS and bacon, cooked on Jessica's salvaged hot plate. Lamont couldn't remember what he'd eaten at his last meal, but he doubted that it had been anything like this. This was hunting-camp fare at best.

He took in the tiny apartment: the stained walls, the plastic window sheeting, the threadbare furniture. He was embarrassed by his bare feet, and by the angry black-and-blue bruise above his right ankle. A gentleman never appeared like this in mixed company. But at the moment, his silk socks were in the bathroom, soaking with his Egyptian cotton shirt. And even under these circumstances, dining with mismatched

flatware and tin cups, his table manners
were impeccable.

"My compliments," he said.

"You're too kind," said Jessica.

Throughout the meal—such as it was—
Lamont kept glancing over at Maddy, sitting
to his right. In profile, she reminded him a little of Margo. Maybe it was just the blond hair.

"I guess you have a lot to catch up on,
Lamont," said Jessica, as Maddy cleared the
plates.

"Things are . . . confusing," admitted Lamont.

"He wouldn't have lasted an hour without
me," called Maddy from the tiny kitchen.

"Probably true," said Lamont. "Even though
you're a terrible driver."

"*Driver?*" said Jessica. She stared at Lamont.
"You let Maddy drive your car?" Maddy
popped back in from the kitchen.

"Grandma, please—never mind," said
Maddy. "It's not important."

Lamont jumped in to change the subject.

"I can't believe what's happened to the
city," he said. "The Depression was bad. But
this is *worse!*"

"Not quite the way you remember, is it?" said Jessica.

Lamont shook his head.

"Not quite the way I remember it either," she said, waving Lamont and Maddy over to the sofa. The lights blinked again and then settled to a yellowish glow. The bulbs gave off a soft buzz.

"Come," Jessica said gently. "Night school is in session."

Maddy settled in against Jessica's shoulder, Bando lay on the floor in front of them. Lamont leaned against the opposite arm of the sofa.

"Where do I start?" said Jessica. From Maddy, Lamont already knew about Gismonde. But only the basics. Now Jessica told him the whole story—about the economic panic that had brought the world to its knees over a decade ago, the growing distance between the haves and have-nots, the last gasp of the United Nations, the new office of world president, and the Alignment—the new world order designed to keep people in their place.

"Who allowed *that* to happen?" asked Lamont.

"It was meant to be temporary," said Jessica, "an emergency measure, for global stability. But it just went on and on—and things got worse and worse. There were riots. But they got suppressed. After a while, for most people, it was easier to accept than resist. The people on top got theirs, and nobody cared about the rest." She pulled a worn blanket up to her waist. "And now, it's gone so far that it feels impossible to change. *Impossible.*"

Maddy had clearly heard this history before. Too many times. She closed her eyes, exhausted from the long day. In a few moments, she was asleep. Jessica brushed a tendril of hair from Maddy's face and kissed her gently on the forehead.

"Now, Lamont," she said softly. "Tell me about Margo. I want to know *everything.*"

CHAPTER 28

ACROSS TOWN, NEVA Lyon held her twins by the hand as they waited in line at the Beautiful Day Mission near the Hudson River. Noah, as always, was a fidget machine, but Brie was quiet and calm. The seven-year-olds hadn't eaten any real food for more than twenty-four hours, only the thin soup at the camp yesterday afternoon. For Neva, it was more like thirty-six hours. She was feeling weak—light-headed and desperate.

"Go to the mission," people had said. "They have free food Friday nights."

"Go early," they added. "There's always a line."

For Neva and the twins, early meant arriving at six a.m. Even at that hour, they found themselves at the end of a huge winding queue. It had been a very long day. At seven p.m., the doors opened. Right on time.

It was another two hours until Neva and her kids even got close. At one point, Noah said he could smell grilled cheese, but Neva said it was just his imagination. Peanut butter and jelly would be more like it, she thought. Or oatmeal. Whatever was cheapest to make in vast quantities.

"Are we really getting food, Mommy?" said Brie, stuffing her small hands into her mother's frayed pockets.

"I hope so, sweetie," said Neva. "Just a little longer."

They shuffled a few paces closer. A few yards ahead, Neva saw a family of five squeeze through the doors. She could already hear low murmuring from inside. Two more families ahead of them in line. Then it would be their turn. Neva leaned over and kissed the top of each twin's head.

"Remember," she said. "'Please' and 'thank you.'"

The kids nodded.

"And when a grownup says, 'Have a beautiful day,' what do we say?"

"'And you as well,'" said the kids in singsong twin unison.

One more family through. This was it. They were next!

The door opened again, but just a crack this time. A man in black overalls stared out from the inside. Behind him, Neva could see narrow tables arranged in long neat rows, family-style. The aroma of tomatoes and browned beef wafted out in a momentary tease. Noah and Brie tugged forward. But the door did not open any wider.

"Sorry," the man said. "We're full for tonight. Try next week."

The metal door slid shut, followed by the sound of a heavy latch falling into place on the other side. Neva was stunned, then furious.

"Next *week*?" she shouted. "What do you mean, 'next week'?" She pounded her fists on the door. A chorus of shouts rose from behind her. *"Feed us! Feed us!"* A second later, the crowd rushed forward in a fury. The strongest stayed on their feet. The weak were simply plowed under. Neva was crushed up against the metal door. She felt her children being ripped away from her in the frenzy. She heard Brie scream.

"Brie! Noah!" she shouted, barely able to turn her head.

Neva thrust her arms straight out, pushing away from the door with everything she had. Slowly, she muscled herself sideways through surging bodies toward the sound of her daughter's voice.

"Brie! Noah!" she called again.

"Feed us! Feed us!" The chant grew in volume as it spread through the hundreds of people behind her, nearly drowning her out. She shoved her way past men twice her size, twisting this way and that, her eyes wide and searching. "Mommy!" Noah's voice.

She saw them low to the ground, huddled together like stones in a stream as the crowd charged around them. With one final shove,

Neva managed to duck down and grab her children.

"Stay with me!" she said, her arms tight around them.

Together, they half stumbled, half crawled to the edge of the crowd, until they broke free and collapsed on the fringe. The crowd milled around the front of the feeding center like a herd of crazed animals, shouting and pounding on the metal door.

"Can't we eat tonight, Mommy?" asked Brie softly. Neva wiped a streak of dirt from her daughter's face.

"Not right now, sweetie," said Neva, and then, trying to put her best spin on it, "Who cares? It's too crowded here anyway."

They stood up and began the long walk back to their camp. Neva held her kids close. Somehow, she managed a hopeful smile and a squeeze for each of them.

"We can do better," she said.

CHAPTER 29

SONOR BREECE DETESTED field research. Too many variables. Too little control. He preferred precise calibrations to crude estimates. Here, the only accurate piece of equipment was the vintage stopwatch in his pocket.

The Beautiful Day Mission was located in a Quonset hut, repurposed from an industrial farm upstate. Inside, curved panels arched up to a central beam. The floor was a mixture of raw dirt and sawdust. The air was filled with the aroma of fresh stew and intense body odor. Around the interior walls, guards were stationed at even intervals. They could hear muffled pounding and shouts from outside, but they weren't expecting any trouble in here. The people who made it through the doors were only interested in one thing. Being fed.

At the head of each table, a uniformed server held a tray of tin bowls, steaming in the cool air. Breece had emphasized how important it was that everybody be served at the same time. Now the servers all looked to him, like musicians to their maestro.

Breece gave the signal. The bowls went down in quick succession all down the line on every table. In his pocket, he pressed the stem of his stopwatch.

The guests grabbed plastic spoons and plunged in hungrily. Seconds before, there had been a low hum of conversation and anticipation. Now the hangar-like space was virtually silent, except for some noisy slurping. One large man abandoned his spoon altogether. He lifted his bowl to his mouth, drinking in the stew like water and letting his red beard catch the spillover.

He was the first to react.

As soon as his empty bowl hit the table, his eyes rolled back and a trickle of white foam began to spill over his beard. He rocked slightly. A small girl across the table pointed and laughed—but only for a second. Then she began spewing white bubbles of her own. The effect was sudden and devastating.

Up and down the rows, people collapsed wordlessly to the ground, where the rough sawdust absorbed leakage from their mouths. The servers and guards stood motionless.

At Breece's nod, the servers began to pick their way through the twitching bodies to the far end of the building, where the doors ran almost the whole width of the structure. As the heavy panels were rolled back, they revealed three trucks idling outside, their massive steel beds empty and waiting.

Breece walked through the dining area. His rubber boots did not suit his sense of style, but they were a necessary precaution against the mess. Here and there a hand reached up as if to claw at his heels, but for the most part, it was over quickly.

"Have a beautiful day," he said, looking around. There was no response.

"What's the count?" Breece called out.

"Seventy-five!" one of the guards shouted back.

Breece surveyed the still forms around him. He clicked his stopwatch and pulled it from his pocket. The red sweep hand was stopped at 30.

Seventy-five people. Thirty seconds. Breece sighed.

He could do better.

CHAPTER 30

HOURS AFTER DINNER, Lamont was still energized. But he was the only one. Maddy was in deep dreams on the sofa with Bando curled around her feet. Jessica had handed Lamont a pile of blankets and a pillow before retiring to the tiny alcove that she called her bedroom. The long talk had worn her out, she said.

Jessica had been so curious about Margo, and Lamont had been eager to share their whole history. He told her how he and Margo had teamed up to fight crime and corruption in the 1930s. How their work relationship had evolved into romance. And, of course, about that horrible night. At least as much as he could remember.

"She was *with* me," Lamont told Jessica. That much he was sure of. "I had her in my *arms!*" And then, "Wherever she is, whatever happened to her, I have to find her."

"You will. I know it," Jessica said. She had sounded so certain. Just before turning in, she had squeezed Lamont around the shoulders.

"For now," she had whispered, "I'm just glad Maddy found *you.*"

The apartment was quiet now, except for the muffled sound of voices coming through the wall from next door. Lamont couldn't make out the words, only the mood—weary and hopeless.

He saw his tux hanging on the outside of the bathroom door. He felt the cuffs and lower legs. Still damp. Then he noticed a small lump in the right pocket of his tuxedo pants. A coin? A key? He reached in. As his fingers touched the object, his heart started to pound.

Slowly and carefully, he pulled out the object—an exquisite diamond ring.

Lamont fell back against the wall. Ever

since he'd been revived, he'd been running on pure instinct and filaments of memory. But this was something else. In one second, a wash of feelings came back, and this time he remembered every detail.

The ring had come from his favorite Forty-Seventh Street jeweler, an expert who had vouched for the stone's cut, clarity, color, and carats. Lamont remembered putting the black velvet box in his jacket pocket before he left for the restaurant, and then realizing that the shape of the box would be a dead giveaway to somebody as observant as Margo. So instead, he'd slipped the bare ring into his pants pocket, within easy reach when the perfect moment arrived.

Lamont's mind flashed to Margo's face— first radiant and smiling, then pale and terrified. He saw a blur of toys on a ceiling, plates on a floor, stunned waiters, and the elegant maître d'. The flashes were fleeting, but they left Lamont perspiring and short of breath.

He tried to focus his mind by concentrating on the present. Where he was right now, at this moment. He stared across the room at Maddy, her blond hair strung across the sofa cushion. He heard Jessica snoring from the next room. Then his mind started tumbling in crazy directions again. Why was Jessica so interested in Margo? It was almost as if she'd known her too. Then, the craziest thought of all: Was it possible that Jessica *was* Margo? There was some resemblance in the features and in the personality. By some miracle, had she somehow been revived before him? Had she been waiting for him all this time? That would explain the difference in years. Was she toying with him?

No. Not possible. He would recognize Margo when he saw her. Even a very *old* Margo. He had no doubt of that.

Lamont began to pad around the apartment slowly, trying to absorb everything. The detective in him took over. The *Shadow* in him. He ran his hands over shelves and walls, as if searching for a secret passage. He moved silently, still in his bare feet. When he looked out the window down onto the street, he saw shapes moving along the sidewalk in the darkness. To the north, he saw small patches of bright lights—the enclaves of people who were rich and privileged. Like he used to be.

As Lamont crept around the partition into the tiny kitchen, his hip bumped into a battered credenza with a single center drawer. He wrapped his fingers around the worn knob and pulled the drawer open, inch by inch. Inside, he saw a corner of pale yellow under a jumble of small white candles. He moved the candles aside to uncover an envelope—so old that it looked ready to crumble.

Maybe it would give him some clues. Anything was better than nothing.

Lamont lifted the envelope and pressed the sides to widen the gap at the unsealed end. He held the opening up to the light and peered inside. The envelope held a single thick sheet. Lamont slid it partway out, and then dropped it as if he'd been burned.

It was a photograph of Margo.

CHAPTER 31

THE NEXT MORNING, Saturday, Lamont was up early. The blankets on the floor had not made for a very restful night's sleep. And he couldn't get the picture of Margo off his mind. He slid on his now dry silk socks and dress shoes, slipped out into the hall, and went down the stairs, moving slowly and quietly.

When he pushed open the door to the sidewalk, the smoky air filled his nostrils again, but he was almost used to it by now. The important thing was that his appetite was returning. He needed food. And coffee!

The street was mostly deserted, but there was a buzz around a small shop on the corner. Lamont saw people coming and going, some emerging with small bundles and paper bags. He walked to the end of the block and pushed open the dirty glass door. A small bell tinkled. A gaunt man in a ratty vest sat on a stool behind the counter.

The shelves were dusty and sparsely stocked. A few large bins sat on the floor in the middle of the shop. Lamont watched a woman reach in and pull out a carton of eggs and a small container of milk. She walked to the counter and put down a crumpled bill and a few coins. She looked up at the counterman. He hesitated for a second, then gathered the money in his hands.

"Close enough," he said, waving the woman out the door with her purchases.

Lamont paced the narrow aisles. He saw simple bags of flour, sugar, and salt. Wooden baskets held a pitiful assortment of fruit, just some spotty apples and a few misshapen pears. A magical, timeless aroma wafted from a metal machine on a small stand in the corner with a sign reading FREE COFFEE WITH PURCHASE.

Lamont opened one of the coolers and pulled out eggs, milk, and butter.

He grabbed small bags of sugar, flour, and salt from a shelf, then a jar of strawberry jam. He poured himself a coffee from the carafe and took his first delicious sip. It was only when his arms and hands were totally full that he realized that he had no money to pay for anything. Not one cent.

The counterman had his back to the counter, unloading goods from a cardboard box. Then he caught something out of the corner of his eye. When he turned around, he saw fifty dollars' worth of food items somehow floating out the door.

"I'll pay you back double, I promise!"

A man's voice. From nowhere.

CHAPTER 32

LAMONT WAS ONLY a short distance from the shop when he felt the quick tingle that told him he was visible again. He was suddenly drained and exhausted. The effect had been perfect, but it hadn't lasted. What happened? Had the chemicals in his body messed with his abilities? Or was he just out of practice? In the old days, he could stay invisible for hours with no effort. Now quick getaways seemed to be all he could manage. Was he losing that old Shadow magic? Maybe he needed to ration it. Emergency use only.

The climb up the apartment stairs had him huffing and puffing. When he got to the top, Maddy was waiting. She was not happy.

"Where the hell did you *go*?" she asked. Her hair was untamed and her eyes were still puffy from sleep, which made her look even more annoyed.

"I needed some provisions," Lamont answered. He was unused to accounting for his whereabouts. Or being trapped in a hovel, for that matter.

"You know the whole city is looking for you, right?" said Maddy. "There's probably a bounty on your head. You could have led them right to us!"

Lamont flushed slightly. He knew Maddy was right. It was stupid of him to put the others in danger. He needed to be more careful.

"Everybody okay?" Jessica peeked out from behind the door, wearing a thin robe and pom-pom slippers.

"Safe and sound," said Lamont, with his best smile. He held up his armful of supplies. "Anybody hungry?"

He glanced at the credenza as he walked in. He had put the photograph right back where he'd found it the night before, and he was an expert at making things look untouched. Of course, he was eager to ask about it, but he wanted to pick the right moment, when he could get Jessica alone.

But right now, what he truly needed was some cooking equipment.

"Is this all you've got?" he asked, looking at the stained and blackened hot plate on the counter.

"What more do you want?" asked Jessica, sounding a little irked.

"Maybe a fry pan and some utensils?" said Lamont.

"Oh," said Jessica, "we're going first class."

She reached into a small cabinet and pulled out a cast iron skillet and a metal spatula. Maddy reached above her head and pulled a large glass bowl off a shelf.

"Okay, I'm in business," said Lamont. "Now *scoot*, both of you. Too many cooks, etcetera…"

Jessica and Maddy retreated to the sofa as Lamont unloaded his supplies onto the counter. Bando hovered around his feet, sniffing his shoes. Lamont turned on the hot plate, and then started measuring and mixing from memory. It had been a while, obviously.

"What are you *doing* in there?" asked Maddy, as a warm, buttery aroma started to waft through the living room.

"Don't rush me, please!" Lamont called back from the kitchen.

In fact, his recipe didn't take long at all. He had stolen it from a chef in a Paris café, and it had never failed to impress his overnight guests. The preparation required a little finesse, but it was worth it.

"Plates?" Lamont called out.

Maddy hustled into the kitchen and pulled three chipped dishes from a cabinet. Lamont moved quickly now, spooning streaks of strawberry jam onto thin circles of golden batter. With a few deft flips of the spatula, he was done. He brought the plates to the table as Jessica and Maddy pulled up their chairs.

"*Bon appetit!*" he said.

It was the first time either Maddy or Jessica had ever tasted crêpes Suzette, and they were just about speechless. Maddy devoured the first delicate wrap in about two bites. Jessica was only slightly more restrained.

"Sorry I couldn't find any Grand Marnier," said Lamont.

"What?" said Maddy, her mouth full.

"Liqueur," he said. "One of the classic ingredients."

"Doesn't matter," replied Maddy. "These are amazing!"

Jessica smiled at Lamont. She hadn't seen Maddy this enthusiastic about a meal in a long time.

"Did you invent it yourself?" Maddy asked, licking her fingers.

"It was invented by the French," said Lamont. "In the 1800s."

"*Vive la France!*" said Jessica, polishing off her portion and smiling at Lamont.

"So how do you make it?" asked Maddy.

"Sorry," Lamont said. "Secret recipe."

"Don't make me beg," said Maddy. "*Tell* me!"

Lamont put down his fork. He sensed a vibration in the very center of his brain. He knew Maddy wasn't really trying to pressure him. She was just a kid in a good mood, having fun. But she had something powerful inside her—more powerful than she realized.

Lamont felt it to his core.

CHAPTER

TWO ORANGE-BREASTED European rob-
ins inched tentatively from their perch onto
Sonor Breece's narrow wrist. Their tiny feet
felt like tickles against his skin, their bodies
almost weightless. The birds chirped nervously. Breece moved slowly. The last thing
he wanted to do was startle them into flight.

With the birds on his hand, Breece eased
over to his worktable. He rested his arm on
the oak top, next to a small dish of water. After a moment's hesitation, the birds hopped
from his hand onto the wood surface. Breece
remained still, his face at the level of the
tabletop, observing. He liked robins, especially this species.

So colorful. So cheerful.

The birds took a few seconds to adjust to the hard, flat surface. They chirped brightly and craned their necks in every direction. Then, one after the other, they moved to the rim of the dish and dipped their beaks into the clear sugar water. They tilted their heads back, letting gravity carry the sweet liquid down their throats.

"Pretty birds," said Breece softly.

In less than two seconds, the birds were both lying on their sides, with tiny bubbles of white foam spilling from their beaks. Breece waited a few seconds more, then reached out and hovered a palm lightly over each bird, feeling for signs of life. There were none.

He was so intent on his experiment that he didn't hear the soft steps behind him. "Has it improved?"

Gismonde.

Startled, Breece stood up sharply and pulled his hands back to his sides.

"Yes, no doubt," said Breece. "The new formula is even faster. More efficient."

"This is predictive?" Gismonde asked, eyeing the tiny lifeless forms on the table.

"Well of course, we need further testing at scale, but I have every confidence—"

Gismonde cut him off. "Test it tonight," he said. He turned toward the stairs and then paused. "And what about Mr. Cranston?" he asked. "Do you have him yet?"

Breece flushed. He had issued the search order, of course. But he had been too preoccupied to follow up. A mistake. And now he was forced to cover up with bluster.

"The squads are out," Breece said firmly. "We'll have him soon, without fail."

Gismonde didn't respond. He just stared. Breece met his gaze for a moment, then dipped his head in a reflexive bow. The look had been enough to shake him. When Breece lifted his eyes again, Gismonde was gone.

Breece pressed a button on a console at the end of the table. A guard appeared in the doorway.

"Open the Hudson mission tonight at five," said Breece. The guard nodded once and started to turn as Breece completed his instructions.

"And add twenty more tables."

Breece took a ruler and carefully pushed the robins into a bin.

CHAPTER 34

I'M TRYING TO talk sense into Lamont, but it's no use. Now that breakfast is over, he wants to go outside and explore the city, looking for Margo. As if she were just going to be walking down the street on a Saturday stroll.

"Lamont, you're a *fugitive,* remember? You escaped from the police! That's no joke!"

"Look, I'm not going to find her by hiding out in this apartment," he says. "If you won't go with me, I'll go out by myself!"

I can tell he's not going to be reasonable about this. So I reach into a drawer and pull out two plastic animal masks. One panda. One raccoon. If he wants to go roaming the streets in the middle of the morning, we need cover.

"Take your pick," I tell him.

"Don't be *ridiculous*!" he says.

"Lamont, there are cameras *everywhere*! FR can pick you out in a crowd of a thousand people!"

Lamont looks puzzled.

"FR? Who's that?"

"FR," I say. "Facial recognition." I try to think of something he might be able to relate to. "It's kind of like a Wanted poster—but electronic—and it's everywhere. *This* is how we beat it." I hold up the masks. He shrugs, and picks the panda. Looks like I'm the raccoon.

A minute later, we're on the street. We walk one block and already there's a bottleneck. On weekends, there's a different rhythm in the city. More kids running loose. Bigger crowds. More unapproved gatherings. More potential for crackdowns.

Up ahead, I see a platform in the middle of the street with two men standing on it. I recognize them from posters. Franklin and DeScavage, two local councilmen.

"I won't compromise on this!" Franklin is shouting.

"You don't have a *choice!*" DeScavage shouts back.

They're arguing about the location of a med clinic. It happens all the time. Since the only hospital in the city is reserved for government officials and rich people, the rest of us have to make do with paramedics and bandages. Sometimes where the clinics end up depends on who can raise the rowdi-est crowd.

"What's this?" asks Lamont. "What's going on?"

I pull him off to the edge of the crowd. "Medical stuff," I tell him. "They're arguing about healthcare."

Usually speakers bring portable micro-phones to these events, but these two are just shouting at each other from ten feet apart. I can hear them from where we're stand-ing. Franklin yells that his district has more seniors. DeScavage yells back that his district has more pregnancies. The crowds on both sides are getting more agitated, shoving closer to the stage. I can see that DeScavage's crowd is younger and more charged up.

The DeScavage side starts to shout Franklin down. He's getting angry and red in the face.

All of a sudden, a huge guy from DeScavage's crowd jumps onto the platform. He shoves Franklin backward and knocks him off his feet. Now the *other* side moves forward. People start kicking and punching. Women are screaming. Faces are getting bloody. It's total chaos.

I tug on Lamont's sleeve.

"We need to go," I say. *"Now!"*

We duck between two buildings and find some space in an alley. The inside of my mask stinks like melted rubber. I figure it's safe to take it off back here. The second I pull off my mask, Lamont pulls his off too.

"It's unbelievable!" says Lamont. "This place has turned into an insane asylum!"

"It's like the Third Reich under Hitler," I mumble. It takes Lamont a second to absorb the name.

"*Adolf* Hitler?" he asks, as we head down the alley.

"Finally!" I say. "Somebody besides Roosevelt that you've actually *heard* of!"

"Hitler. With the goofy mustache?" Lamont asks.

"That's the one," I say.

"Yes! I remember," says Lamont. "He was that creepy little guy who was getting Germany all riled up!" I can see him getting excited, picking up steam, proud that he's remembering.

"He did more than that," I say.

"It got *worse*?" says Lamont. "What happened? What did he do?"

"Lamont," I say, "I don't even know where to start."

CHAPTER 35

THAT NIGHT, LAMONT took a walk by himself, heading south on Eleventh Avenue.

Walking had always been a way for Lamont to clear his mind. But now his brain was turning nonstop. Maddy had spent the day filling his head with all the evil he'd missed while he was sleeping. Not just Hitler. Stalin. Mao. Pol Pot. Milosevic. Hussein. Bin Laden. Al-Assad. And all the rest. It was hard to keep them all straight—along with their assorted crimes against humanity. The world had truly gone mad!

And now on top of everything else, the city seemed to be sinking under his feet. To the west, what used to be Twelfth Avenue was now underwater. And even on Eleventh, he had to step around deep puddles and small streams that appeared out of nowhere. Lamont heard a low rumble, strong enough to make the sidewalk shake. For a second, he thought the pavement was about to collapse.

Suddenly, a huge armored patrol vehicle turned the corner behind him. Lamont angled his head just enough to see the outriders leaning off the side platforms, rifles ready. A searchlight on the roof swept the street in a steady back-and-forth pattern. Lamont's heart began to pound. In another few seconds, he'd be caught in the glare. Without his panda mask.

The truck was even closer now, just yards away. The searchlight swept back in his direction. At the last possible instant, Lamont closed his eyes and concentrated. He waited for the rush. The truck rumbled past him. The guards looked along his side of the street and saw . . . nobody at all.

Lamont leaned back against a wall. He saw the searchlight rake the vacant storefront just past him. He exhaled slowly, exhausted and totally visible again. No question about it. His superpower was totally out of shape. Maybe it was permanent, or maybe he was just out of practice.

As the patrol turned the corner ahead, Lamont stayed close to the shuttered shops. A half-block ahead, he saw a man and a woman heading for a belowground staircase. The woman was slender, with blond hair. Lamont felt his pulse quicken. Could it be? He headed for the staircase. When he got closer, he saw a dim light from below. At the bottom of the stairwell was a thick metal door. He hurried down the steps.

"Hold it!" A heavyset woman emerged from the dark corner of the stairwell. She was pointing a gun five inches from La-mont's face.

"Turn around," she ordered.

"I don't have any money," said Lamont, holding his arms out. "I'm totally broke."

"You and me both, honey," said the woman. She passed her hands over him in an amateurish body search, then slapped him on the shoulder.

"You're fine. Go ahead in if you want." She nodded toward the door and stuffed the gun back into her waistband. "But things don't really get hopping until after two."

Lamont reached for the door handle and pulled it open. The air from inside hit him in a thick wave, filled with smoke and the scents of beer and sweat. The small room was packed, mostly with young people. Lamont craned his head over the crowd, looking for the couple he had followed. There! At the bar. At least he thought so.

The woman turned toward him. Petite. Pretty. Blond. But not Margo. Maybe she *wasn't* the one he saw. He tried to push his way toward the back of the room, but it was no use. Too packed.

Lamont had been in plenty of speakeasies, but this was something else. Cables from a generator near the door led to a small stage, where a man with a thick body and broad smile was pacing. A fringe of long, wiry hair surrounded his bald spot, which reflected the beam of the spotlight whenever he turned his head.

He moved with the authority of a preacher and spoke in a deep, raspy voice. Lamont only caught every other word—but from what he'd heard from Maddy, just about everything this guy said could get him arrested. Because it sounded like he was making fun of the authorities. His punchy phrases were answered with hearty laughs and cheers from the audience.

In a miserable, unhappy city, this was the last thing Lamont expected.

A comedian.

"In or out!" said a voice from behind. A new group of patrons was pressing through the door behind him. Lamont stepped aside to let them pass. He made one last scan around the room, but he was getting faint from lack of air. Slowly, he edged his way back out into the stairwell.

"What is this?" he asked the greeter with the gun. "What's going on in there?"

"Comedy club," she said. "Totally illegal. But that's what makes it fun."

"Does this happen every night?" Lamont asked.

"Until they lock us all up," she replied. "Or kill us."

Lamont headed up the stairs. "I'll come back soon," he said. "I'll bring a friend."

He suspected that Maddy could use a little comic relief.

CHAPTER 36

LAMONT WAITED FOR a few minutes before darting across the street back to Maddy and Jessica's apartment. He watched. He listened. When the street was deserted, he crossed. But as he approached the door to the building, two men emerged from the adjacent alley. Lamont froze.

The men were both weaving, and slurring their words. In a split second, Lamont decided he couldn't take any chances. Not this close to home. The men looked up. Lamont took a breath. He concentrated. He vanished.

The men saw Lamont. Then they didn't. They stood unsteadily in the middle of the street, too pickled to notice the door to the building nearby opening on its own.

One man squinted into the darkness. "Did you just see...?"

"I...uhh...nope," said his buddy. It wasn't the first time his eyes had played tricks on him after a long night. "Damned hooch," he muttered.

Inside the vestibule, Lamont rested a few minutes to catch his breath before tackling the stairs. He was hoping Jessica would be awake so he could ask her about the photo of Margo. But when he got to the top and opened the door, Maddy was the only one still up.

"Make any new friends?" she asked, with a sarcastic edge. She hadn't been pleased when Lamont insisted on going out alone. And like a nervous parent, she'd waited up.

"Is your grandma asleep?" asked Lamont.

"Snoring like a chainsaw," said Maddy. Bando stirred from his blanket and scurried over to nuzzle Lamont's leg. Lamont gave him a long scratch on the head.

"Come with me," said Maddy. "I need to show you something."

Maddy led him to her sleeping area, a space smaller than one of Lamont's old walk-in closets. It was separated from the living room by a flimsy fabric curtain. Maddy reached under her bed and pulled out a battered cardboard box.

"My private collection," she said.

Maddy sat on the bed, the box on her lap. Lamont sat down next to her. Inside the box was a stack of yellowed magazines, each with the same header in bold type: *The Shadow.*

Maddy pulled the top magazine from the pile. The cover illustration showed a swarthy man in a black leather coat and a wide-brimmed hat. A long red scarf covered his lower face. He brandished a heavy-duty pistol.

"So," said Maddy. "That's *you?*"

Lamont shifted awkwardly on the bed. He remembered those stories, and they embarrassed him. Dime store trash. He'd only read a few.

"*Inspired* by me, obviously," said Lamont, choosing his words carefully. "But I never dressed like that. Never even owned a hat. Never carried that ridiculous gun. I guess they had to jazz things up to goose their sales."

"Okay, then," said Maddy. "What about *this*?" She dug under the jumble of magazines and pulled out something that looked like a compact radio. Maddy pressed a button marked play. A somber organ melody played, and then a man started speaking, his voice clear and resonant, even through the tiny speaker:

"The Shadow is in reality Lamont Cranston, a wealthy young man about town. Years ago, in the mysterious Orient, Cranston learned a magical secret—the hypnotic power to cloud men's minds so they cannot see him. Cranston's friend and companion, the lovely Margo Lane, is the only person who knows to whom the voice of the invisible Shadow belongs!"

The radio show. Lamont remembered that, too.

"Also inspired by me," he said. "And Margo, of course."

Lamont recalled that at first he'd been flattered that a radio show would be based on his detective business. But he'd also been worried about the publicity interfering with his actual cases. It was hard to be discreet with your name on the radio every week. On top of that, the announcer's voice drove him up the wall.

"Why do you *have* all this stuff?" he asked.

Maddy pressed pause. "I told you. I'm a huge fan of *The Shadow.* I figured you were too. I assumed that's why you chose the name. I mean, who just decides to call himself Lamont Cranston?"

Lamont bristled.

"I *am* Lamont Cranston!" he said, trying to keep his voice down. "How many times do I have to tell you?"

Maddy pressed play again. "Okay, Lamont," she said, "what about *this*?" It was the same man's voice again, now even more dramatic.

"Who knows what evil lurks in the hearts of men?" A pregnant pause, and then—*"The Shadow knows!"*

The announcer gave the word *Shadow* a distinctive inflection, the verbal equivalent of a knowing wink. Then, after another pause, he added a low, maniacal laugh. Lamont scoffed.

"I never laughed like that in my life," he said. "Total showbiz nonsense!"

Maddy slapped the magazine on top of the machine and held them both up in front of Lamont's face.

"So you're telling me that *this* guy is made up, but you're real?" said Maddy. "Why should I believe that? Why shouldn't I think you're just a crazy rich guy who thought he found a way to live forever and picked a famous name so nobody in the future would know who the hell he really was?"

Lamont had to admit it all sounded absurd. A fictional detective with magical superpowers. Who was actually based on a real person. Who somehow came out of a deep sleep after more than a hundred years! If one of his old clients had told him that tale, he wouldn't have believed it either. Lamont reached over and pushed the cardboard box aside.

"Put that junk away," he said. "I'll tell you the real story."

CHAPTER 37

LAMONT CLEARED HIS throat and pressed his fingers together, not sure where to begin.

"This is going to sound strange," he said.

"Stranger than a dead body coming back to life?" said Maddy.

"I wasn't dead," said Lamont.

"I know, I know, just cryogenically decelerated."

Lamont leaned forward. "Look. The lab, the research, the equipment—all mine. I paid for it. It was a gamble, pure and simple. I had no way of knowing if it would actually work."

"Were you really poisoned?" asked Maddy.

"Absolutely," said Lamont. "And I knew who did it. And I knew nobody would have the antidote—not back in those days. The plan was always that if something happened to me and Margo, we would be preserved until there was a way to bring us back."

"Wait." said Maddy. "You *know* who poisoned you?"

"Yes. Without a doubt," said Lamont. "It was Khan. My archenemy."

Maddy stared at Lamont. She blinked hard. She bit her lip.

And then she burst out laughing.

"Your *archenemy*?" Maddy squeaked. Just saying the word set her off again. She rolled back on the bed, knees to her chest, red-faced, almost out of breath.

Lamont sat quietly, just looking at her. Maddy finally inhaled deeply and sat back up, holding her belly. She tried to settle herself.

"Khan?" she asked. "*Shiwan* Khan? The evil villain from the Shadow stories? *He's* the one who poisoned you?"

Lamont nodded. "No question."

At this point, Maddy was pretty sure she had a lunatic on her hands. Or the world's most extreme prankster. Maybe it had all been a setup—the lawyer's letter, the warehouse, everything! Maybe the whole frozen-body scene had been fake! But why play such an elaborate trick? And why make her the patsy? It made no sense.

"Maddy," said Lamont, "look at me."

She did. He was calm. Calmer than she'd ever seen him. Instantly, all her silliness ceased. He stared into her eyes, persuading her. Convincing her. Not with thoughts or words or sounds. It was as if he were letting her absorb *his* memories—transferring them to her in a single blast. Not hypnosis. Not deception. In fact, it was the opposite. It was total clarity.

Maddy exhaled slowly, stunned by the fast-motion movie that had just unspooled in her mind.

"Oh my God," she said softly. "It's all true."

And then she passed out.

CHAPTER 38

LAMONT TUCKED MADDY'S legs under a blanket and put a pillow under her head. He was pretty sure she wouldn't come to until morning. Bando sniffed around the room. He looked at Maddy, and then at Lamont. He whimpered and pawed the floor.

"Okay, pal," said Lamont, "I guess I could use another walk."

The night air had gotten cooler. Within a block, Lamont was wishing he'd brought a jacket. But then he remembered that the only jacket he owned was the top half of a tuxedo. Come to think of it, a leather coat might be nice. And a stylish scarf.

Lamont looked around to make sure he

was alone. He cleared his throat. Then he spoke out in his best imitation of a radio announcer voice.

"The *Shadow* knows!"

He tried it at different speeds and volumes. "The...Shadow...*knows*!" "THE SHADOW KNOWS!"

Then he tried it with the laugh. He felt ridiculous.

Luckily, only the dog was around to hear it.

As they walked, Bando roamed from garbage pile to garbage pile, sniffing at the trash and gnawing at the occasional discarded bone. At the bottom of a utility pole, Bando lifted his leg and released a thin stream. Lamont heard a man's voice, muffled, coming from the other side.

"*...and let us all remember that the marks of a superior society are safe streets, clear rules, and mutual consideration...*"

Lamont walked around to see a small screen—the same kind he'd seen in midtown. And now he was getting his first close-up look at the man who was speaking. World President Gismonde. His face filled the frame.

"Surely we can agree that the comfort of all depends on the efforts of all. When times are hard, it is the small gestures that lift us up…"

Suddenly Lamont felt a bright flash in his brain, stunning and painful. He saw Gismonde's image replaced by the face of a fawning maître d'.

"Everything to your liking, Mr. Cranston?"

His mind reeled back a hundred and fifty years. And in that instant, it came to him. He'd seen Gismonde before. A long time ago.

Gismonde … was Khan!

Lamont stooped over, holding his throbbing head. Was it possible? There was a time, more than a century ago, that Lamont thought he had eliminated this evil creature, and now here he was again, staring him right in the face.

Just then, Bando starting yipping. Somebody was coming.

CHAPTER 39

BANDO'S BARKING SNAPPED Lamont's attention back. He turned. Footsteps were approaching fast from around the corner. Seconds later, two young men burst into view, one stocky, the other tall and gawky. Both breathing heavy, eyes wild.

"Let's go! Let's go!" said the stocky one. But his companion hesitated, bent over, chest heaving.

"I can't!" he wheezed. "No more! I *can't!*"

"They'll kill us this time," his friend said. "C'mon! *Move!*"

When Lamont stepped out from the other side of the utility pole, the men looked up, terrified, as Bando kept barking. Lamont heard the tromp of heavy footsteps in double-time rhythm from the darkness behind them. Disciplined. Relentless. Close.

Lamont looked to the left. A huge metal garbage bin sat at the edge of the sidewalk, angled back from the pavement. He stepped forward and scooped Bando up in his arms. He looked one man in the eyes, then the other.

"Don't run," he said calmly. He pointed to the bin. "Hide there."

The men stared back at Lamont. Then, without a word, they hurried to the side of the massive container. The chunky man lifted the heavy rubber lid. The bin released a powerful stench of decay and filth, but neither man flinched. The stronger one cupped his hands and hoisted his skinny buddy over the edge. Then he muscled his way up and swung himself over.

Lamont stood in the middle of the sidewalk with Bando in his arms. Within seconds, flashlight beams hit him square in the face, so bright he could barely make out the men behind them. He raised his hand against the glare. Now he could see that there were four of them. Black uniforms. Black helmets. Black guns.

"Which way?" the lead officer shouted.

Bando growled. The officer stepped closer. Lamont could see himself reflected in his dark helmet visor.

"Two men!" the leader said. "Which way?"

Lamont tightened his grip on Bando. He pointed down a dark side street.

Bando growled again. The lead officer aimed his pistol directly at his snout. "Control your animal," he said to Lamont. Then he followed the rest of his squad into the darkness.

After the police disappeared, Lamont walked back and knocked gently against the bin. He lifted the lid partway and looked inside. The men had burrowed into the garbage. Their now filthy faces stared back like doll heads from under the stinking refuse.

"They're gone," said Lamont, flipping the lid open. "Have a beautiful night."

"And you as well," came two voices in unison.

Lamont headed back toward the apartment. Bando skittered ahead, sniffing everything and anything on the way. The wind was kicking up. Lamont's head was still throbbing. But he realized that there was probably a lot more pain in store. Because if he knew about Khan, the odds were that Khan knew about him, too.

CHAPTER 40

WHEN I OPEN my eyes the next morning, Lamont is sitting on the floor of my room, reading one of my Shadow magazines. My head feels sore and scrambled.

Lamont looks up. "Are you okay?"

I don't know how to answer. What do you say to somebody the morning after he's reached into the depths of your brain? But now I understand a few things for sure: Lamont Cranston is real. The Shadow is real. And they're the same man. And he hasn't just been around for a hundred and fifty years. He's been around for *ten thousand years*!

"I'm sorry," says Lamont. "I know that was a lot to absorb. But it would have taken me all night to explain it. This was way more efficient."

"Ten thousand years?" I ask. That's how much history I have crammed in my head right now.

"These powers have existed even longer than that," says Lamont.

"But why did *you* get them?" I ask.

"I *worked* for them," says Lamont.

"In Mongolia," I say.

"Correct," says Lamont. "The Kharkhorin valley."

"The Kagyu monks!" I blurt out. This is insane! How do I suddenly *know* all this stuff? This was definitely *not* from the radio show.

"My parents raised me," says Lamont. "But the monks trained me. Martial arts. Invisibility. Everything. But there was another student there at the same time. A *better* student. An orphan from the mountains."

"Shiwan Khan," I say. There's no doubt. I know I'm right.

Lamont nods. He puts the magazine down. He looks worried, like there's a new weight on him.

"And now he's here," Lamont says.

"What do you mean, 'he's here'?"

"Khan. He's here. He's in the city right now."

"Where?" I ask. I'm picturing some dark, mysterious cave. Lamont nods toward the window, looking north.

"He's living in my house."

It takes me a couple of seconds to put it together.

"Your house? Wait. You mean Nal Gismonde is Shiwan Khan?"

"One and the same," says Lamont.

Suddenly Grandma pops her head through the curtain in my doorway.

"Enough gabbing, you two! Time for breakfast!"

CHAPTER 41

WHEN WE COME out of my little nook, Grandma is shuffling around in her robe and slippers. Sunday breakfast is already on the table. Nothing fancy. Just some fruit, bread, and hard-boiled eggs. We all sit down.

I hardly know where to start. Or *if* I should start. I'm not really the same person I was before last night. And now I know that Lamont is something way different from anything I thought he was. I'm not sure Grandma can handle it. But this isn't something that I can keep to myself. So here goes...

"Grandma, you know all those Shadow books and radio tapes I've been collecting since I was ten?"

"You mean all your illegal contraband?" Grandma says. "What about it?"

I look at Lamont. Then I reach out and put my hand on Grandma's arm.

"Grandma," I say, "I don't know how to put this, but the Shadow is real. And Lamont ... is the Shadow!"

Grandma smiles.

"I know, dear," she says. "Have some fruit."

What's going on here? Am I nuts?

"Grandma!" I shout. "What do you mean, you *know*? Detectives with ancient super-powers don't just show up out of nowhere! They don't just sit down to Sunday break-fast! Why are you acting like what I'm saying is *normal*?"

"I didn't say it was normal," says Grandma. "I just said it was a fact. Lamont and I had a long talk the other night. Frankly, dear, I'm surprised it's taken you this long to catch on."

The teakettle starts whistling. "Be right back," says Grandma, "There's something else."

Something else? I press my fingers against my temples. I'm not sure I can deal with anything else right now.

Grandma comes back from the kitchen with a cup of hot tea and a yellow envelope. I see Lamont sit up straight in his chair. Grandma drops the envelope in front of me.

"What's this?" I ask.

"I found this in my father's desk after my parents died," she said. "No name. No date. No explanation. I was going to show it to Lamont the other night, but I think he might have found it on his own. I know *somebody* was in that drawer."

I can see Lamont getting nervous across the table.

I pick up the envelope. It feels like it might fall apart in my hands.

"Go ahead," says Grandma. "Open it."

I reach into the envelope and pull out what's inside—a cracked black-and-white photograph of a young woman. Big eyes. Blond hair. Movie-star beautiful.

My heart starts pounding. I've never seen her before, but it's like I've known her all my life. I put the photo down on the table.

"This is Margo Lane," I say. "The real one."

Grandma looks over at Lamont.

"Is that right, Lamont?" she asks, "Is this Margo's picture?"

Lamont doesn't say anything. He just nods.

"Well then," says Grandma, "I'm so happy I saved it."

CHAPTER 42

SIXTEEN HOURS LATER, I still have Margo Lane on my brain. Obviously, she was beautiful. And from what Lamont says, she was a really brainy investigator. I also know that she was way more than just a "friend and companion." That's just a line from a radio script. I can tell Lamont really, really loved her. I mean, *loves* her. Present tense. Because he swears she's still alive.

That's why we're on our way to some secret club, where he thinks he might find her. Margo loves nightlife, he says. But there's another reason for going there too.

"Trust me," says Lamont. "You need this."

We're in a part of town where everybody

carries a knife or a bat for protection. Some-times both. Especially at two in the morning.

"It's right over there," says Lamont.

The next thing I know, we're going down a dark staircase.

"Welcome back!" A voice from the bottom of the stairwell. I see a woman who looks tough enough to break me in half. She gives Lamont a nod.

"You've been here *before*?" I ask him.

"Just briefly," says Lamont. He pushes the door open and BAM! It all hits me at once. The heat. The music. The smell. The cellar is tiny. I don't think two more people can even fit. But Lamont steers me in. As soon as we clear the door, the crowd closes around us. No turning back.

The noise level is insane. The only light in the whole place is pointed at a dinky little stage. I have no idea what's going on.

"I hope this isn't another healthcare de-bate!" I shout into Lamont's ear.

"Just watch!" he shouts back. I can see him scanning over my head, searching the crowd.

The music dips a few decibels and a man's voice blasts out.

"Ladies and gentlemen! Please put your hands together for the most dangerous man in New York City—Danny Bartoni!"

A sturdy young man hops up on stage with a handheld microphone. The crowd claps and howls like crazy. He gives a little bow, which shows off the bald spot on the top of his head. He doesn't wait for the noise to die down. He just beams a big smile and plunges right in, pacing back and forth on his little stage.

"Thank you!" he shouts. "And welcome to the end of civilization as we know it!" Loud cheers. "My name is Danny Bartoni and I'm here to make you all forget your arrest records for the evening!" Big laughs. He stops in midstride and stares at a patron sitting near the edge of the stage. He leans down.

"Sir, it's okay—you don't need to wear your mask in here!" He pauses. "Oh. Sorry. You're not *wearing* a mask! Must be the lights!" His victim is either a good sport or too drunk to care. He laughs along with everybody else.

"So let's get started!" Bartoni says. "Anybody do anything *illegal* today?"

The crowd goes wild. He lowers his voice. "I mean, other than being *here*." More laughs and whistles. Whoever this guy is, the audience loves him.

I can't believe what I'm seeing and hearing. For one thing, everybody is drinking, which means the booze must be stolen, since the government controls the supply. I've never seen or smelled or stepped in this much beer in my life.

For another thing, this guy Bartoni is making fun of the government—one joke after another about stupid police, filthy streets, and crooked officials. Is he crazy?

Now he's holding up a poster with two photographs. My God! One photo is of Gismonde. The other is of Sonor Breece, the chief of staff. "And how about *these* two guys?" Bartoni says. "Beauty and the Beak, right?" The crowd noise dies down. People look at each other. There's an uncomfortable shift—like maybe he's going too far. You don't mock the two most powerful people in the world. You just *don't*. But he's not stopping.

"World President Gismonde!" Bartoni says, patting his own wiry head. "Can I please have your hair-care secret?" Murmurs and mumbles. "And Sonor Breece!" he shouts. "When this guy loses his can opener, no problem! He just uses his *nose*!"

BANG!

A bright flash and loud explosion from the back of the room. Then screams. I see lights and helmets and guns pouring through the back door.

Oh, shit.

Bartoni drops the mic and tosses the poster aside. Fans reach up to pull him off the stage. But a squad of TinGrins are already on him.

Somebody cuts the power. The place goes totally dark. The screams get louder. Gunshots blast into the ceiling. Lamont grabs my arm and pulls me forward. I feel strong hands around my waist. I try to wrestle away. A woman's voice says, "Don't fight me. Just move!" It's the lady bouncer, pushing me toward the entrance. Then another blast blows the front door off its hinges. More TinGrins pour in.

In a split second, we change course. I'm in a human sandwich between Lamont and the bouncer lady. We push through the crowd and end up behind the bar. There's a hatch in the floor with a big metal ring. The bouncer pulls it up. I see stairs leading down.

"Go!" she says. A rifle pokes over the bar, pointed straight at me. The bouncer grabs the barrel and shoves it away. A spray of bullets hits a mirror. I can feel Lamont right behind me. The hatch closes with a thud over our heads.

The passage below is narrow and pitch black. We work our way through for about twenty yards—heads down, breathing hard—and then, we're out, somewhere behind the club. We can see police vehicles left and right. But we slip straight through.

"Keep moving," says Lamont. "Do not look back."

A half block down, we back into a doorway.

"You okay?" asks Lamont.

"No holes. You?"

"Fine."

We peek around the corner. All clear. We head back uptown, walking fast.

I can still feel the adrenaline pumping.

"I'm sorry," says Lamont. "It was stupid to put you in that kind of danger."

That's true, of course. On the other hand, it was pretty exciting! It made me feel alive.

"No, you were totally right to bring me," I say. "I needed that."

CHAPTER 43

THE NEXT NIGHT, it's my turn. Different nightspot. *Way* different.

"Where are we going?" asks Lamont.

"You'll know when we get there," I tell him.

It's midnight. We're walking north in midtown. We take a long detour to avoid the Presidential Residence, then wind past Columbus Circle and cross over into the wilderness. Lamont perks up.

"This is Central Park!" he says.

"Used to be," I say. "Watch your step."

We start making our way up an abandoned roadway. The pavement is cracked. Curbstones gone. Plants sprouting in potholes. And most of the trees are missing their lower branches. Taken for firewood.

I haven't been back here in years. Not since things got really bad. But up ahead there's this big rock I remember that's great for climbing. It's craggy and rough with plenty of good footholds. Rat Rock, they used to call it. And not for the shape. The rats are still here, but if you make enough noise, they just scatter.

I stamp my feet a couple times when I get to the base, then I start making my way up. "C'mon!" I call to Lamont. He follows me. Pretty agile for a guy his age. Even in dress shoes. From the top of the rock, the park looks like a jungle. Everything is thick and overgrown. In the distance, we can make out the turret of an old castle.

"Why don't I see any police?" asks Lamont.

"They don't even bother to patrol here at night," I say. "Whatever happens, happens. Murder, rape, suicide. They just come in and pick up the bodies in the morning."

We climb down off the rock and keep heading deeper into the park, farther north. Toward the place I need Lamont to see.

Lamont and I haven't talked much about

Margo tonight. I know she's always on his mind, but I didn't bring him here to stir up memories. I brought him here to show him reality.

"Almost there," I say.

Up ahead we can already see the glow.

We work our way through one last stand of trees, and there it is. A city within the city. Tents and shacks as far as we can see. And barrel fires—thousands of them. We can hear babies crying and people shouting in about a hundred different languages. On old maps they call it the Great Lawn. Not so great now. Now it's basically one big refugee camp.

"Good God!" says Lamont. "It's like a shantytown from the thirties! Who *are* these people? Where did they come from?"

"From everywhere," I say. "This is where you end up when you don't have anyplace left to go."

We work our way around the camp and end up on the west side, keeping close to the inside of the park border. Suddenly, right ahead of us, we see a bunch of people, maybe eight or nine, sneaking outside the railing.

Probably looking for food or a missing kid. It happens all the time.

A large black van is waiting by the curb, with a squad of police behind it. The TinGrins avoid the park, but they're always hiding around the edges, watching for stragglers to pick up. The police have a nightly quota and this is an easy way to fill it. Before the refugees can run for cover, the police surround them.

I pull Lamont down behind a hedge. The police grab the prisoners and shove them into the van, one by one. Mostly men. A couple of women. I can feel Lamont straining.

"I can't watch this!" he says.

"Let's go," I say. I try to pull him backward into the park.

"No!" he says. "Not this time." He's dead serious.

Before I can stop him, he creeps forward and picks up a couple broken hunks of cement.

"Lamont! Don't be crazy!" I whisper. I duck back down.

I see Lamont move up past the van. He winds up and heaves a rock at the escort vehicle parked in front. The rock doesn't even make a mark in the armor, but it makes a loud bang.

The TinGrins spin around toward the sound. Now Lamont is in the middle of the street. He heaves another rock. This one ricochets off the rear window. The TinGrins spin around again. They're all in crouch positions, looking for a sniper. Now Lamont is on the entry step of the van. He leans in. What the hell is he *doing*?

Suddenly, I see the prisoners slip out the door of the van. They make a run for it— across the street and back into the park. There's no way the TinGrins will follow. They'll just grab Lamont.

But they don't. They totally ignore him. They sling their rifles back over their shoulders and go back to leaning against their vehicles.

Lamont walks back to where I'm hiding. He seems wrung out, but really proud of himself. "How about *that*?" he says. "A little justice at last!"

I pull him down low. I grab him by the shoulders and shake him.

"How could you be that stupid? How did you not get *shot*?"

Lamont looks puzzled.

"How could they shoot me?" he asked. "They couldn't *see* me."

"What do you mean, they couldn't see you?"

"I was invisible," he says. "I'm the Shadow, remember?"

"I know that now," I say. "But I could see you the whole time."

This brings Lamont up short. He wasn't expecting it. And I'm not sure he really believes it.

"You *saw* me?" he asks. "Even when I was invisible?"

"Yes! Every second! No question. You were never invisible. Not to me."

Lamont sits back on the grass. He blows out a long breath.

"Impossible!" he says. "There is no way that could happen."

"Sorry, Mr. Shadow. It just did."

This definitely adds a new wrinkle to our relationship.

CHAPTER 44

ONE A.M. JESSICA held Bando by the leash as they made their final trip around the block. Recently, Lamont had been taking doggy duty, but he and Maddy were still not home from their trip to the park, and Bando could not wait. Jessica didn't mind. These Bando walks were a good time to collect her thoughts. About Maddy. About Lamont. About everything.

The power to the neighborhood was out again—third time this week—so even the video screens were black. That was fine with Jessica. She'd heard enough of Gismonde's evening homilies for a lifetime. And she had no problem navigating the neighborhood in the dark. It had been her home for almost twenty years, since before Maddy was born. She knew every building, every shop, every vehicle.

So when she got close to her apartment steps, she realized instantly that the van on the corner had not been there on her last circuit. She pulled on Bando's leash, tugging him closer. She backed up and started to head down a side street, just in case.

She never made it.

The back of the van suddenly burst open. Ominous blue light illuminated the interior, silhouetting the helmeted figures moving in her direction. In an instant, they had her. She felt the leash being ripped from her hands as one of the police bent her right arm up behind her back.

"Bando!" Jessica shouted.

Another officer leaned in, the cold jaw plate of his helmet pressing against Jessica's ear.

"Shut your mouth," he commanded. "Do not resist."

Jessica heard Bando growling. When she looked down, she saw him circling the booted feet of the officers, nipping at their thick leather heels.

"Bando! Stop!" Jessica shouted. A thick glove covered her mouth. She struggled to break free, but each man outweighed her by at least a hundred pounds. It was like wrestling with bags of cement. She heard a thick thud and a whimper as a boot connected with Bando's rib cage. He cowered and ran off a few yards. As he circled back, she saw a gunshot explode the pavement just behind his rump.

"No!" shouted Jessica, her voice muffled by the glove. She was almost in the back of the van now, propelled forward, her feet barely touching the ground. There were two officers waiting to pull her in. Then she was on the floor. A gag was wrapped around her mouth. She heard loud laughs from the two men still outside the van.

Then two more shots.

CHAPTER 45

WHEN LAMONT AND Maddy returned from the park at two a.m., they paused in Lamont's usual spot across the street from the apartment. Lamont looked left and right. When the street looked clear, he tapped Maddy on the arm.

"Okay," he said. "Let's go."

As they started to move toward the building, Lamont heard a jangly sound from around the corner. He pulled Maddy back. Suddenly, Bando ran between his legs, his leash dragging behind him.

"Bando!" yelled Maddy. She bent down to rub his belly and felt something sticky in his fur. When she pulled her hand back, it was streaked with crimson.

"Lamont!" she cried out. Lamont gently lifted Bando off his feet and rolled him onto his side, revealing an angry-looking red stripe across his belly. Maddy screamed. "No!"

"Gunshot," said Lamont. "But just a graze."

Bando whimpered as Lamont pressed lightly along the length of the wound, feeling for fragments. All clean.

Maddy felt her stomach sink and her chest tighten.

"If he was out, Grandma was with him!" Maddy stood up and shouted, "Grandma!" Lamont pulled her down.

"Quiet!" he said. "We'll check out the direction he came from. Stay close to me."

Maddy picked Bando up in her arms, careful not to press his wound as she nuzzled his head. "Shhh, baby," she said. "We're going to fix you up. We just need to find Grandma first, okay?"

They peeked around the corner. Nothing moving. It didn't mean there was nobody there. They moved slowly across the street, peeking into every stairwell and doorway. At the curb, Lamont's foot kicked a small piece of metal in the street. He picked it up. A shell casing. He sniffed it. Recently fired.

There was a rustle from behind a row of garbage cans. Lamont pushed Maddy and Bando behind him. Slowly, a head popped up in silhouette over the metal containers.

"Don't shoot!" a voice said.

"No guns," said Lamont, holding his hands up. "Who are you?"

Slowly, a man emerged from behind the battered containers. He had sores on his face, fingerless gloves on his hands, and plastic sandals on his feet. As he approached, a wave of stench preceded him. Garbage, urine, maybe worse.

"Is the little guy okay?" he asked, angling his head to look at Bando.

"He got shot," said Maddy, holding Bando close.

"I know," said the man. "They did a little target practice on him. But he's quick, that one." He reached out to pat Bando's head. The stench was overpowering. Maddy pulled back. Lamont stepped in between them.

"Someone was with him," Lamont said. "A woman. Sixties. Small. Feisty."

"Yeah," said the man. "They got her."

Maddy rocked back. "They *shot* her?"

Lamont leaned down, right into the man's face. He could smell the decay wafting from his mouth.

"Did they?" asked Lamont slowly. "Did they shoot her?"

"The lady?" said the stinky eyewitness. "No. They wanted her alive."

CHAPTER 46

I'M HOLDING BANDO down on the kitchen table. Lamont is dabbing at the clotted blood on his belly.

"Why would they take her?" I ask Lamont. "Grandma is the most law-abiding citizen ever."

"They were looking for me," says Lamont. "The police, one night, they saw me with Bando. Maybe they made a connection. If they didn't kill her, it means they want her for leverage. I'm the one they want."

"We have to find her!" I say.

"First," says Lamont, "I need to get some answers."

"What answers?" I ask. "From who? Where?"

Lamont has been quiet since the incident in the park. I can see his brain working. And now he thinks he has an answer.

"We're going back where you found me," he says. "The warehouse. That's where it all started. I think Fletcher knows about Margo."

I can feel myself losing it. How am I supposed to care about some mystery woman I've never met when my grandmother just got dragged away?

"Lamont!" I yell. "They took Grandma! She needs to come first!"

"You don't understand," says Lamont. "It's all connected. Margo. Your grandmother. Me. You. Once we find Margo, we'll go find Jessica. I promise."

An hour later, Lamont is banging on the door of the warehouse. I can't believe I'm down here again. At four in the morning, the place is even creepier. The fires are still burning, but there's nothing moving but us.

"Open up, dammit!" Lamont is out of patience. He picks up a big rock and gets ready to heave it against the door. Then the door opens. Just a crack.

I can see Fletcher's frizzy head peeking out. He squints at Lamont, then at me.

"I'm impressed," says Fletcher. "He's still alive."

"I'm better than ever," says Lamont. "Let's talk."

"Look," says Fletcher. "I did what I was paid to do. I brought you back. You left. I'm done."

I step up and nudge Lamont aside.

"Dr. Fletcher," I say. "Open the door. Right now."

So he does. Lamont gives me an approving look.

"Well done," he says.

"I've been practicing," I say.

Once we're inside, Lamont goes into full exploration mode. His eyes are darting everywhere. I'm noticing things I missed the last time I was here. Like the scruffy little cot in the corner where Fletcher's been sleeping.

"Anybody else here?" Lamont asks.

"Just me," says Fletcher, scratching his head. "And by the way, it's four in the morning."

Lamont points down the dark corridor that leads off the main lab. "What's down there?" he asks.

"Storage," says Fletcher.

But when Lamont starts to move in that direction, Fletcher tries to block his way. Lamont has had enough. He points to Fletcher's battered chair.

"Go," says Lamont. "Sit."

Fletcher obeys.

Lamont feels for a light switch at the entrance of the hallway. A small ceiling bulb pops on. It casts about as much light as a match. But it's enough for us to see that the corridor branches off in two directions, left and right.

"You go that way," says Lamont, pointing down the left passage. "Be careful." He heads right.

After about ten yards, it looks like my route is pretty much a bust, just brick walls and a dusty wood floor. The light from behind me is almost running out. I keep my hand on the wall and look down toward the end of the corridor. I think I see a staircase.

"Maddy! Back here!" It's Lamont.

When I find him, he's standing in a little alcove with three doors leading off it. He's tried them all. All locked.

"Get Fletcher!" he says. "And tell him to bring his keys."

On my way back to the main lab, I have a better idea. I know Lamont is the professional detective here, but I decide to just cut to the chase.

Fletcher is slumped in his chair, his head in his hands. He looks up.

"What?" he says. He's tired. He's nervous. Maybe scared.

"Julian," I say. "Take me to the lady."

Fletcher gets up from his chair and walks to his desk. He pulls out a fat ring of keys. No cards or pass codes in this place. He looks like an old-time jailer.

When we get to the alcove, Lamont is still tugging on the door handles, one after the other. The doors are solid. They don't even budge.

"Open these doors!" Lamont shouts at Fletcher. "All of them!"

"We only need one," I say.

Fletcher walks to the center door. He inserts the key. Pushes the door open. A light inside pops on automatically. We're in a room identical to the one where I found Lamont. Same walls. Same floor. Same hatch.

Lamont is angry now.

"Is she here?" he shouts. Everything echoes.

Fletcher is silent, looking down at his feet.

"I said, is she here?"

I walk over to the hatch. I look at Fletcher.

"Open it," I tell him.

Fletcher reaches up and pulls down on the lever. The hatch door drops down. My heart is pounding. I look at Lamont. He's barely breathing. His hands are balled into fists.

Fletcher grabs the drawer handle and leans back. The drawer eases out.

In one glance, I know it's her. It's Margo Lane.

As pretty as her picture.

CHAPTER 47

LAMONT TOOK A deep breath. He leaned in over Margo's body. The last time he saw her face, she had looked so scared. Now she looked serene, like she did when she was sleeping. He brushed her hair with the back of his fingers. Lamont felt tears brimming in his eyes and a tightness in his throat. He shook it off. He looked at Fletcher.

"Let's get started," he said. "Bring her back."

"That's not possible," said Fletcher.

"What do you mean?" said Lamont. "You brought *me* back! Do what you did for me!"

"I'm sorry," said Fletcher. "I was told that

the lady was dead. The contract stated 'care in perpetuity.' I've never been in this room. I never even knew her name."

Maddy stepped forward. She pointed to the tubes and electrical wires.

"So why are the infusion lines still running? And the power?"

"I don't know," said Fletcher. "Look. I've never seen her before. She's been in here since before I was born. I only know what I was told—there's a lady back there. She's deceased. Just leave her."

"I don't believe it!" said Lamont. "*Look* at her! She can't be . . ."

Apart from the stains on the bow of her dress and some makeup smears, Margo looked like she was resting after a night at the ballet.

Maddy looked at Fletcher.

"Get everything ready," she said. Lamont looked defeated and destroyed. Maddy could see how much he loved this woman. How much he needed her. How much he wanted her to be alive.

Fletcher was back with his controller and

two bags of saline solution. He looked anxious. Beads of sweat were popping on his forehead.

"I'm telling you," he said. "This won't work."

Maddy tugged at Lamont, trying to nudge him out of the tiny room.

"Lamont," she said. "Wait outside. You don't want to see this."

Lamont didn't move. He looked at Fletcher.

"Do it," he said calmly.

Fletcher connected the controller to the table base, and then hung the bags of saline at the head of the table. He connected a syringe above the IV tube running into Margo's ankle.

Maddy pulled Lamont by the elbow.

"Stay back," she said. "He's going to give her a jolt."

Lamont moved back, but only a step. His eyes were locked on Margo's face. Fletcher looked at Maddy. Maddy nodded. Fletcher cranked the control dial.

Margo's body arched off the table and settled again. Lamont flinched, but didn't move. Fletcher set down his controller and pressed the plunger on the syringe.

"Saline going in," he said.

He waited a few seconds and then cranked the controller dial again. Margo's body vibrated on the table from head to toe. Fletcher cut the power and waited.

Nothing.

"I'm sorry," he said. "Like I told you, she's not really here anymore."

Lamont slumped back against the wall and slid to the floor. He covered his head with his hands and began to sob. Maddy knelt beside him, her hand on his shoulder. Fletcher unplugged the controller.

Maddy could feel Lamont's body heaving. Slowly, he regained his breath. He pressed back against the wall and struggled to his feet. He walked the few steps to the side of the table. He rested his palms over Margo's bare shoulders and lowered his face toward hers. Gently, very gently, he kissed her cheek.

Maddy took a deep breath. She felt a heaviness in her chest. Then she noticed something. Margo's left toe. It was twitching.

"Lamont!" Maddy shouted. "Do exactly what I tell you! Right now!"

Lamont looked up, stunned and confused.

"Do what?" he asked numbly.

"Breathe into her mouth!"

"What?" he said. "What are you talking about?"

Maddy brushed past Fletcher and moved to the head of the table. She reached over and gently pressed Margo's cheeks until her lips parted.

"Don't touch her!" said Lamont.

"Do it!" said Maddy. "Put your lips over hers, hold her nose, and push some air into her lungs!"

Lamont hesitated. Then he leaned forward. He gently pinched her nostrils. His closed his lips over Margo's lips. He exhaled slowly.

Margo's chest rose and fell. But that was just mechanics, not a sign of life.

"Again!" said Maddy. "Faster! More air!"

Lamont tipped Margo's chin up for a better angle. He pressed in and gave her two more quick, forceful breaths. He pulled back, waiting. Suddenly, Margo's eyes popped open. She blinked.

"Lamont!" she said with a scratchy voice.

"Margo!" Lamont said softly. He leaned in close to her, laughing and crying at the same time.

Fletcher dropped the controller. This was finally too much for him. He stepped around the perimeter of the room and backed out.

"Everything's okay," said Lamont. He hovered over Margo, gently stroking her hair. "Don't be afraid. I'll explain everything."

Lamont squeezed Margo's left hand, feeling the warmth return to her fingers. Her head was still resting on the foam support. She didn't have enough strength to lift it yet.

"Khan poisoned us," said Lamont. "At the restaurant. But I managed to get us here, to the lab. Fletcher was ready. The process worked. We're alive. It's unbelievable! We're both alive."

"How long since . . . ?" Margo asked.

"A long time," said Lamont softly. "A very long time."

"I don't remember anything," she said.

"You will," said Lamont. "Trust me. Things come back. Sometimes in pieces. But they come back."

Slowly, Margo lifted her head, Lamont put his arm under her shoulders to support her. She looked slowly around the room and saw Maddy standing against the wall across from the table. Margo squinted, trying to bring her into focus.

"Who's that?" she asked.

Lamont waved Maddy closer. She took a couple tentative steps toward the table and leaned her head forward.

"Margo," said Lamont, "this is Maddy. She's a friend."

Maddy moved another step closer and gave a small wave.

"Maddy," said Lamont. "Meet Margo Lane."

"I've heard a lot about you," said Maddy. "How do you feel? Can I get you anything?"

Margo gave her head a small shake as the color began to seep back into her cheeks. She sat up a bit and took a deep breath.

"How about a cocktail?"

CHAPTER 48

I DECIDE TO give Margo and Lamont a few minutes alone. I step out of the vault and wander back down the hall into the lab. Nobody there. Fletcher didn't just leave the room. He left the building. The front door is half open.

I walk slowly around the lab table. I pick up one of Fletcher's notebooks and start leafing through it. It's filled with page after page of calculations and diagrams in really bad handwriting. There's a small table with a coffee machine in one corner. In the opposite corner there's a file cabinet. Just like the one in Poole's office. Same vintage brand. Tempting.

I ruffle through the cords and papers on the table. I see a flash of metal.

The key ring! Fletcher must have dropped it when he came back to get the controller. I scoop up the ring and walk over to the cabinet. But I can tell right away that none of the keys is small enough to fit into the lock.

I find the next best thing—a paper clip. A nice thick one. I bend the clip open so that one end sticks out like a probe. I stick it into the lock and wiggle it back and forth, up and down. Then it snaps off.

"Dammit!"

I pat my pockets. I pull out a pencil stub, a few pennies, and then—a metal pin for my scooter! I always carry a spare in case a wheel comes loose. I use the end of the scooter pin to pry out the broken paper clip. Then I stick the pin into the lock and give it a twist.

I feel a little resistance, then a click. I hold the pin in place with one hand and give the file drawer a tug with the other. Success! The drawer rolls open. Inside, there are more notebooks and a stack of manila folders with handwritten labels: CONTRACTS. FORMULAS. DESIGN. SECURITY. Most of the files are all bent and frayed. But there's one that stands out. Like it hadn't been touched in a very long time. The label says PROCEDURES.

I pull the folder out. It's filled with with medical notes and anatomical diagrams, like a hospital chart. I flip through the pages. I recognize plans for the hatch and the slide-out table. There are lots of electrical symbols and weird chemical formulas. And here's the design for the controller. Pretty cool.

The last sheet in the folder catches my eye because it has the initials "M.L." at the top. It doesn't take a famous detective to guess whose initials they are. I look down the sheet. It's an intake form. "September 6, 1937. Female. Age mid-20s. Height 5'5". Weight 115 lbs. Comatose. Ingestion of toxin / unknown origin. +/- 1 hr."

I flip through to the last page, where I see a diagram of a female body in a black line drawing. There are notes all over it. Hard to read. I turn the page sideways to read what they're about.

Oh my God.

"Maddy!" Lamont's calling from the back room. "Where are you?"

I fold the paper, slide it into my pocket, and close the drawer.

"Coming!"

Take it slow, I'm thinking. Lamont is back. Now Margo is back. Count your blessings. That's two medical miracles in a row. And maybe the notes were wrong or mixed up. I should probably put what I just read out of my mind.

Because what it said is not possible.

CHAPTER 49

WHEN I GET back to the vault, Margo is standing. Not too steady, but at least she's on her feet. Lamont has one arm around her waist.

"My shoes," says Margo. "What happened to my shoes?"

"Sorry," Lamont replies. "Lost in the shuffle."

"The floor is so cold," says Margo.

Lamont sweeps her up into his arms.

"Better?" he says. Margo smiles warmly and nuzzles his neck.

"My hero," she says. She winks at me. "He really is."

"Yeah," I say. "He kind of grows on you."

"Lamont, I want to go home," says Margo,

flicking the stained black bow over her chest. "I need to get out of this filthy dress."

"Don't worry about that," says Lamont. "Maddy will find you something to wear."

Margo looks me up and down. I can only imagine what's going through her mind. The kind of dress she's wearing only exists in the rich sectors, and in old movies. Definitely not in my collection.

"Margo, we can't go back to your place right now," Lamont explains. He didn't have the heart to tell her that her stylish midtown apartment was probably occupied by squatters. "And Maddy's apartment is too dangerous."

"What about your mansion, Lamont? I have some clothes in the closet there."

Lamont looks at me.

"Lamont!" says Margo. "Don't tell me you've *sold* it!"

"Of course not," says Lamont. "It's just... not a good place for us at the moment. For right now, until you get stronger, we need to stay here."

"I found some stairs down the hallway,"

I say. "I'll see if there's any room on the second floor."

"Don't be long, dear," says Margo. "I have a terrible chill."

I head back out into the hallway and take the branch off to the side where I was exploring before. When I get to the stairs, I can see daylight coming down from above. The sun must be rising. Partway up, there's a landing with a dirty window. At the top of the stairs there's a metal door. I give it a shove. It doesn't move. I put my shoulder into it and it swings open. Suddenly, I'm looking at a warehouse floor the size of a soccer field. I could fit Grandma's apartment in here about ten times!

I can see a few walled-in spaces at the far end. Maybe storage rooms or offices. There's a row of windows running along one whole side. The windows must be facing east, because the morning sun is pouring in. The ceilings are about two stories high. I can hear birds fluttering around somewhere in the rafters.

This is one hell of a hideout. I think the Shadow will approve.

I run halfway back down the stairs and call out.

"Lamont! Margo! Come on up!"

I hear Lamont's footsteps on the stairs and then see him come around the corner. Margo is walking on her own now, still in her bare feet. At the top of the stairs, I pull open the door.

"Take a look!" I say.

Lamont and Margo step to the doorway and peek in.

"Excellent," says Lamont. "This will do."

"Lamont!" says Margo. "You *cannot* be serious!"

"It's just for a while," says Lamont, "until I figure some things out."

"Please," says Margo. "Figure it out quickly. I'm not a factory girl."

CHAPTER 50

RIKERS ISLAND WAS barely an island any-more. Tidal water now covered all but a few acres of the original prison compound, along with the narrow causeway. Most of the out-buildings and facilities had succumbed to rot and rust. But the cell blocks, designed in the 1920s, had been built to last. And where others saw ruin, World President Gismonde had seen opportunity. What ruler wouldn't want his own private penal colony?

Jessica's six-by-ten-foot cell had a bare tile floor, white cinder-block walls, a metal cot with a thin mattress, a steel toilet with a square sink above it, and a single barred window.

She was wearing a scratchy prison jump-suit. Bright yellow. Her own clothes were in a bin somewhere. Probably burned by now, she figured. Jessica had barely slept in the past twenty-four hours. By now, she had become attuned to every sound on her corridor. The clanging echo of metal doors. Long intervals of silence punctuated by sudden shouts and screams. Overnight, she'd heard a man singing loudly in what sounded like Russian. That ended around dawn. Now the only sound came from the boots of the guards as they patrolled slowly back and forth.

Then she heard something new. A low, growing murmur from the far end of the corridor, and the echo of footsteps moving with purpose—in her direction.

A jailer appeared at her cell. He shouted back down the corridor, "Open C-Thirteen!" Jessica's cell door rolled back with a hard clang. She stood up from her cot. A man in a somber black suit entered the cell, flanked by the jailer and a huge guard. Jessica recognized the man at once. Who wouldn't? But he still felt the need to announce himself.

"Mrs. Gomes," he said. "I'm Sonor Breece."

"I know who you are," said Jessica. "Why am I here? What do you want? When can I leave?"

"So many questions," said Breece, lifting his imposing nose into the air. "Perhaps you'll do me the courtesy of answering mine first."

"Well, if you're asking about the accommodations," said Jessica, "the mattress is uncomfortable, the toilet is backed up, and the view could be better."

"Do you take this for a joke, Mrs. Gomes?" Breece replied. "I assure you, it is not."

"Did I forget to clean up after my dog?" asked Jessica. "Because I think a simple fine would have been appropriate. Maybe just a warning."

The guard shifted nervously, adjusting the grip on his rifle.

"Or did I litter?" Jessica wouldn't quit. "Did I add another scrap of paper to your trash heap of a city?"

Breece held up a hand, his patience at an end.

"Lamont Cranston," he said evenly.

Jessica pursed her lips and tilted her head. Her heart began to thud in her chest.

"Odd name," she said.

"I agree," said Breece. "Quite old fashioned. Of another time."

"What's he have to do with me?"

"Exactly my question, Mrs. Gomes!" said Breece. "That's what we want to know. We know that Lamont Cranston is in the city. And we assume that he has been in contact with you."

"Why me?"

"Another excellent question," said Breece, leaning in. "Who are *you* to Lamont Cranston?"

Jessica folded her arms over her chest, afraid that her heartbeat would show through the jumpsuit.

"Old boyfriend?" she said. "Hard to know. There were so many."

Breece took another step forward, his lower jaw thrust out, eyes flashing, his face only inches from Jessica's.

"Listen to me, you bitch!" he said.

"I'm listening," said Jessica, not moving. She stared him right back. She concentrated.

Suddenly, Breece's knees buckled. He fell to the floor in a dead faint.

The jailer caught him just before his head hit the tile. The guard flipped his rifle up and put the green laser dot in the middle of Jessica's forehead.

"He'll be fine," said Jessica. "Probably just low blood sugar. Tell him we'll talk more when he's feeling up to it." She stepped forward so that the muzzle of the rifle pressed into her skin. "I'm sure he'd tell you that executing a valuable prisoner would put a big black mark in your file."

The guard lowered his rifle and helped to drag Breece out of the cell. He slammed his palm against a button to close the cell door behind them. Jessica heard a hubbub from down the hall as other guards scurried to help.

"Have a beautiful day," she called out.

When the noise receded, Jessica collapsed backward on the cot. She was exhausted and scared. Her heart was still pounding hard. But she was proud of herself too.

"Still got it," she said softly.

CHAPTER 51

"LAMONT! GET ME out of these rags!" shouted Margo. "I smell like mothballs."

Maddy had raided her grandmother's meager closet that morning when she'd gone back to retrieve Bando. She figured that Margo and Grandma were about the same size. But nothing in the selection came close to Margo's fashion standards. Not the housecoat. Not the pom-pom slippers. And definitely not the threadbare flannel nightshirt she was reluctantly wearing.

"Your dress is still drying!" Lamont called back. He had rinsed the delicate frock the best he could in the industrial sink. Now it was hanging from a crude clothesline strung between two massive wooden posts.

Seeing Margo in her grandmother's clothes gave Maddy a pang of guilt. As if she'd given up on finding Jessica again. Which she hadn't. But since finding Margo, she'd been helping make a new home out of nothing. And now it was too late to go out searching. Too late and too dangerous.

They had all settled into the warren of small rooms at one end of the vast upper floor. Lamont had pulled desks and chairs out of an office to clear a private space for himself and Margo. It was furnished only with a flashlight and a pile of thick packing blankets. Maddy had created a nook of her own against the wall on the opposite side of the floor under a clouded skylight.

Lamont headed for the door. "I'm going out for wood," he said.

The wood was for the massive factory stove that sat at the back of the warehouse space. Early in its life it had been fed with coal, but Lamont had discovered that it burned scrap lumber just as well.

After Lamont's footsteps receded down the stairs, Margo waved Maddy over to the corner where she was sitting. She sat down next to Margo, with Bando nestled between them. Maddy had told Margo all about her grandmother and how scared she was for her. And now it seemed like Margo was trying to take her mind off it a little bit.

"So. Maddy," Margo said. "Lamont tells me you're a woman of many talents."

Maddy shrugged. "Pretty good with scooters," she said. "Not so great with cars."

"So I heard," said Margo. "But I'm talking about *mental* skills. The power of the mind."

"You mean getting people to do what I tell them to do?" said Maddy. "Yeah, I've always had that. My little mojo."

"It's called mind control, darling. And it's nothing to sneeze at."

Maddy realized that other than Grandma, she'd never really had another woman to confide in, and Margo seemed eager to listen. Sharing felt nice.

Maddy moved a little closer.

"There's another weird thing about me," said Maddy, "and Lamont."

Margo tilted her head, curious. "Go on," she said.

Maddy cleared her throat, then paused. She felt awkward.

"Okay," she said. "When Lamont turns invisible..."

"Yes?" said Margo, leaning in. "I'm listening."

"Well," said Maddy, "I...I can see him the whole time."

Margo sat back. She tapped her chin.

"Now that *is* interesting," she said. "God knows *I* can't." She turned this new information over in her mind, then reached out to hold Maddy's hand.

"Have you ever tried it yourself?" she asked.

"What?" said Maddy.

"Invisibility."

Maddy scratched her head. "Uh...no. Never. Lamont's the Shadow, not me."

Margo stood up and pulled Maddy to her feet. She placed her hands on Maddy's shoulders.

"Stand straight," said Margo. "Get balanced."

Maddy rocked her hips and shifted her feet a few inches farther apart until she was in a solid stance.

"Now," said Margo. "All I know about this is that it has to come from inside you. You have to *will* it. You have to *feel* it. You have to *believe* it."

Maddy felt awkward, not really sure what was going on.

"Wait," she said. "You want *me* to try to turn invisible?"

"Why not?" said Margo.

"Right now?" replied Maddy nervously. This felt ridiculous.

"No time like the present," said Margo. "It's about accessing a part of your mind that you've never touched before. Maybe it's possible for you. Maybe it's not. But you won't know if you don't try."

"Okay," said Maddy. "Then I'll try."

She closed her eyes. She concentrated on disappearing. She *pictured* herself disappearing. She whispered the word "disappear" over and over. She felt her mind straining, like trying to remember a trig formula. She clamped her eyelids even tighter. She let out a slow breath.

"Well," she asked. "Am I gone? Am I invisible?"

Margo patted her on the shoulder. Maddy opened her eyes.

"Sorry, dear," said Margo. "You're still here."

They heard Lamont's shoes tromping up the staircase.

"The noble woodsman has returned!" Margo called out. Lamont walked in with a stack of flooring strips in his arms. He dumped them on top of the pile near the door and brushed the wood dust off his sleeves.

"What are you two up to?" he asked.

"Just girl talk," said Margo.

"I tried to turn invisible," said Maddy.

Lamont raised an eyebrow. "And...?"

"No go," said Maddy. "I guess I don't have the genes."

CHAPTER 52

IT'S SUPPERTIME. WE'RE eating macaroni soup out of coffee mugs and drinking water from tin cups.

"Lamont," says Margo. "This cannot go on!"

"Apologies," says Lamont. "Fletcher didn't leave a great assortment in the pantry."

"And no alcohol, I assume?" asks Margo.

"Only some methyl hydrate," says Lamont. "Intoxicating. But fatal."

The stove is crackling behind us and the sky outside the window is totally black. Bando is curled up beside me. Margo and Lamont are sitting next to each other on the other side of the crate. Margo's wearing her freshly cleaned party dress, and Lamont is wearing his tux jacket and white shirt. If it wasn't for the soup can and tin cups, they'd look like they were at a fancy party in the last century.

I've tried to imagine what their life must have been like back then. Nothing like this, I'm sure. Earlier, when I was heating up the soup, I heard them bickering about invisibility. Now they're at it again.

"I'm telling you, Lamont, it's mass hypnotism, pure and simple. You don't actually dematerialize. You just create the *illusion* that you're invisible. It's all in the mind of the beholder."

"The power to cloud men's minds?" says Lamont. He wiggles his fingers in front of his forehead. "Nonsense! That's just some bunk the radio writers made up because they had no other way to explain it."

"So what is it, really?" I ask. "How does it work?"

"Well," says Lamont. "There's technique, of course. Things that can be taught and practiced. But first you need the predisposition, like perfect pitch. 'Being attuned' is how the monks described it. *Zokhikh yos.*"

"Now, don't start throwing Mongolian at us, Lamont," said Margo.

"Look," said Lamont. "You can call it the spirit of the universe, you can call it black magic, one of the dark arts—call it whatever you want. But I assure you, it's physical. It's real. And it's been around for longer than you can imagine."

"Then explain something," says Margo. She nods toward me. "Why can Maddy see you when nobody else can? Not even me."

"You talked about that?" he asks.

"Among other things," says Margo.

Lamont looks at me.

"The truth is," he says, "I'm not sure yet. There's a lot about Maddy that I haven't figured out."

Margo gives me a little smile. "Don't worry," she says. "It took him a while to figure *me* out too."

"*Years!*" says Lamont, pretending to be serious.

"And worth every minute!" says Margo. She leans over and snuggles against him. He puts his arm around her shoulders. For a second, their cheeks touch. I swear I can see actual electricity in the air. I start blushing. Suddenly I feel like a total third wheel. I put down my mug of soup and get up from the so-called table.

"I think I'll take Bando out for a walk," I say. "Just down to the river."

Margo stretches her long arms out over her head and yawns. I mean, *pretends* to yawn. I can tell the difference.

"I might just turn in early," she says.

"Me, too," says Lamont. "I'm exhausted."

I snap my fingers. Bando gets up and follows me to the door. It just got a whole lot warmer in here. And not from the stove.

CHAPTER  53

THE SECOND MARGO heard Maddy close the latch, she moved her hand to Lamont's lapel and pulled him closer. She tilted her head and closed her eyes. Then she kissed him. Lightly at first, then slow and deep. He pressed against her, one hand cradling her head, his fingers laced through her fine blond hair. He could feel the warm breath from her nostrils on his cheek. She broke the kiss off slowly and opened her eyes. Deep blue against her ivory skin.

"I missed you," she whispered.

"Missed you, too," he replied.

Lamont pulled Margo close, one arm around her narrow waist. He leaned in to kiss her softly on the neck, moving up to a spot just below her ear.

Margo trembled.

"If you do that again," she said. "I'm going to need to lie down." He did it again. She intertwined her fingers with his and pulled him toward the abandoned office that was now their bedroom.

As they passed through the doorway, Lamont swept Margo up in his arms. Then he knelt gently and laid her down on the big pile of blankets in the corner.

Margo pulled Lamont's jacket off. "How long does it take to walk the dog?" she asked softly.

"Maybe he'll find a rat to chase," said Lamont. His hands went under the hem of her dress. She lifted her hips as he tugged it up. When it reached her waist, she leaned forward and pulled it over her head. It didn't take long from there. Just a few more snaps and clasps and straps, back and forth. His pants. Her slip. His briefs. Her bra. Margo pulled a loose blanket over her naked torso. Lamont gently slid it back off.

"My God," he said. "You are so beautiful."

"You are too," she said, lifting her lips to his. "Have I told you how much I love you?"

"Actually," said Lamont, "it's been a while."

"I can't *believe* how long it's been," she said. He kissed her shoulder and ran his palm down her body, following the curves. She was everything he remembered. Soft. Smooth. Warm. Perfect.

Margo pulled him close and pressed her lips against his ear.

"Lamont Cranston," she whispered, "don't you dare disappear on me."

CHAPTER 54

EARLY THE NEXT morning, Margo woke up to the smell of freshly brewed coffee. "That smells heavenly," she called out.

"Warehouse blend," replied Lamont from outside their alcove. "Only the best." For a second, she imagined that she was nestled in Lamont's four-poster bed on Fifth Avenue. Instead, she looked down to see that the quilted pattern on the packing blankets had left a matching impression on her thigh.

"Terrific," she muttered. "I look like a waffle."

Lamont poured a cup for himself and took a sip. Satisfied with the strength, he poured another for Margo, then added four and a half—not five—teaspoons of sugar, just the way she liked it. With a cup in each hand, he walked slowly back into the sleeping area. He handed the cup to Margo and settled beside her on the pile of wrinkled blankets. Margo cradled her cup in two hands, inhaled the steam, and took her first sip.

"Not heaven. But close," she said, tugging a cushion up to her neck. Then, lowering her cup, she said, "Lamont, darling, you know you can't keep me in this place forever. I'm not some princess in a tower. We need to find Maddy's grandmother. I can help. I'm a good detective, remember? But I need to get out of this warehouse and into the city. I know it's different. But I have to see it for myself."

She was right, of course. But, as always, Lamont's first instinct was to protect her. He didn't even want to *think* about losing her again.

"You can't believe how dangerous the city is," said Lamont. "The rich have gotten richer, and they all have their protected estates, but the rest of the city is in total chaos. Uncivilized. Evil everywhere."

"Is it really so different?" Margo asked. "We

dealt with some pretty evil things in our day, remember?"

Lamont *did* remember. He remembered ruthless crime lords, weapons dealers, mad scientists, and international spies. He and Margo had defeated them all. But all of them put together didn't come close to the evil that he knew was controlling the world right now. The same evil that came close to killing them both. He'd been revealing things to Margo in small doses, but now it was time to tell her the truth.

"There's something else you need to know," Lamont began.

Margo set her cup aside. "Don't tell me we're out of macaroni soup."

"Khan," continued Lamont. "He's here."

"*Khan?*" Margo tugged the cushion up to her neck again and shifted under the covers. Even with the warmth of the coffee, a chill shot through her. "I thought we outlived that bastard! I thought that was part of the plan—to wake up in a world without him. Better. Safer."

"I thought so too," said Lamont. "But

it's almost like he's been waiting for us to come back. And from what I've seen, he's more powerful than ever. He's got the whole damned world under his thumb. And people have no idea what he's capable of. *None!*"

They heard scratching on the floor, and then Bando hopped around the partition and into their space. He trotted over and crawled up onto Margo's covers until his head was nestled under her chin.

"Your replacement has arrived," said Margo.

"Maddy!" Lamont yelled. "Come retrieve your beast!"

"Lamont, it's fine," said Margo. "He just needs a little morning attention."

Margo and Bando had known each other for less than forty-eight hours, but they were already very close.

"Maddy!" Lamont shouted again. He walked across the wide-open floor to Maddy's alcove. Morning light was streaming in from the window and dust particles were dancing in the bright rays. He tapped on the partition that separated Maddy's sleeping space from the rest of the room.

"Hello?" he said. "Maddy? I think Bando needs to go out."

Lamont peeked around the corner of the partition. He saw a pile of blankets. Rumpled. Empty.

He walked briskly to the bathroom just behind Maddy's sleeping area. He knocked on the door.

"Maddy? You in there?" Nothing. The hairs on his neck stood up.

"Margo!" shouted Lamont. "She's not here!"

Margo peeked out of the bedroom in her slip. "Maybe she went for a walk."

"Then she should have told us!" he said, sounding like a grumpy parent.

Margo started scanning the loft for clues. She looked along the wall. The scooter was gone. As she passed the crate that served as their dining table, she noticed a scrap of yellowed stationery sitting on top.

"Lamont!" She held up the paper. "Look!"

Lamont grabbed the paper out of Margo's hands. It was Maddy's scrawl for sure. But with a very unexpected message.

"Good morning!" it said. "Went to school."

CHAPTER 55

"DID YOU GUYS miss me?"

It's my little joke. Or at least my attempt at one.

I'm in the school courtyard, talking to a bunch of kids who couldn't care less about whether I came back at all. So what? I can't keep my mouth shut any longer. If the government took my grandmother, they can take anyone. I have to speak up. If I had a picture of Grandma, I would have found a way to print up some Missing flyers. But maybe I can at least recruit some people to help me search.

But I'm not having much luck.

"We got cleaning detail because of you!"

said Lisa Crane. I can tell she's really pissed off, and so are the other kids. Obviously, my daring escape had not gone unnoticed. And I know the whole class sometimes gets punished for one kid's offense.

"Look, I'm sorry," I say. "But cleaning duty is the least of our problems. It's getting worse out there. More TinGrins. More roundups. It's only a matter of time before they come for everybody!"

"This is a school!" says Lisa. "We're safe here as long as we follow the rules—until somebody like *you* messes it up for everybody!"

"Open your eyes, Lisa!" I say. "This isn't a school. It's a holding pen! Someday you're going to wake up and realize that we should have done something while we had the chance!"

I've never been much of a speech maker, but I had to warn people. Even people who think I'm a loner weirdo delinquent.

Just then, I see a face in the doorway that leads to the courtyard. It's Renny Zale, the politician's daughter and permanent teacher's pet. The last person I wanted to run into.

Sure enough, two seconds later, there's a teacher in the doorway too. And she's pressing a button on her pendant.

Shit. This is not good.

I hear the pounding of boots from the hallways, heading this way. This time, they won't give me a second chance. They'll ship me off to a school where cleaning is pretty much the whole curriculum. Or they might just execute me on the spot, as an example.

Guards rush into the courtyard from all sides, like an invading army. The other kids scatter, but the guards don't even make a move to stop them. There's only one person here they're interested in, and that's me.

"Maddy Gomes!" I hear my name, but I can't really tell who's talking. The guards' voices come through speakers in their chest plates and the words echo around the courtyard walls. "You are under arrest for inciting insurrection!" They always make a show of announcing the charge. It's like a warning to everybody else. Inciting insurrection is no joke. It's a capital offense. Coming back here was a huge mistake.

The guards are closing in. I can hear their equipment rattling. I can see green laser sights pointed at me. My stomach is burning. I feel like I might throw up. Forget mind control. I can't even think. And there are too many guards to control anyway. I see Renny standing with the teacher in the doorway. She gives me a sick little "bye-bye" wave. It's like everything is moving in slow motion.

Concentrate, Maddy!

The rifles are almost touching my chest. I close my eyes. Ready to accept whatever happens. One of the guards reaches for me. Almost touching me.

And then I feel it. A rush in my head—like I'm falling, then floating.

The guards start spinning around like tops, pointing their guns every which way. I back away, but nobody's looking in my direction. I'm expecting somebody to grab me and throw me to the ground. But nobody does.

Then I realize why.

Omigod, it happened.

I'm *invisible*!

There's a light buzz in my brain, but my

thinking is clear. Clearer than ever. Even my vision seems sharper. This is crazy!

I pick up a stone and throw it against a window across the courtyard.

When the stone hits the glass, the rifles all turn in that direction. The Shadow strategy!

I can see my way out—right behind the column where Renny is hiding. She doesn't want to get shot by mistake.

I move across the courtyard on tiptoe, trying not to make any noise. Not that it would matter. Kids are screaming and the guards are shouting orders at one another. On my way out, I do one last thing. I can't resist.

I knock Renny Zale onto her skinny rich ass.

CHAPTER 56

AT THAT SAME moment, Margo Lane was getting her first taste of Manhattan in a hundred and fifty years.

"Don't say I didn't warn you," said Lamont.

As they wandered the streets beyond the warehouse, Margo was stunned by what she saw. It was worse than any slum her low-life clients had ever taken her to. Worse even than Lamont had described. But one thing bothered her more than anything else.

"Lamont," she kept saying, "the *smell!*"

From the warehouse, they had roamed west through the empty canyon of Wall Street and across Trinity Place to the new shoreline of the Hudson River. Margo remembered seeing the

Hudson from the window of her first apartment, watching as it turned from green to blue-green to gray in the sunset. Now the color was dirty brown, and it stank like a sewer.

Lamont kept his eye out for police and for anything that looked like a prison compound. Anyplace they might be holding Jessica. But it was a big city. He realized that she could be anywhere.

As they rounded a corner, they saw what looked like a group of kids playing soldier. But as they got closer, they realized it wasn't a game at all. The two tallest kids, maybe eighteen or nineteen, had three younger kids pinned against a wall. And the gun that one of the older kids was holding wasn't pretend. It was real. The other kid was wielding a bat. The smaller kids had been carrying food in cloth sacks, maybe old pillowcases. But now everything was scattered on the ground. Bread. Apples. Rice. The older kids wore masks—a rabbit and a fox. Their victims were bare-faced and terrified.

"See what I mean?" Lamont said. "In broad daylight!"

He nudged Margo into the entryway of an abandoned store.

"Wait here," he said.

He headed down the street toward the kids. Margo tried to grab him.

But it was no use.

"Lamont!" she said. "He has a gun!"

"Not for long," Lamont replied.

Margo backed into the doorway, just her head peeking out. As Lamont walked briskly down the street, she saw him suddenly disappear into thin air. Her heart was pounding fast, and a little thrill went through her whole body. She was terrified and excited. It had been a long time since she'd seen the Shadow in action.

"Oh, Mr. Bunny!"

The kid in the rabbit mask heard a mocking voice. He turned, but there was nobody there.

"Hippity hop!" said the voice. Now on the other side.

The rabbit spun around, pointing his gun in the direction of the sound.

Suddenly something knocked him backward. As he stumbled, the gun was ripped from his hands. Now it was floating in mid-air. The fox lowered his bat and watched, stunned. First the ammo magazine separated from the gun and flew into a water grate near the curb. Then the gun itself went spinning up onto a nearby roof.

The little kids were still pressed up against the wall, shaking. No clue what was happening. Then the smallest kid heard a man's voice, right next to his ear.

"Go!" the voice whispered. "Take your food and go!"

The kids scooped up their supplies and dashed around the corner. In seconds, they were out of sight.

The fox and the rabbit were now back to back, turning in a slow circle, looking high and low. The fox had his bat raised. But there was nothing to swing at.

"What the hell is going on?" he asked, his voice dry and cracking.

"Shut up!" said the rabbit. "Stay ready!"

Suddenly the fox felt his legs being swept from under him. He fell hard on his back and heard his bat clatter onto the side-walk.

"Shit!" said the rabbit. Now the bat was in the air, coming at them, waving in a menacing arc.

The fox scrambled to his feet and followed the rabbit at top speed down the street. Just as they reached the intersection, a four-man patrol of TinGrins rounded the corner.

From her hiding spot, Margo watched as the two teens yanked off their masks and pointed back down the street. She saw the officers stiffen and raise their rifles, moving slowly in her direction. The rabbit and the fox ran off, leaving the masks in the middle of the street.

Margo took a breath, composed herself, and stepped out of the doorway, having acquired a new accessory. She was now carrying a huge, orange-flecked tabby cat. When she reached the middle of the street, the four officers formed a cordon in front of her. She stopped.

"We had a disturbance report," said the lead officer. "Did you see anything?"

"Nothing at all," said Margo. "I'm just out for a stroll." She smiled and waved her hand as if shooing flies.

"Coming through, boys," she said, stroking the cat gently between the ears. The cordon parted.

"Have a beautiful day," the lead officer said.

Margo kept walking.

"Go suck a lemon," she said under her breath.

Margo turned the corner and exhaled slowly. She stooped and put the fat cat down on the pavement. When she stood back up, Lamont was standing beside her and the cat was gone. Margo was incredulous.

"Shape shifting?" she said, hands on her hips, eyes wide. "Where in God's name did *that* come from?"

"Not sure," said Lamont. "Maybe all that time while you were just resting, I was evolving some new skills." He took her by the arm as they walked down the empty street—toward the flooded plain that was once Battery Park.

"Any other animals in your repertoire?" Margo asked. "Or is it just the cat?"

"I thought you'd be more impressed," said Lamont.

"Lamont," said Margo, "you know I hate cats."

CHAPTER 57

LAMONT LED THE way through the alley between two warehouses as he and Margo headed back toward their makeshift abode. It was still the middle of the day. No sense in being out in the open this close to home. The path was a narrow obstacle course of puddles, trash, and broken bricks. At the end of the alley, the vista of the East River was framed like a picture—a picture of rot and desolation. A ghost barge floated past a half-submerged pier, where a few lonely souls hauled water out of the river with buckets. The water would need to be boiled, of course, and even then it would retain a tang of decay.

Suddenly they saw a figure streak across the frame like a missile.

Maddy!

Lamont and Margo hurried to the end of the alley just in time to see her hop off her scooter in front of the warehouse. She turned and saw them at the same time.

"Maddy!" yelled Lamont. "Are you all right?"

"Lamont! Margo!" Maddy called back. She hurried over, trembling with excitement.

"I have to tell you something!" she said. "There was this incident at school! But guess what? Guess *what*?" She didn't wait for a reply. "I did it! I went totally invisible! That's how I got out of trouble! It was *amazing*!"

"What kind of trouble?" asked Margo.

Maddy's words spilled out, rapid-fire.

"So I kind of snuck into school between periods without telling any of the teachers I was there, and I was trying to get kids to understand what we're up against. I told them about the TinGrins taking Grandma and all the other roundups around the city, but nobody was really listening. And then the guards came and I almost panicked but then I just..."

"Disappeared?" said Lamont.

"One hundred percent!" said Maddy. "I couldn't *believe* it!"

"Maddy," said Lamont. "You have to be more careful. You can't just go around the city spouting off and showing off your powers. It's dangerous."

"But you do it all the time," said Maddy.

"I'm experienced," said Lamont. "You're not."

Lamont's reaction stung. Maddy thought he'd be proud of her. She definitely didn't expect to be scolded. Margo saw the hurt in her eyes. She pulled Maddy close and put her arms around her.

"Are you sure you're okay?" she asked. "How do you feel? Any after-effects?"

"I feel fine," said Maddy, now subdued, her chin hooked over Margo's shoulder. Suddenly, Margo felt Maddy tighten and push away. Maddy was looking at something in the distance. Margo and Lamont turned to look too.

Coming down the row of warehouses, just

fifty yards away, was a squad of TinGrins. The officer in front held a small video device, and the others were doing a visual sweep of every doorway and alley. This was no random patrol. It was a search party. The bucket people returning from the river froze in their tracks. The TinGrins ignored them and walked by.

Margo stared at the officer with the video device. She looked at Lamont.

"They're coming for you," she said.

Maddy grabbed Lamont by the sleeve.

"Lamont!" said Maddy. "*Do* it! Just disappear!"

"No," said Margo firmly. "Everybody act normal. For once."

The TinGrins were only yards away now. The lead officer had obviously locked on to the three figures in front of him. He raised his compact video screen higher. It showed a grid pattern over a frozen image from a surveillance camera at the World President's Residence. Lamont's image. The officer waved the device over the three people in front of him. The scruffy teenager. The slender blonde. When he reached Lamont, the grid on the screen turned from gray to red.

"Match!" the officer called out. Behind him, a half-dozen rifles came up into shooting position. Margo linked arms with Maddy and Lamont.

"Everybody just hold still," she whispered. "And Lamont?"

"What?"

"No cats."

The lead officer stepped forward until his helmet was just a few feet from Lamont's face. "Lamont Cranston?" he asked. "Is that your name?"

Margo wedged herself between them and stared into the black visor. She couldn't see the officer's eyes, but it didn't matter. She was close enough.

"Lamont Cranston is not here," she said. "Your device is improperly calibrated. You need to keep looking. Farther uptown."

The officer turned and circled one hand in the air. The patrol did a slow about-face and began working their way back up the row of warehouses.

"Have a beautiful day," said the officer as he turned on his heel.

Lamont waited until the officer's back was to them.

"And you as well," he said, lifting his middle finger.

Margo put her arm around Maddy as they walked back toward the warehouse.

"I'd almost forgotten," said Margo, "mind control is a beautiful thing."

CHAPTER 58

TWO HOURS LATER, I'm getting my first full lesson in superpowers.

"Maddy, I need you to pay attention," Lamont is saying. "This is important. Life or death, actually."

There's a warm fire in the stove. Lamont and Margo are sitting in matching office chairs.

"This is great!" I say. "I always wanted to be homeschooled!"

"Be serious," said Lamont. "No fooling around."

I straighten up and focus.

"Sorry," I say. I can never resist making sarcastic comments in class.

But never in my wildest dreams had I ever imagined sitting in a class like this. I'm getting a lecture on invisibility, from the Shadow himself.

"The first thing you need to understand," says Lamont, "is that invisibility has a limited range of projection. For one thing, it can't project through metal. All that stuff about the Shadow running around with matching forty-five pistols was nonsense. I never even wore a belt buckle if I could help it. Invisibility will project through clothes, as long as they're not too baggy. Too much loose fabric can be a problem if it moves outside the field."

"Lamont usually wore a tux," said Margo. "Ivory or Bakelite buttons. No zipper. Custom tailored."

"So what about all those pictures of the Shadow with a cape and scarf?" I ask.

"Ridiculous," says Lamont. "Way too much fabric. That's all some artist's crazy imagination."

"Speaking of too much fabric," says Margo, looking at me. "Do you have anything in your wardrobe that's a little more...form-fitting?"

"Form-fitting?" I ask.

"Tighter. Closer to your body. Less like a feed sack."

I tug on my shirt. It is a little baggy. That's the way I like it.

"I don't know," I say. "Bike shorts, maybe?"

"Bike shorts?" says Margo. "You mean bloomers?"

"What the hell are bloomers?"

"Never mind," says Lamont. "Margo's right. Why don't you go see what else you've got. It might make things easier."

"Okay, okay, I'll go look." I go back into my sleeping space. I've got a bag full of clothes that I brought back from the apartment. I dump everything onto the floor and start sorting through the options. Almost every-thing here is loose and baggy, the way I like it. Except maybe for the bike shorts. And one T-shirt. I do a quick change and walk back into the main room. But I'm walking funny. The shorts pinch me in all the wrong places, and the T-shirt is about two sizes too small. I feel like a sausage. This is a fashion disaster.

"Well, my dear!" says Margo, "Don't you look *nice*!"

"I *hate* this!" I shout. "Nobody saw my clothes when I disappeared at school!"

"You don't know what people saw or didn't see," says Lamont. "Sometimes in the confusion, you can get away with things. But you need to be careful, especially when you're starting out. Stick to the rules. No mistakes."

"I remember once," Margo says, "Lamont had to disappear while he was wearing a terrycloth robe. I could still see the loose end of his little belt flopping around in midair."

"Ugggh!" This is totally humiliating! Maybe I should just stick to mind control. I just want to be gone. Then I feel it—the rush in my head, the rise in my belly, the clarity in my mind.

Then—guess what?—I disappear.

CHAPTER 59

CREIGHTON POOLE HAD absolutely nothing to do. Sometimes he wondered why he even showed up in the office. Force of habit, no doubt. And the need to keep some filament of his faded career glowing. There was also the possibility that the phone would ring with a call that would move him into some government ministry, where he might have a flicker of power, or at least a way back up the ladder.

The last thing he expected on a quiet Thursday was a buzz on his intercom. He instinctively turned to call out to his assistant, then remembered that he no longer had one. He pressed the button on his desk console.

"Creighton Poole," he said. "Who's there?"

"Mr. Poole!" A familiar voice came through the speaker. "It's me. Maddy. Maddy Gomes." Poole pressed the button again, this time with annoyance.

"What do you want?" he asked. His last meeting with Maddy Gomes had not exactly gone according to plan. This girl was wily— not to mention some kind of sorceress.

"We need to talk," said Maddy.

"About what?" asked Poole.

"I have an assignment for you," said Maddy. "I have money."

The magic word. Poole pressed the buzzer.

Still no elevator. While waiting for guests to walk up thirty flights, Poole usually lit a cigar. The little ritual relaxed him. But this time, he wanted to keep his edge. Whatever this crafty brat wanted this time, he would play hardball. No tricks. In the meantime, he paced.

A few minutes later, he heard a knock on the outer office door. He opened it a crack. And there she was. Same attitude. New wardrobe.

"No skateboard today?" he asked.

"Scooter," she corrected him. "The sun was so warm, I decided to walk."

Poole opened the door wider for Maddy. Suddenly, two other people—a man and a woman—stepped in from the sides. Before Poole could react, all three were standing in his outer office.

Poole looked perplexed. He looked to Maddy for answers.

"I'm sorry . . ." he stammered. "Who are . . . ?"

"Mr. Poole," said Maddy, "this is Lamont Cranston."

"My pleasure," said Lamont, extending his hand. Poole shook it gingerly and squinted at Lamont's face.

"Dear God," said Poole.

"You look surprised, Mr. Poole," said Margo, holding out her hand as well. "Margo Lane."

"Margo Lane?" said Poole, taking her hand limply. Now his mind was reeling. "But you're . . ."

"I know," said Margo. "Dead."

"Check out this view!" said Maddy. She

was already in Poole's inner office, standing at his wall of windows. Margo brushed past Poole to join her.

"You have a balcony!" said Margo. She reached for the door handle.

"Don't open that!" said Poole. "You'll let the smoke in."

Margo opened it anyway. She stepped out onto the narrow platform, put her arms on the railing, and took a deep breath. Poole retreated to the safe space behind his desk and loosened his tie, feeling flushed and nervous.

"What...what do you want?" he asked. "Maddy said something about an assignment?" He cleared his throat. "And money?"

Lamont leaned over Poole's desk.

"The assignment is very simple," he said. "Produce every document in your possession that concerns Maddy and Jessica Gomes. And there is no money."

"Sorry," said Maddy. "I lied a little."

Poole looked down. He felt the tingle of sweat in his armpits.

"We want to know about Maddy's history,"

said Lamont. "Her parents. How she and I are connected."

"Every juicy detail," said Margo, peeking in from the balcony.

"I'll bet it's all in there," said Maddy. She pointed to a metal file cabinet in a corner of the office. Poole looked over at the cabinet and gave it a dismissive wave.

"That's just old firm business," said Poole. "Ancient history at this point. I wouldn't even know where to find the key!"

"That's a real shame," said Margo. She was now closer, leaning over the desk. Poole looked around. Suddenly, he and Margo were the only two people in the room.

"Wait!" he said, looking wildly from side to side. "Where did...?"

He felt himself being lifted by both arms, and dragged toward the open balcony door.

"No! Stop!" he said, looking desperately at Margo. "What's happening?"

"It's called persuasion, Mr. Poole."

Poole flailed, his body jerking around so that his back was to the railing.

Suddenly he felt pressure behind his knees

and then a solid lift. A second later, he was hanging backward over the balcony, upside down, tie flapping in the wind.

He screamed—loud enough to make people thirty stories down look up.

"Maddy's records?" It was Lamont's voice. But it was coming from thin air.

"Sweet Jesus!" screamed Poole. "Don't drop me!"

"My records?" Now it was Maddy's voice, from the other side. Poole's eyes rolled back and caught a blur of buildings, streets, and barrel fires four hundred feet down.

"Yes!" he whimpered. "*Yes!* Put me down!"

He felt a strong hand hook around the front of his belt. With one powerful pull, he was upright again, feet on the balcony, face nearly purple. He felt lucky that he was wearing a dark suit. It concealed that he had slightly peed himself.

CHAPTER  60

POOLE SLUMPED BACK into one of his leather guest chairs, trembling. His face was returning to its usual doughy pallor, but sweat still beaded his forehead. He reached for his pocket square and dabbed at the droplets. He was panting, trying to catch his breath.

In front of him stood Lamont and Maddy, fully visible again. Margo was leaning against the desk, her arms folded. Poole's head swiveled from Lamont to Maddy and back again.

"How did you...?" he said, his voice thin and reedy. "I didn't see..."

"Ever hear of the Shadow?" asked Maddy.

Poole looked confused.

"The Shadow?" he repeated. "Is that...a magic trick? Some kind of illusion? Is *that* what just happened? Was I really just sitting here the whole time?"

"The Shadow was a crimefighter," said Maddy. "He fought evil in the city back in the 1930s."

Poole spun through his mental trivia bank. Crime-fighter. Evil. Big City.

"You mean like...*Batman*?" he asked.

Lamont looked puzzled.

"Who's Batman?"

"Batman," repeated Poole, digging deep into cultural memory. "I think he had some kind of double identity. A rich playboy. He had a mansion. And he came out at night to fight bad guys. Like a bat."

"Goddamned copycat!" said Lamont.

"Not nearly as mysterious as the Shadow," said Maddy.

"Thank you," said Lamont.

Poole wasn't following any of this. What were these two nutcases talking about? Who cared about a couple of made-up super-heroes from the last century?

"Batman was a comic-book character," said Poole. "Not an actual person. He wasn't ... he wasn't *real*."

"Well, the Shadow was," said Lamont. He leaned in close to Poole's face. "The Shadow *is*."

"Oh," said Poole, pressing back into his chair. "I see." He decided it was best to play along. He looked at Lamont. He blinked nervously. "You mean ... *you're* the Shadow?"

"Correct," said Lamont.

Early in his law practice, Poole had deposed a number of defendants with mental issues. He had learned that the best thing was to remain calm and humor their delusions.

"Well," said Poole, sticking his sweaty pocket square back in his pocket, "that must be fascinating."

"The files?" asked Maddy. "That's why we're here."

"As I told you," said Poole, "I have no idea what's in that cabinet. It came with the office. I don't have any clue where the key might be."

"Well then," said Margo. "Why don't we

look?" She moved around to the back of Poole's desk and opened one drawer after another, peeking in, running her hands through the contents. She pulled out the wide top drawer and dumped everything onto the desktop—pens, cigars, paper scraps, pencil shavings, business cards. But no key.

"That cabinet hasn't been opened in decades," said Poole. "If I had a hammer and screwdriver, maybe we could…"

"Hold on," said Maddy. "I almost forgot." She reached into her pocket and pulled out her scooter pin. She walked over and inserted the pin into the cabinet. She gave it an expert twist. There was a metallic clunk as the drawers released. Margo gave Maddy an admiring look.

"You're a safecracker?"

Maddy slipped the pin back in her pocket.

"Working on it," she said.

"Hey!" said Poole, starting to rise from his chair. "Whatever's in there is privileged information. Confidential files. Private property."

Margo looked at Lamont.

"Maybe Mr. Poole needs a little more air?" she said.

"Never mind," said Poole, slumping back into the chair. "Help yourself."

Lamont joined Maddy and Margo at the open file drawer. It had the musty smell of old paper. They started thumbing through the thick sections of manila folders. Halfway to the back, Maddy's finger stopped at a folder with a single word on the label: "Gomes."

"Jackpot," she said.

Maddy opened the Gomes file on the desk and spread out the contents—some loose papers, some stapled together. The various headings were all very official-looking: "Power of Attorney," "Irrevocable Trust," "Legal Guardianship." But there was one thing all the documents had in common.

Every line of legal text had been completely blacked out.

CHAPTER 61

"LAMONT, THIS IS the last place in the universe we should be right now," said Maddy, her voice muffled slightly by the panda mask. After the unproductive visit to Poole's office that morning, Lamont had come up with another angle.

"Do you want to find your grandmother?" asked Lamont from behind the raccoon mask.

"Obviously I do," said Maddy.

"Then we need to know what's going on here," said Lamont. "We need to find out where they're holding people. For all we know, your grandmother could be here."

They were standing across the street from

the World President's Residence, though Lamont insisted on calling it "my place." From
their position, they could see the whole rear
of the house and the small balcony overlook-
ing the back garden, although the garden
itself was hidden behind a cement wall.

It was a warm night, and the neighborhood
was crowded. There were the usual curious
onlookers, a constant stream of official vehicles, and the usual heavy presence of TinGrin
patrols and residential guards. Lamont had
built his mansion to be secure. Now it was a
fortress. And the rear gate was closed.

But not for long.

"There!" said Lamont. He pointed to an
arriving van with an official emblem on the
side. "Let's go!" he said.

They moved quickly to a spot just across
from the gate where the truck was idling. The
driver was having a routine exchange with
a gate guard. ID scan. Manifest check. All
the while, the gate stayed open. Lamont and
Maddy ducked back into an angle formed
by intersecting hedgerows. A blind spot for
security cameras, Lamont had calculated.

"Remember what we talked about," he said, pulling off his mask.

"Stay focused. Stay calm. Don't stretch it," recited Maddy. Her mask yanked at her hair as she slid it off.

"Fifteen minutes, tops," said Lamont. "Anything beyond that is too risky. Ready?"

"Ready," Maddy answered.

They disappeared.

As the gate slid open, two young boys wandered past the small shelter where Maddy and Lamont had been standing. A raccoon mask and a panda mask lay on the ground. The boys scooped them up and ran off down the street.

One thing Maddy had learned about invisibility was the need to adjust her body movements to stay as quiet as possible. She was used to clomping around in heavy boots, but now she wore a pair of supple running shoes. She had learned to watch where she walked, to avoid puddles and dust that would show her footsteps. It wasn't enough for her body and clothes to disappear; she had to remove all signs that she even existed. Part art. Part science.

And then there was the problem of staying out of Lamont's way. When they were both invisible, she could see him but he could not see her. After having her toes stepped on a few times, she learned to synchronize her movements with his, even in close quarters.

But of course, to the guards, the van driver, and everybody else bustling around the mansion, they were both as invisible as air. Lamont and Maddy followed the van through the gates.

"Follow me!" Lamont whispered. He led the way to a set of stone stairs leading down from the parking area—toward the secret entrance he had used hundreds of times.

Back at the warehouse, Lamont had explained it all to Maddy, drawing elaborate diagrams on East River Storage stationery. He had designed the system himself and he was immensely proud of the whole setup: The button hidden beneath the crown of the entryway lamp. The secret door disguised as a stone wall. The complex assembly of gears, cables, and levers that made everything work seamlessly and silently.

"What makes you think any of that stuff is still there?" Maddy had asked. "It's been over a century! We might as well be breaking into King Tut's tomb!"

"Please," said Lamont, insulted. "You don't know anything about quality workmanship!"

The van was backed up near the rear wall of the mansion. Kitchen workers in white uniforms pulled crates and bins from the cargo area as the guards paced nearby.

Maddy was surprised that the antique carriage lamp was still there, mounted on the granite wall to the right of the door. Lamont reached for the top of the lamp, its copper plating now covered with green corrosion. His fingers clamped around the ornamental tip. He tried to turn it, but it was stuck shut. Maddy rolled her invisible eyes.

Lamont picked up a loose rock from the entryway. He held it about six inches from the lamp, ready to give it a solid tap. He looked over as the workers took the last of the supplies from the back of the van. The driver came around and put his palms against the doors. At the exact second he slammed the doors shut, Lamont whacked the stone against the crown of the lamp. The whole top of the lamp flew off, sending an ivory button flying, along with a few screws and a small bunch of brittle wires.

"Any other ideas?" whispered Maddy, her back pressed against the cold stone wall. Suddenly, she felt movement. She turned around. The secret door was opening! Unbelievable.

Shadow's luck.

CHAPTER 62

AND...WE'RE IN! Creeping through the basement. The ceiling is low and the whole place smells like wet dirt. Lamont leads the way, obviously. He knows this place from top to bottom. The basement has passages that lead off in every direction. Here and there, I see signs with old-fashioned lettering—STORAGE, UTILITIES, PUMP, TOOL ROOM. I can picture Lamont designing them himself.

At the end of the corridor is a set of wooden stairs. Lamont waves me forward. Am I still invisible? The only way I can tell is the feeling in my brain. It's like a low-level hum. My personal generator.

When we reach the door to the first floor, Lamont slowly nudges it open. We peek out. The hallway is buzzing with ministers and assistants scurrying back and forth. Even from the little sliver I can see, this place is amazing. The floors are so polished, they glow. The chandeliers look like they're made from icicles. It looks more like a castle than somebody's home.

We wait until the hall is almost empty, then slip into the hall and close the door behind us. My heart is beating fast. I'm still adjusting to the idea that even though I can see Lamont, nobody else can. People coming down the hall look right through him. And me. So weird.

Right away, we can see that the center of activity is a room down the hall.

A bunch of men in suits are huddled together near the doorway. More servants in white uniforms are wheeling in carts of wine.

"This way," whispers Lamont. "The dining room."

I follow close, but not too close. I don't

want to step on his heels. When somebody approaches on our side, we press ourselves against the wall and suck everything in to make ourselves as thin as possible. *So far, so good.*

Now we're at the entry to the dining hall. Inside, through a huge wooden arch, I can see a long wooden table with chairs set all around it. I can hear people talking in a bunch of different languages. Lamont slips into the dining room, staying close to the wall. I follow his route exactly. The center of the table is filled with the kind of food I've only seen in pictures. Enough to feed my neighborhood for a month, with plenty left over. Platters of seafood. Baskets of fruit. Huge piles of bread.

Lamont leads the way to a winding staircase at the back of the room, up to a small balcony that overlooks the table. I'm tempted to reach out and swing from a chandelier, but that would be a dead giveaway. *Stay focused. Stay calm. Don't stretch it.*

Now all the people from the hallway are streaming into the dining room. About twenty people or so, mostly men, just two or three women. I can't understand what anybody is saying. They're all talking at once and I can only pick out a few words.

Suddenly, the buzz in the room goes quiet. A man in a dark suit walks in.

Holy crap! It's Sonor Breece! He moves toward the head of the table and takes the first seat on the right—the second most important seat in the room.

A few seconds later, the host arrives.

I've only seen his face on posters and video screens. He's taller than I expected, and— I hate to say it—better-looking. As soon as he walks in, everybody stands at attention and lowers their eyes. He looks around the table slowly, like he's counting heads. Nobody says a word. Nobody moves a muscle. Total silence. Total fear.

"That's him!" I whisper to Lamont. "That's Nal Gismonde!"

"No," he says. "That's Shiwan Khan."

CHAPTER 63

GISMONDE STOOD COMPLETELY still and let the room absorb his presence. He understood that silence was often the ultimate power play. It made the ministers around the table feel anxious, uncomfortable, off-balance—exactly how he wanted them. At the point where it felt natural to speak, Gismonde held back and let the silence hang a bit longer. He looked from face to face, causing little stings of worry as he went, making each attendee think about possible offenses—a political indiscretion, an unfulfilled promise, a careless alliance.

At Gismonde's first sentence—a soft, simple "I am honored by your presence"—the whole room eased a little. "Please, sit," he continued. The ministers quickly lowered themselves and pulled their chairs up to the table. They sat like attentive schoolchildren, hands on their laps or clasped tightly on the edge of the table.

Gismonde had no need for notes. His message was simple, his thoughts clear and well organized. He spoke slowly and deliberately, letting each phrase sink in before moving on to the next. A total master.

"My friends, I think we can agree that our problem—our *collective* problem—is intensifying around the world. You need only to look outside these very walls for the evidence. The breeding rate has not decreased, in spite of severe austerity measures. Or perhaps *because* of them. After all, what else is left for these people to do?"

Gismonde's lifted eyebrow telegraphed his little witticism, and Breece's smile gave the others permission to titter. But not too much.

"As the masses grow," Gismonde continued, "so does the threat. Tonight, we sit in privilege, as did the Qin dynasty, the

French Court, the Russian czars. Unassailable. Or so they thought. Until—one after the other—they awoke to the sound of the rabble at their gates."

Watching from the balcony, Maddy felt the heat rising in her invisible cheeks. Her hands gripped the balcony rail tighter. *Pompous bastard!* she thought. She looked over at Lamont. His eyes were locked on Gismonde.

The world president's voice was smooth and evenly modulated. But now it began to build in urgency, even as he lowered his volume. An effective technique. The ministers around the table leaned in.

"Tonight," he said, "the people who contribute to the progress of the world must find the strength to move against those who add *nothing*. If we do not act soon, we may not have time to act at all. Those of us in this room must decide—and the moment has come. We have the method. Do we have the nerve?"

Silent nods of support all around the table.

"What's he talking about?" whispered Maddy.

"Murder," Lamont whispered back. "Mass murder."

Maddy had a long history of problems with authority figures. But until now, she had never been face-to-face with pure evil. It radiated like palpable, dark energy from Gismonde's smooth, attractive face. As Maddy listened, her anger escalated. Her grip on the balcony rail tightened and her whole body stiffened. She felt herself losing focus. She wanted to yell something, throw something, *do* something!

"Mr. Breece," Gismonde continued, "will now discuss the particulars of the..." He stopped in midsentence and looked up at the balcony. Where there had been only empty space, he now saw a flicker. The faint outline of a female figure. Gismonde turned toward the hall, his voice now loud and commanding.

"Guards!"

CHAPTER 64

A SECOND LATER, two heavily armed men were in the doorway.

Lamont knew that he and Maddy were in big trouble. He'd known it the instant he saw her begin to flicker back to visibility. They had already been invisible for nearly twenty minutes—longer than any of Maddy's practice sessions, and longer than any of his own short bursts since being revived. In his prime, he could stay unseen for hours at a time. But his powers were eroded. He had lectured Maddy about being cautious, and he had broken his own rule. Before he could think or do anything about it, he turned visible too.

As two massive guards charged up the staircase toward them, Lamont pulled Maddy to the opposite side of the balcony. He vaulted over the edge, dangling from the railing before dropping the extra six feet to the floor. Maddy was right behind him.

"They can see us!" said Maddy. "*Both* of us!"

"Looks that way," said Lamont. "Move!"

Lamont pushed against a panel in the rear dining room wall. It swung open into the huge main kitchen, where white-uniformed cooks huddled over steaming pots. The cooks looked up, wide-eyed, as Lamont and Maddy raced past.

"C'mon!" said Lamont, glancing over his shoulder as the two guards burst through the kitchen door. He pulled Maddy through a back exit into a service corridor—a maze-like passage where butlers and servers could move unseen behind the walls of the mansion.

"There's a staircase ahead!" said Lamont. Maddy followed at a dead run. They ducked down a short passage that ended abruptly in a thick plaster wall.

"Dammit," said Lamont. "They remodeled!"

They could hear the guards approaching the last turn behind them. They huddled in the short hallway as the guards rushed past. Lamont looked up. There was a metal hatch in the wall, about three feet off the floor.

"The dumbwaiter!" said Lamont.

"The what?" said Maddy.

Lamont yanked open the door to reveal a stainless steel compartment, about the size of a large suitcase.

"Get in!" he whispered.

"You're kidding," said Maddy.

"Now!" said Lamont.

Maddy folded herself into the tight cabinet, her knees bent up against her chin. Lamont closed the hatch and pressed a button on the wall. When he heard the motor and cables begin to whine, he stepped out carefully into the main corridor.

When the tiny lift lurched to a stop on the second floor, Maddy shoved the door open and tumbled out into a small alcove barely big enough for a serving cart. Lamont was already there. The relocated service stairs had led him to the same spot. He kicked at a corner of the baseboard in the alcove. A section of the wall spun open. Maddy's eyes popped.

"Who was your architect?" she asked. "Houdini?"

Lamont pushed her through the opening into the next room. The false wall spun closed behind them. They heard guards passing by in the hallway outside, but nothing behind them.

Lamont was breathing hard. Running from villains had never been his forte. He always preferred to use his wits and his powers of deception. But now he felt drained—and guilty. He had pulled Maddy into another bad situation that could get them both killed. She needed more practice. And obviously so did he.

"Where the hell are we?" asked Maddy.

The room was huge, with floor-to-ceiling windows and a lush Oriental carpet. At the far end was a massive four-poster bed. Seeing it gave Lamont a jolt. The last time he saw that bed, he and Margo were lying in it.

"It's my bedroom," said Lamont. "Or *was*."

A small table near the marble fireplace held a tray with a wedge of cheese, a tin of olives, and a split of champagne. Maddy grabbed a small bag from a dresser top and started filling it with the fancy provisions.

"What are you doing?" whispered Lamont.

"Habit," said Maddy. "I see food, I take it."

Lamont moved quietly to the long side of the room opposite the windows. It was lined with wide closet doors. He opened the first door to reveal a row of expensive suits. The style was too European for his taste, but he knew exquisite tailoring when he saw it. The floor of the closet was lined with equally elegant shoes. At the far end of the hanging rod, past the suits, Lamont caught a flash of color. He shoved the row of suits aside to expose an impossibly beautiful robe. Not the kind you'd wear to the bathroom. The kind you'd wear to rule an empire. The collar was ermine, and the clasps were pure gold.

The noise from the hallway got louder. Suddenly, the main door to the bedroom burst open, slamming back against the wall as a squad of huge guards rushed through. Once again, Maddy was staring at the green beams of laser sights. But this time the men holding the weapons were not everyday TinGrins. They were elite palace guards. The best and the biggest. Well trained and terrifying.

Lamont moved quickly to the center of the room. He pulled Maddy behind him so that the laser beams danced across his chest instead of hers. He'd been in tight spots before. He'd faced down plenty of evildoers with guns. It came with the job. But now he had somebody else to protect—somebody who'd never planned on this kind of life, or this kind of danger.

And at the moment, he was fresh out of secret powers.

CHAPTER 65

THE GUARDS ADVANCED into the room, sweeping it high and low with their rifle barrels. But two rifles stayed trained on Lamont and Maddy.

"On your knees! Now!" one of the guards commanded.

Lamont turned to Maddy. For the first time since he'd known her, he saw fear in her eyes. All her bravado was gone, and she looked like exactly what she was—a teenager who was in way over her head. His fault.

"Maddy," he said softly. "Do exactly what they say."

She slowly crouched down until her knees touched the carpet. Lamont knelt beside her.

As the two lead guards moved forward, one pulled a small device from his belt. He held it up in front of the captives, waving it close to Lamont's face.

"We've got him," he called out to the rest of the squad. "We've got Cranston."

Now all the guards moved in to surround them. One of the guards wrapped a set of plastic ties around Lamont's wrists and pulled them tight. So tight that they bit into his flesh. Then two guards grabbed him under the arms and started dragging him toward the doorway. Two other guards kept their rifles on Maddy.

"What about the girl?" asked one, the green dot of his sight on the back of Maddy's head.

"She's all yours," said the guard in charge. "Then dispose of her."

The two guards dropped their rifles onto the carpet. One grabbed Maddy around her rib cage. The other slid his arms under her knees. Maddy arched her back and twisted furiously.

"Don't touch me, you goddamn robots!" she shouted.

Maddy thrashed with every fiber of strength in her body, but the men were too much for her. Solid muscle, surrounded by solid armor. They tightened their grip and started carrying her toward the bed.

"Lamont!" Maddy cried out.

Lamont was at the doorway now, pressed between his two handlers. He kicked against the door jamb.

"Stop!" he shouted. "Leave her alone!"

The guards threw Maddy roughly onto the bed and climbed on top of her. One pinned her arms over her head while the other swung his legs over hers.

"Get off me!" screamed Maddy. "I'll kill you!"

The guards pulled Lamont halfway into the hallway as he struggled against them. He twisted his head to look back.

"Maddy!" he shouted.

"Wait!" said one of the guards, grabbing Lamont roughly by the shoulders and pinning him against the doorframe. "Maybe we should let him watch."

"Leave her alone!" Lamont shouted into

the guard's visor. "I'm the one you want! Not her! Let her go!"

Maddy felt a gloved hand hook under the waistband of her shorts. She screamed again. No words. Just sounds, muffled by the thick glove over her mouth.

Lamont leaned his head back and screamed too—something wild and primal, from a place so deep inside him he didn't know it even existed. He strained at the plastic ties. He bent his head and went silent, as if giving in. For a few seconds, it was as if time stood still. He felt warmth in his hands, then heat. The plastic cuffs started to bubble and melt, forming red welts around his wrists.

Maddy rolled her torso furiously from side to side and strained to pull her arms free.

"Hold still, you little bitch!" said the guard straddling her legs. He leaned forward and slapped her hard across the face.

"Don't fight me!" he yelled.

"Lamont!" Maddy cried out again, or tried to.

The guard had his hand back for another slap when the fireball hit him. It struck with the force of a cannon blast, knocking him off the bed and against the wall. He fell in a heap to the floor. Maddy turned to see Lamont standing with his arms free—his right palm stretched forward, melted plastic dangling from his wrist, a strange haze surrounding his whole body. He looked as stunned as everybody else in the room.

The guards surrounding Lamont were rocked back. As they recovered their footing, their rifle barrels came up. Spinning toward them, Lamont gathered the barrels together like flower stems and pressed them between his palms. The rifles melted into a single drooping wad of metal. He swept his arm across the guards, shielding himself with a curtain of flame. He was surging with a force he barely knew how to control.

Maddy twisted free of the remaining guard, shoving him off onto the floor. The guard quickly rolled toward his rifle, lying just a few yards away on the carpet. Maddy flipped herself off the bed and made a flying leap over the guard's back. She got to the weapon first, raised it like an axe, and brought the

stock down on top of the guard's helmet—
so hard that the rifle snapped in half.

Lamont ran to Maddy as reinforcements
poured into the room. With one hand, he
pushed her behind him and thrust the other
out toward the oncoming guards. A swirl of
flame emerged from his open palm and shot
across the room like a meteor. The fireball
blasted the entire squad back into the hallway, helmets shattered, rifles and equipment
flying.

A fresh squad rushed up the staircase. The
guards took positions on both sides of the
doorway, rifles held tight to their breastplates.
On a hand signal, they burst into the room,
stepping over prone guards and weapons
somehow melted into abstract sculptures.

The fugitives were gone.

CHAPTER 66

LAMONT KNEW THAT in a perimeter search, the main entrance often got the least attention. So he and Maddy didn't bother with secret exits. They simply walked briskly out the front door, invisible to the milling guards in the foyer. *Mostly* invisible. The effect was not perfect. Neither of them was close to full strength. But in the chaos, it was enough.

Two minutes later, sitting on top of Rat Rock at the edge of the park, they were both fully visible and completely exhausted. At this time of night, the forbidding park was actually the safest place to be—for them, anyway. No FR cameras. No patrols. And they doubted that the presidential guards would roam this far from the mansion.

They sat for a few minutes, side by side, not saying anything. Just breathing hard. Relieved to be breathing at all. They hadn't found Jessica, but at least they hadn't ended up captured, or dead. Lamont rubbed his wrists, still red and sore. Maddy stared into the dark foliage. The flicker of faraway barrel fires glowed through the leaves. Her wrists hurt too, from her attacker's rough tactical gloves. In fact, now that the adrenaline was fading, her whole body was starting to ache.

Lamont spoke first.

"Maddy," he said, "I'm sorry."

Maddy stared straight ahead.

"Why?" she replied softly. "We're alive, aren't we?"

"It was a careless plan," said Lamont. "I was arrogant. I should have gone in there by my-self. There was no reason to put you in peril. Nothing like that will ever happen again."

"Yes, it will," said Maddy. "I'm in this too."

"No," said Lamont, "the fight with Khan is *my* fight, not yours."

"Not just yours," said Maddy. "You heard him. He's planning to wipe an entire class of human beings off the planet! People like my grandmother. People like me."

Maddy turned her head back toward Fifth Avenue. In the distance, landscape lighting illuminated wrought-iron gates and stately homes.

"Those people with the big houses and fancy lawns? Those are *your* people. Rich people. They'll be fine. Meanwhile, everybody *I've* ever known will be gone."

Lamont didn't say anything. He just listened.

"Look," Maddy continued. "I didn't ask for...whatever it is I've turned into. But now it's part of me. Just like it's part of you. And you can't just leave me out. It's not your decision to make. You're not my father."

Lamont dipped his head.

"You're right," he said. "I'm not."

"Besides," said Maddy, "I obviously still have a lot to learn." She looked down at the welts on Lamont's wrists. Lamont exhaled slowly.

"The fireballs?" asked Lamont.

"Yeah," said Maddy. "Let's start there."

"The truth?" said Lamont.

"Please," said Maddy.

"Apparently I developed some new powers while I was sleeping," said Lamont, rubbing his wrists. "I guess fireballs are one of them."

CHAPTER 67

WE'RE BACK AT the warehouse, and I'm dumping out the bag of goodies I stole from the mansion. Margo is really relieved to see us. And she's very excited about the champagne. She rubs the bottle between her hands.

"Darling," she says to Lamont. "We *cannot* drink Dom Perignon out of tin cups. That is where I draw the line!"

"I agree," Lamont says. "Let me go downstairs and see what I can find."

Margo waits until Lamont is out the door. Then she scoots over next to me and brushes the hair off my forehead. There's a big bruise there, turning into a big red lump. Obviously, she noticed it when we came in.

Along with the red mark on my cheek. And the welts on Lamont's wrists.

"What in God's name happened to you two tonight?" she asks.

Lamont's been pretty quiet about the whole episode since we got back, and I'm not sure he wants Margo to know just how close we came to not coming back at all. All he told her was that something big and dangerous was up and that he'd explain later.

"I banged my head on one of Lamont's secret doors," I say.

Margo smiles.

"Oh, I know all about those," she says. "One night, coming home late, I got my dress caught on one of those damned hinges. Almost stripped me bare!"

"Victory!" Lamont's voice comes booming from the doorway. He's holding up three medium-size laboratory beakers.

"I hope you washed the hydrochloric acid out of those things!" says Margo.

"Fresh from the box," says Lamont. "Pristine Pyrex."

"Pour away!" says Margo.

The three of us gather around our little crate table. Lamont pulls the foil off the champagne bottle. Underneath, there's a little wire cage around the cork. Lamont looks at me with his eyebrow raised. He taps the foil and the wire.

"Good thing nobody was looking too closely," he says. How was I supposed to know there was metal on a champagne bottle? Lamont unwraps the wire, then presses his thumbs against the bottom of the cork.

POP!

The cork shoots across the room and bounces off a wall. Bando barks and chases after it. A stream of bubbles spurts out of the bottle.

Lamont pours some champagne into Margo's beaker, then some into his. He looks at me.

"What's the legal drinking age these days?" he asks. "Still twenty-one?"

"Sixteen," I say. "Twelve if you work on a farm or a fishing boat."

"Are you making that up?" asks Lamont.

"Yes, I am," I say.

Lamont pours some champagne into my beaker anyway. I hold it up to my nose, then tip the beaker back and let the champagne touch the tip of my tongue. My first taste of champagne. It feels fizzy and sweet. I gulp down the whole beaker. The bubbles burn my throat.

Then I burp. Can't help it.

"Goodness gracious, Maddy!" says Margo. "Sip! Don't guzzle!"

"This tastes...amazing!" I say. What's even *more* amazing is the feeling in my head right now. A little numbness right above my eyebrows and a warm buzz at the top of my skull.

Margo shaves off a slice of cheese with a butter knife and holds it out to me. "Try this," she says.

The cheese is so close to my face, I practically have to cross my eyes to look at it. There are little brown flecks all over it. My nose wrinkles up.

"What's in there? Flies?"

"Truffles, darling," says Margo. "Gift of the forest!"

"*Tuber melanosporum,*" says Lamont, slicing a piece for himself. "Delicious!"

I take a little nibble, then a little bite. The cheese is creamy and the truffle bits taste like...*omigod*! They taste like *dirt*! I spit out the cheese and wipe my tongue on my shirt-sleeve. *Ugh!* I hold out my empty beaker to Lamont.

"Refill! Now! I have to get rid of this *taste*!"

Lamont pours me what's left in the bottle. I drink it down in one gulp. Dirt taste gone. And then...here comes that little buzz again. So nice. Suddenly I'm not as achy anymore. Just a little sleepy. I move over toward Margo. In this light, she glows like an angel. I rest my cheek against her shoulder and kind of slide down her arm until my head is resting in her lap. So warm.

I look up at Margo's perfect chin and then over at Lamont.

"Tell me everything," I say.

"About what?" asks Lamont.

"About Shiwan Khan."

CHAPTER 68

THIS PART REMINDS me of nights when I was really little, after I was all tucked into bed. That's when Grandma used to tell me stories. Fairy tales. Ancient mysteries. Greek myths. Sometimes the stories would blend in with my dreams and things that happened in my life and pretty soon I didn't know which parts were real and which parts were made up.

That's how I feel right now. My head is fuzzy from the champagne. I'm really tired. And I'm hearing the kind of story that sounds like it could never be true. Even if it actually is.

"Shiwan Khan is a golden master," says

Lamont, "descended from Genghis Khan himself. Direct line. The legend says that Genghis died when he was struck by lightning. His followers kept his battle spear, which was supposed to hold his spirit. After a while, they built a monastery to keep his spirit alive. When Shiwan's parents died, the monks in the monastery took him in. They protected him. They taught him. They trained him. They passed on all their secrets. But Shiwan had powers even the monks couldn't understand."

I'm snuggled tight in Margo's lap. She's rubbing my head gently. It feels good, but it's making me even sleepier. I'm drifting in and out. But still listening.

"We ran into Khan back in the 1930s," says Margo, "when he was building his own private army. Lamont tracked him down and discovered his stockpile of weapons."

"Khan tried to escape in one of his experimental planes," said Lamont. "The plane crashed in the river. I thought he was dead."

"But . . . he wasn't?" I say.

"No," says Lamont. "He survived. Or maybe

he was never in the plane in the first place. Maybe it was all some kind of illusion. Anyway, that's when he came back to poison me and Margo."

"Luckily," says Margo, "Lamont had a plan to keep us around."

"I'm glad you're both still here," I say.

Or maybe I just mumble it.

Right before I fall asleep.

CHAPTER 69

WHEN I WAKE up the next day, my head is filled with Mongolian chants and exploding fireballs and a million other things I don't really understand. And there's a stabbing pain right between my eyes.

"It's called a champagne hangover, honey," Margo says. "Get some air."

Sounds like a good idea. I grab my scooter and head outside. I promised to wear a mask. But I break that promise right away. I walk to the closest street and start rolling uptown. As I head up the Bowery, I'm passing video screens with Gismonde's face, spouting his usual platitudes. I can't listen to his babble anymore. Especially after what I heard last night.

I see a small crowd gathered in front of a construction wall. They're looking at a poster tacked to the plywood. Two government workers are putting up the same poster on every available space. I roll up to take a look. One of the workers glances at me.

"Have a beautiful day!" he says.

"And you as well," I answer. "Dickhead," I add under my breath. More people start crowding in behind me to read the poster. It must be something good. I scoot up close to get a look.

"The Most Beautiful Day Feast" says the poster headline in fancy, friendly lettering. Underneath, in smaller letters—"Free Food! Gather & Enjoy! Monday." That's just three days away.

The crowd is all excited, practically jumping up and down. Could this be real? Actual generosity from the government? It sounds too good to be true. I feel a chill shoot through me. It *was* too good to be. It was a lie. I know it.

I hear air brakes hissing behind me. It's

a bus, rolling to a stop across the street. Suddenly, the crowd scatters. The people without masks look down or turn their heads away. No wonder. It's a prison bus. I can see suspects pressed up against the bars on the windows.

I turn my face back toward the poster, pretending that I'm reading. When I hear the air brakes release, I shove off on my scooter to follow. I know Lamont and Margo wouldn't approve, but I can't help myself.

Wherever this bus is headed, I'm headed too.

CHAPTER 70

AS THE BUS rolls up First Avenue, I stay a safe half-block behind, weaving around cars and motorcycles. Suddenly, I hear the blast of an air horn behind me, so loud that it makes my ears ring. I wobble on my scooter and turn around. A huge trailer truck is about three feet from my rear wheel. I bank to the side and let the truck pass, but now the huge box of the trailer is blocking my view. I give a couple hard kicks and swoop out in front again. But now the bus is out of sight.

Dammit!

I look down on the river side of the street. I see a huge culvert pipe running alongside the roadway—another abandoned city project. I slide down the incline and roll my scooter into the empty metal tube. It's so tall that I only have to duck my head a little bit. About twenty feet ahead, the light fades out. Spooky for sure, but it looks like a pretty good shortcut.

The floor of the tunnel is pretty smooth, a lot smoother than asphalt. I kick my scooter along, picking up speed. I can see the seams on the sides of the tunnel zipping by and I hear the rattle of my wheels echoing against the concrete walls. It's like gliding through a space warp. A few blocks ahead, I see a circle of light and bright flashes. The tunnel is ending!

I shoot out of the tunnel like a cannonball past a couple of scrappers with acetylene torches. The sparks shoot across the opening as I fly past. I sail through the air and land hard on the ground, my face planted in the dirt.

I hear the scrappers laughing and applauding.

I look up. At the top of the incline, just a few

yards away, I see it. The bus. It's stopped to pick up more prisoners. My shortcut worked!

I drag my scooter behind a cement piling and toss a few pieces of scrap lumber on top. I climb up the slope to the street. The bus door is open. Just outside, three TinGrins are herding the new prisoners up the steps. Inside, I can see another guard shoving people into empty seats. Nobody fights back. What's the use?

I take a breath. I concentrate. I feel the rush. I disappear.

I slip into line and step onto the bus. I take a seat on the aisle.

The last in line is a lady in a bright red turban. She walks up and tries to slide into the seat I'm already in. We bump hips. She turns around. I hold my breath. "Hey!" she says, waving to the guard and pointing to the seat. "I can't . . ."

"Quiet!" he says. "You don't like that seat, take another!"

With his gun, he points her toward the seat across the aisle. The woman takes it, but keeps staring across the aisle. I know she can't see me, but it feels freaky anyway. Freaky and risky.

The bus takes off again up the east side of Manhattan. A few minutes later, we turn onto a narrow bridge. In the distance I can see the abandoned airport. The bridge leads to another island. A smaller one.

I stare out the window at the end of my seat row. My heart is racing but I concentrate on holding still, not moving my feet. I'm aware of every sensation in my body. I know I'm probably headed for trouble, and this time I can't let my focus wander.

I look down the aisle toward the front of the bus. Over the head of the driver there's a yellowed sign from the old days. Better days.

It says RELAX & ENJOY THE RIDE.

CHAPTER 71

THE CITY HALL subway station had been closed since the middle of the last century, but it retained an air of majesty— vaulted brick arches, decorative patterns in Guastavino tile, and elaborate leaded glass skylights. The sun was pouring through those skylights now, illuminating a buzz of activity on the platform that had been extended to cover the abandoned tracks.

The station had the look of a Roman bath, but the aroma of an industrial kitchen. The air was steamy from the heat of a hundred pots, sitting on massive gas stoves against the interior walls. A dozen white-jacketed cooks stood at their stations, slicing mountains of onions, peppers, and tomatoes and shaking sizzling skillets of ground beef. The prepped ingredients were dumped into huge simmering pots, then swirled with stirring paddles the size of small oars.

Sonor Breece walked slowly up and down the line, hands folded behind his back. Between his fingers he dangled a long-stemmed tasting spoon, which flicked out behind him like a thin silver tail.

The aromas that filled the space were a bit crude for his senses. He preferred more subtle seasoning and, as a rule, he avoided meat. But scale and economy were the objectives here, not haute cuisine.

He wandered over to the side of the cook in the center of the line and dipped his spoon into the bubbling mixture on the burner. He touched the spoonful to his lips to test the temperature. Then he took a small nibble and let the flavors expand in his mouth. He worked the mixture lightly between his molars for a few seconds, then leaned forward and spit the half-chewed wad back into the pot.

"Too thin," said Breece. "Start again."

The cook's eyes never lifted from the stove in front of him.

"Right away, sir," he replied, his voice barely audible. The sweat on his forehead was from the heat of the stove. But the sour odor of stress rose from beneath his jacket as Breece watched him tip the forty-quart pot by its handles and dump the steaming contents into a large garbage bucket.

"More texture this time," said Breece, wiping his spoon on a clean towel.

The loud squeak of metal wheels echoed against the curved station walls. Breece looked up to see a crew moving toward the station on a small electric cart made to fit over the ancient steel rails. The three men riding the cart wore rubber bib overalls and heavy gloves.

Two of the men climbed a small ladder onto the end of the platform and began to unload their cargo—dozens of small metal containers, each marked with an abstract stencil of a bird's head. The third man, the foreman, just watched. Breece pulled a pair of rubber gloves from a workstation and walked toward the workers.

"Gently, please," he said. "Gently."

The words of caution were unnecessary. The heavyset men were already handling the containers as if they were precious jewels, stacking them carefully in a neat pyramid. Breece picked a container from the top of the growing pile. He used the narrow stem of his tasting spoon to pry off the tight-fitting lid. Inside was a clear liquid with the consistency of cough medicine.

Breece carried the open container over to the sweating chef in the center, now furiously chopping up a fresh load of produce. Breece dipped his tasting spoon into the container, picking up a small dollop of syrup on the tip.

He held it up to the chef's mouth.

"Taste," said Breece.

The cook rested his knife on the cutting board as Breece lifted the spoon to him— almost like feeding a baby. Instinctively, the cook sniffed. No smell. He wrapped his lips around the spoon tip and took a small dot of syrup onto his tongue. He rolled it slowly in his mouth. He swallowed.

Suddenly, the cook spun back against his stove, his body stiff, eyes wide. Breece saw him try to scream, but his vocal cords were already paralyzed. The gas flame from the burner flared onto his jacket pocket, singeing it. The cook reached for his throat as white foam began to pour from his mouth. He dropped hard onto the cement platform as an almost comical waft of smoke rose from the side of his jacket—like a cartoon character after grasping a live wire.

Breece tossed his tasting spoon into the garbage along with the chef's failed recipe. He looked at the foreman.

"Perfect," he said.

CHAPTER 72

TO ALL APPEARANCES, the bus was now empty, parked near an arched entryway at the prison gate. Outside, guards shoved and sorted the prisoners on a bare pavement slab. Another guard rested his rifle near the front door of the bus and started sweeping the aisle for stowaways. It was not unusual for prisoners to hide under seats, praying not to be noticed.

From her aisle seat, Maddy watched the guard's black helmet duck down, one row after the other, all the way to the bench that ran across the rear of the bus. Maddy knew from the hum in her head that she was still invisible, still safe, but for how long? The guard walked to the front of the bus and leaned out the front door.

"Clear!" he shouted. The squad leader outside nodded.

Maddy moved down the aisle behind the guard and waited for him to exit. As he stepped down onto the ground, she followed. Suddenly, the guard wheeled around and started back up the steps to retrieve his rifle. As Maddy spun sideways to dodge him, she felt the hard ballistic nylon of his sleeve brush against her leg. She held her breath. The guard grabbed his rifle and stepped back out of the bus.

The prisoners had already been separated by gender, men to the left, women to the right. The only juvenile on this load was a boy about eleven years old, who was roughly pushed in with the men. The woman in the colorful turban stood quietly at the end of the female line. At a signal from the lead guard, the solid metal gate in front of the prisoners rose like a garage door—the eight-ton, bomb-proof variety.

Maddy slipped into the line behind the

turban lady. She glanced over her shoulder to make sure the guard in the rear was maintaining a comfortable gap as the column moved forward. *Stay focused. Stay calm. Don't push it.* She had already been invisible for fifteen minutes.

As the prisoners moved through the bleak prison vestibule, they passed an unmanned kiosk with an automatic camera. At a guard's command, each prisoner turned to face the camera for his or her official mug shot. When Maddy reached the camera, the sensor saw nothing. Maddy posed anyway. She gave the lens her most charming smile, and *both* middle fingers.

After passing through two more electronically controlled doors, the columns of people reached the core of the prison. Everything here was metal—metal bars, metal pipes, metal ducts, metal railings, even metal floors, in the form of grated platforms that ran around cell blocks stacked three stories up. The men's column turned left and disappeared down a long corridor. The guards herded the women toward a wide staircase.

When they reached the third level, the column halted. The guard at the rear saw something flicker right in front of him. Or *thought* he did. Barely a blink. He looked up at a wire-covered light fixture on the wall. He tapped it with his rifle barrel. It flickered. He shrugged. That must have been it. Either that, or he needed his eyes checked.

"Come forward!" the lead guard called out. "One at a time!"

The prisoners advanced until they were spread out along the cell row, one woman in front of each cell door.

"Open Row C!" the guard shouted.

There was a loud buzz and rattle as twenty cell doors slid open in unison. Prodded by rifles, each woman stepped into her new home.

"Close Row C!" the guard called out.

Twenty doors slid shut with a loud clang. Maddy pressed her back against the outside railing as the guards moved back past her toward the control station. She felt a tingle. None of the guards noticed her flicker this time, but she knew she had to hurry. She had a whole cell block to search.

As soon as the guards were clear, Maddy turned and slipped back down the stairs to the second level. In the cell just across from the staircase, a lone guard was flipping the mattress and banging on the window bars as the occupant stood trembling in the center of the floor.

When he finished his inspection, the guard stepped back into the corridor and shouted toward the control room.

"Close Number Twelve!"

The cell door slammed shut. Maddy stepped in behind the guard as he moved to the next cell in the row.

"Open Number Thirteen!" he called out.

The door to Number 13 rolled back. Maddy heard a rustle from inside the cell and then . . . a woman's voice.

"How many times do I have to say it?" the voice said. "It's too early for turn-down service."

Maddy's heart did a flip.

Grandma!

CHAPTER 73

IT TOOK ALL Maddy's strength to hold back a shout. She fought every instinct to run forward and wrap her grandmother up in her invisible arms, guard or no guard. Instead, Maddy silently followed him into Cell 13 and pressed herself up against the front bars.

Jessica's yellow prison jumpsuit practically swallowed her small body. Her silver hair was pulled back into a tight bun. She stepped to the middle of the cell as the guard grabbed her mattress—nothing more than a thin pad—and tossed it onto the floor. He used his rifle butt to test the window bars and tapped at a few chipped cinder blocks in the middle of the wall.

"You caught me," said Jessica. "I was chewing my way out." The guard ignored her sass and turned toward the door.

"Replace your bedding," he said as he stepped back into the cell corridor.

"Close Number Thirteen!" he shouted.

The door clanged shut.

"Open Number Fourteen!" yelled the guard, moving on to the next prisoner, the woman in the red turban. For some reason, she had been allowed to keep her headwear. It created a bold contrast with the mustard color of her prison uniform. She stood holding her mattress in her hands, shaking it vigorously.

"Thought I'd save you some time," she said.

"Drop it!" said the guard. He was in no mood for attitude. Besides, he'd been warned that a mattress could conceal a length of wire or a sharpened shard of stone.

Suddenly, a scream came from the previous cell. Number 13.

"Help!" the woman was shouting at the top of her lungs. "There's something in here!"

Rat! was the guard's first thought. They

usually stayed hidden until dark, but sometimes the inspections stirred one from the
nest. He pulled a short club from his belt. A
rat wasn't worth a bullet or the risk of a rico-
chet. One solid whack would take care of it.

He moved back to Cell 13. The old woman
was sitting on the metal bed. But something
else was happening. Something very strange.
Her mattress was floating in midair—waving
and rippling like a magic carpet.

"What the hell?" said the guard. He shoved
the club back into his belt loop and turned
toward the control room.

"Open Number Thirteen!" he shouted.

The cell door began to clatter. When the
guard looked back into the cell, the mattress
was lying still on the floor. But now, he saw
two people in the cell. The old lady in the
jumpsuit. And a teenage girl in shorts and a
T-shirt. The guard flipped his rifle into firing
position.

"Who the hell are you?" the guard asked
Maddy. "How did you get in here?"

"Is there a policy against guests?" asked
Jessica.

The guard was young and new to prison duty. A veteran would have called a code eight immediately, bringing a riot team to the scene in seconds. But this kid was green enough to think that he could resolve the problem on his own. It was an old lady and a girl his age, after all. No big deal.

Then the girl said, "Step into the cell and take off your clothes."

CHAPTER 74

JESSICA'S COUGH WAS very convincing. The security detail at the end of the cell block didn't question the guard escorting her, especially when they heard the magic word in a low, firm voice.

"Infirmary."

The last thing they needed was a tubercular crone on their block. Stuff like that spread like wildfire. A buzzer sounded. A metal gate opened. The guards went back to their small talk, not noticing that the escort's uniform was a particularly bad fit.

As she moved forward, Maddy could barely see. The helmet kept shifting on her head and the visor gave everything a dark cast.

It was like being inside a bucket. She held the rifle at hip level and followed Jessica through the open gate and then down a short, windowless corridor.

"Are you sure that safety is on?" whispered Jessica, feeling the rifle barrel tap the small of her back.

"Yes, Grandma, I checked. Twice," said Maddy. "Keep moving. Look sick."

One more guard station to go. Once again, Maddy tucked her chin down and tried to force her voice as low as possible. She thought of that Shadow announcer on the radio.

"Infirmary," she spoke into the grill at the front of the checkpoint kiosk. Jessica hawked up a nice wad of phlegm and spit it onto the cement floor. The guard quickly pressed his button.

Maddy and her prisoner reached the main gate just as the massive door was lifting. Outside, an idling bus was unloading a new crop. Maddy tipped her head toward one of the guards and gave Jessica a hard poke with the rifle.

Jessica produced another wet cough. The guard stepped back.

Maddy and Jessica walked through the scrum of guards and fresh prisoners near the entryway, then moved behind the bus, blocking themselves from the activity on the other side.

The roadway that led in and out of the prison passed straight through the entryway arch, just high enough for a bus to pass under. Beyond the arch, Maddy and Jessica could see the rippling water of the broad bay that bordered the road and, in the distance, the long bridge to the mainland. They walked quickly under the arch and around the outside of the wall, keeping their backs against the stone.

Suddenly a tall guard appeared from around the corner.

"Hey!" he called out. "Infirmary's that way!" He pointed over his shoulder toward a red brick building on a small rise on the other end of the island.

Maddy gave him a thumbs-up and nudged Jessica in that direction.

"Damn rookie," she heard the guard mumble as they walked past. He turned and walked back under the arch.

"Walk faster," said Maddy, tapping the gun between her grandmother's shoulder blades.

"Easy, soldier," said Jessica. "I'm sick, remember?"

A new busload was rolling toward them on the road from the bridge. It slowed to a crawl as it approached the archway. Maddy waited until the bus was halfway past them, blocking them from the main building. She grabbed her grandmother's arm and pulled her down a steep incline at the edge of the roadway. They lost their footing on the wet grass and slid wildly to the bottom of the slope. Halfway down, Maddy's helmet flew off. The rifle spun away in another direction. Maddy and Jessica dug in their heels and stopped their slide just short of an ancient barbed-wire fence—the last barrier before the ragged shoreline. They rested with their backs against the damp slope for a few moments, catching their breath.

"You okay?" asked Maddy.

Jessica nodded. She pointed at the fence.

"You think it's electrified?"

Maddy clambered up to retrieve the rifle from where it had lodged in the grass. She tossed it against the wire, barrel first. No sparks.

"It's our lucky day," she said.

Maddy held two rusty strands of wire apart with her gloved hands as Jessica crawled through. They were now about ten feet below the road, sheltered by the embankment— but trapped by the bay. The opposite shore was at least a half-mile away.

Maddy ripped at the Velcro fasteners on the muddy uniform. She pulled off the pants, then the vest, then the jacket, until she was down to her T-shirt and shorts again, now soaked with sweat.

The bus, empty again, was heading back toward the bridge. Maddy and Jessica flattened themselves against the muddy slope and waited for it to pass above them.

"There's no way we'd get across that bridge without somebody stopping us," said Jessica. "Too visible."

They stared out at the brackish water. Near the shoreline, the water was patched with green algae. Farther out, the ripples were speckled with brown scum and dotted with floating bottles and disposable diapers.

A loud claxon sounded from behind the prison walls.

"They found our bare-assed guard," said Jessica. "Let's go!"

Before Maddy could say anything, Jessica was in the water up to her thighs. Maddy waded in after her grandmother until they were both shoulder deep, their feet sinking into a thick sludge on the bottom. They heard boots pounding on the roadway above them. Together, they pushed forward and started breaststroking their way toward the green park in the distance. Maddy didn't want to think about what they were swimming through. She looked over at her grandmother, who was matching her stroke for stroke.

"Just grit your teeth," said Jessica, "and filter out the big stuff."

CHAPTER 75

BACK ON THE main island, Gismonde's armored entourage crept up West Drive toward Transverse Road, making its way along the far edge of the Great Lawn refugee camp. Sonor Breece sat beside Gismonde in the plush rear seat. The driver was moving so slowly that children felt bold enough to approach the vehicle. The tinted one-way windows kept them from seeing in, but Gismonde could definitely see out. And even through the bulletproof glass and armor plating, he could hear their high-pitched chatter.

"Filth," muttered Breece, staring out at the crowd on his side.

The bodyguard in the front seat bristled as

small hands began pounding on the doors
and hood of the vehicle. He raised his short-
stocked automatic weapon.

"No," said Gismonde. "Not today." The
car rolled forward. The windows were like
picture frames filled with dirty, hungry faces.
Gismonde closed his eyes.

*A young boy in a gold robe stood in the
opening of a high stone window, looking
down. In the distance, snow-capped mountains loomed over flat steppes.*

*Below the window, a mob of peasants
pressed against the high metal gates of the
palace compound. The peasants looked skele-
tal and desperate. They spotted the boy in
the window and began to shout at him in
fury, hurling stones in his direction.*

"Food!" they cried out. "Feed us!"

*A young woman in a colorful gown
snatched the boy from the window as a
rock shattered against the ledge. Below, the
force of the mob bent the gates down far
enough for the boldest to climb over. Within
seconds, the whole crowd spilled across the*

manicured courtyard, trampling flower beds and splashing through koi-filled ponds.

In the high-ceilinged chamber behind the stone window, the woman pulled the boy to a safe spot, out of sight from the mob. She brushed his fine black hair back from his face. There was fear in the boy's eyes, and he could read it in hers, too. The woman reached into her pocket and pulled out a small glass vial.

"I'm sorry we can't both live," the woman said softly, "but if it has to be one, it must be you."

She put the vial to the boy's lips. He drank in the warm liquid. The boy's eyelids fluttered, then closed. He fell limply into the woman's arms. The sounds of the crowd had moved from the courtyard to the stone-lined corridors below. It was like an angry hum, rising up the staircase now. The woman moved quickly to the far end of the room, carrying her son.

With one hand, she lifted a wooden shelf. But it was not actually a shelf. A lever.

A section of the stone wall opened. Inside

was a small chamber with a child-size bed, covered in thick velvet. The woman laid the boy down and smoothed his hair against the pillow. She stepped out and lowered the shelf back into position. The door swung closed.

The woman heard the pounding of a hundred footsteps in the hall outside, then rhythmic, heavy ramming against the door. She backed against the wall. As the door splintered in the middle, rough hands wrenched it off its hinges. The door fell with a loud bang onto the stone floor.

Inside his secret chamber, the boy's chest rose and fell slowly. He was unconscious now, beyond hearing, oblivious to his mother's final screams. It would be many years before he woke again. And when he did, he would be hungry too. For many things.

"Have a beautiful day!"

Gismonde was startled by the loud sound of his own voice. The driver had switched on the vehicle's PA system, broadcasting the recording from powerful speakers concealed behind the armor.

"And you as well!" came the reply from the crowd outside.

"Have a beautiful day," Gismonde's voice repeated as the vehicle moved forward.

"And you as well" came the response from a new section of the crowd.

The pattern of call and response went on, repeated every few seconds or so, as the entourage moved through the masses.

Breece looked over at Gismonde.

"You will have the poor with you always," he muttered with a sneer.

"Who said that?" asked Gismonde.

"Jesus," Breece responded, "the Nazarene."

Gismonde remembered the man, of course, just not all of his pithy sayings.

"Jesus was naive," said Gismonde, looking out the window at the multitude. "Even 'always' has its limits."

CHAPTER 76

AT ABOUT ONE p.m., Bando started yipping excitedly.

"That'd better be her!" said Lamont. It was long past the time when Maddy should have returned from her scooter run, and Lamont was both angry and anxious. He had just returned from searching the neighborhood with no results. Margo had been pacing around the warehouse the whole time. Between stretches of worry, she pondered suitable punishments.

"We should saw that damned scooter in half!" she said.

Bando's nose was practically touching the door when it flew open. Maddy burst in, her clothes wet and soiled with brown slime.

"Maddy!" shouted Lamont.

Margo ran to greet her but was stopped short by the smell. She rocked back, her hands over her nose and mouth.

"My word!" she said. "Did you fall into a *sewer*?"

"Kind of," said Maddy.

"What the hell happened?" asked Lamont. He tried to sound angry, but he was really just happy to see her alive.

At that moment, Lamont and Margo both noticed the slight figure behind Maddy. She was dressed in mustard yellow, splotched with the same ugly slime.

"Jessica!" yelled Lamont as she stepped into the room beside her granddaughter. Lamont wrapped his arms around both of them. Jessica looked down at Bando, who was circling happily, tail wagging.

"Bando!" said Jessica. "I thought the bastards killed you!"

"He's faster than he looks," said Lamont.

Jessica unwound herself from Lamont's hug and walked over to where Margo was standing.

"My God," Jessica said softly, "it's you."

"You must be Jessica," said Margo. Margo held both of Jessica's hands and smiled. For a few moments they just stared at each other. Margo was feeling something that she couldn't really understand, something buried deep.

Everything she felt from Maddy, and maybe more.

Jessica turned to Maddy, tears in her eyes.

"You weren't going to *tell* me?"

"I wanted you to be surprised," said Maddy.

Jessica turned back to Margo.

"How did...?"

"Lamont and Maddy found me," said Margo. "They brought me back."

Jessica couldn't stop staring at Margo's face.

"Margo," she said, "can I hug you? Would that be okay?"

In spite of the slime, Margo said yes.

CHAPTER 77

I NEVER KNEW a shower could feel so good. I had to show Grandma how the system worked—the industrial hose rigged to the post over the big metal tub at the back of the warehouse. Not fancy, but it does the job. Like me, she's just happy to be clean again. I found her coziest robe, which she really appreciated. Now she's settled in with us around the stove. We're sharing what's left of last night's bean stew.

"Is this where you two used to live?" Grandma asks Margo.

Margo almost chokes on her beans.

"Jessica, please!" she says. "I hope you think I have better taste than *this*!"

"I thought it might have been nicer," says Grandma. "You know... back then."

"This place has never been less than *dreadful*," says Margo. "A warehouse is a warehouse."

Lamont looks at me. I can tell his mind is working. Earlier, he scolded me for running off. Now he wants to know what I know.

"You said you saw something," he says. "What was it?"

I tell him about the food posters going up all over the city, and the people crowding around.

"The Most Beautiful Day," I say. "I think that's when it's going to happen."

"That's Monday," says Grandma.

"Most Beautiful Day?" says Margo. "What's that?"

"It's the only holiday left," says Grandma. "At least, the only one allowed. It's the one day when people can gather without worrying about getting arrested, let off a little steam, share whatever food they have. It's the one day a year when people can feel good."

"And this is the first time the government has promised free food for everybody," I say.

"Free food?" says Margo. "Nonsense. Sounds like an excuse to round everybody up."

Lamont looks at me. "I think it's worse than that."

"Well, Lamont," says Grandma, "does the Shadow have a plan? Can we help?"

"Jessica," says Lamont. "Aren't you the same person who just escaped from a top-security prison? It might be a good idea for you to lower your profile for a while."

Grandma doesn't have a comeback, which is rare. I think the long day is finally catching up to her. Her chin is tipped down and I can see from the way she moves that her whole body is sore. Lamont sees it too.

"We'll talk tomorrow," he says. "You two should get some sleep."

Margo leans over and wraps her arms around Grandma's neck.

"I'm glad you're here," she says.

"I'm glad you're here too," says Grandma.

Lamont and Margo head off toward their nook. That leaves me and Grandma in front of the stove, with Bando snoring at my feet. When I think about what happened in the past twenty-four hours, my head starts to spin. There were so many things that could have gone wrong. But today, I felt like I had no choice. I would have taken any chance to find Grandma and save her. I would have given my life.

"Were you scared, Grandma?" I ask.

She reaches over and brushes the hair out of my face.

"I was afraid of not seeing you again," she says. "Nothing else."

The heat from the stove is cozy, and it's making me tired. I lean up against Grandma. She rubs my head, like she did when I was a little girl. It feels nice.

"Whatever it took to find you, I was going to do it," I say. "No question."

Grandma puts her arm around my shoulder and squeezes me tight.

"So, my brave, darling girl," she says. "I'm learning so much about you. You can make yourself invisible. You can swim. You can bring half-dead people back to life. Is there anything else I need to know?"

"Just one thing." I lean my head against hers. "I love you."

CHAPTER 78

MARGO WAS EXHAUSTED. She collapsed on the packing blankets without even bothering to take off her dress. Seconds later, she was asleep. Lamont was tired too—but his mind was also buzzing with worries. He was relieved to have everybody together. They were safe here for the moment. But he knew the moment wouldn't last. Nobody was truly safe anywhere. Not as long as Khan was in power. Not with whatever plan he was hatching.

Lamont leaned against the wall and gazed out the small window in the sleeping area. The window looked out over the front of the warehouse, with the ever-expanding river a short way off. The moon was full, and through the yellowed window glass, the bleak empty lot below almost glowed. Lamont closed his eyes. His mind reeled back to that same empty lot on another moonlit night—many, many moons ago.

He stumbled through the warehouse door, holding Margo in his arms. White foam dribbled from their mouths and stained their elegant evening clothes. Fletcher, the white-coated scientist, stepped aside to make room for them. His eyes were baggy, his frizzy hair wild and uncombed.

"Please!" he said to Lamont. "Let me take you to a hospital!"

Lamont could barely speak, but he forced the words out.

"No hospital has the antidote," he croaked. "Activate the plan! That's why we're here! That's why you're here!"

Fletcher rolled out two metal gurneys. He took Margo from Lamont's arms and laid her down gently on the first one, straightening her dress to cover her pale legs. He

helped Lamont onto the second gurney. La-
mont craned his head toward Margo.

"Do not die," he whispered. "Do not die!"

His body was stiffening and every move-
ment brought burning pain. He pressed his
shaky right hand against his side and felt the
small round shape of the ring in his pocket.
His secret.

Lamont opened his eyes and exhaled
slowly, his heart pounding from the memory. He walked over to the thin metal pipe
where his tuxedo was hanging. He reached
into the pocket and pulled out the ring. He
held it up to the window. The facets of the
diamond reflected the moonlight in small
bright splinters.

He looked down at Margo's face on the
bunched-up blanket she used as a pillow.
She was so beautiful, and he loved her more
than ever. But a proposal? Marriage? Did
those concepts even make sense anymore?
Marriage meant a home and comfort and
security, and none of those things seemed
possible right now. And children. Marriage

meant children. Why would anybody want to bring a child into this filthy, miserable world? Lamont put the ring back. He lay down beside Margo and wrapped his arms around her.

CHAPTER 79

TEN BLOCKS AWAY, Julian Fletcher had been drinking—a lot. In the three days since leaving the warehouse, he'd been roaming from shelter to shelter and visiting the ad hoc bars that popped up in the part of the city that used to be called Tribeca. For a brief era in the last century, this neighborhood had been a thriving art district, its gritty apartments and lofts occupied by striving young filmmakers, musicians, and sculptors. But that was long before creative expression was banned except for government posters and videos.

These days, quality liquor was as hard to find as an original painting. But Fletcher was persistent. And when he found a reliable watering hole, he patronized it for as long as it survived. He was already on his third bourbon of the evening. If the liquor hadn't been so watered down, he would have been thoroughly drunk. As it was, he was just grumpy. He lifted his glass and let the last drop of warm liquor drip onto his tongue.

At some point in the far distant past, this place must have been a drugstore. The white countertop still had partitions made for consultations with the pharmacist. Long rows of shelves that once held pills and lotions were now drying racks for a sparse collection of glassware. Fletcher waved to the young woman behind the counter, down at the far end.

"Leena," he called out. He wiggled his empty glass.

Leena had green-streaked black hair, and dark eyes that peeked out through her sequined mask. Like everybody who served stolen liquor in the city, she was part barkeep, part lookout, part escape artist. At the first hint of a raid, she would simply whisk her small collection of bottles into a padded cooler bag and disappear into the alley. A few days later, she would reemerge to set up shop somewhere else. Anyplace with a counter and a few chairs would do.

"Same?" she asked, hoisting the bottle of amber liquid. Fletcher nodded.

As Leena started to pour, Fletcher saw her eyes flick up. Then he felt a firm hand clamp over his shoulder. Leena quickly dipped the bottle down below the bar.

"Julian Fletcher!" a booming voice said.

Fletcher turned to see a stout man in a dark suit.

"Creighton Poole," said Fletcher, with a slight slur. "How did you find me?"

"Not easy," said Poole. "This might as well be Budapest."

Down here below Forty-Sixth Street, Poole's business wardrobe stood out like a clown costume. Leena eyed him suspiciously.

"Is he government?" she asked Fletcher.

"Worse," said Poole, leaning over the counter. "I'm a lawyer."

Leena half smiled at his little joke. "Drink?"

she asked, hoisting the bottle back into view. Poole waved it away.

"Let's try something you haven't cut," he said.

Leena eyed Poole with new respect. She reached under the counter and pulled out a nicer bourbon. She tipped the neck toward him. Poole examined the wax seal around the cap. He tossed a few bills on the bar and grabbed the bottle. He motioned for two glasses. Leena handed them over. Poole headed for a small table in the corner. Fletcher got up slowly from his stool and followed him.

When they got to the table, Poole set down the glasses and twisted the bottle cap. Small flakes of red wax fell onto the table. Poole poured two fingers into each glass. Fletcher took a deep swig of his fresh drink. The burn of the full-strength booze made him wheeze.

"I wasn't ready," he said.

"For what?" asked Poole.

"For any of it," said Fletcher. He took another quick gulp. "My whole life, I felt like I was working in a graveyard. And then all of a sudden I was shocking people back to life like some kind of mad scientist."

"You *are* a mad scientist," said Poole. "You are the *definition* of a mad scientist. So what? The process worked. Now it's time we both got something out of it."

"I should publish a research paper," said Fletcher. "'Modified Cryogenic Suspension and Revivification.' I could be famous."

"Sure you could," said Poole. "And then people would go right out and steal your process. Where's the genius in that? Where's the payoff for Dr. Julian Fletcher?"

Poole leaned in, cradling his glass in both hands.

"Look," he said, "our families have been keeping secrets for generations. We've both been waiting forever. Not doing. *Waiting.* It's time we *got* something."

"Meaning what?" said Fletcher.

"These people . . . these *freaks*," said Poole, "have strange . . . Let's call them 'talents.' Not just Cranston, but his lady friend. The girl, too."

"Mind control," said Fletcher. "I think they used it on me."

Poole took a long sip of his drink. "Not just mind control. *Invisibility!* Maybe more. Maybe things nobody's seen yet."

"Invisibility?" said Fletcher, shaking his head. "No."

"Look," said Poole, "I don't understand it either. Maybe it's some kind of hypnosis or voodoo. Maybe they got into some weird chemicals when you weren't looking. All I know is, people with those kinds of skills could pose a real threat to the powers that be."

"Gismonde?" said Fletcher.

"That's right," said Poole. "And I'm betting that the world president's people would pay a sweet bundle for what we know. You and me."

Fletcher stared numbly over the rim of his glass. Even with the fuzz that coated his brain, he could see that Poole had a point. He'd spent the first half of his life waiting for something he never thought would happen. And now that his job was done, what was in it for him? There had to be something. Something better than this.

"Trust me," said Poole. "We'll make enough to get off this dirty island for good." He drained his glass and slammed it down. "Before the whole damned thing sinks."

CHAPTER 80

BEING A CAT was harder than it looked. For the second time in one night, Lamont almost got himself stepped on. While he was looking the other way, a worker carrying a heavy toolbox nearly tromped on his left front paw. Lamont dodged the boot at the last instant and jumped to the top of a metal trash can. From there, he had a safe, unobstructed view of the Most Beautiful Day preparations.

This shape-shifting power took some getting used to. In some ways, he was finding that being a cat had its advantages over being invisible. He was more agile, for one thing, and he could fit through tighter spaces. But he was still getting the hang of it. And tonight was good practice.

A huge tent had been erected in the middle of Madison Square Park, covering the length and width of the entire block. Lamont had watched the whole operation. As squads of police stood guard, teams of workers hoisted poles, stretched huge sections of canvas, pounded stakes, and tightened ropes. Others unloaded long folding tables and metal chairs from trailer trucks. Meanwhile, two-man crews mounted extra screens on poles and trees around the park.

Lamont was still adjusting to his small, furry body. It felt light, almost insubstantial. Sometimes it was hard to sense his position or gauge distances. But his hearing was incredible. Lamont could pick up voices, movements—even a slight whistle of wind—with unbelievable clarity. And even though his color perception suffered, his vision was amazingly sharp, especially in the dark. As Lamont watched the work proceed at two a.m., everything was as clear to him as daylight.

From the dark corners of buildings surrounding the park, Lamont could see faces
peering out, the temporary tenants of another ruined district. But when he flicked his
ears just the right way, he picked up something unusual—murmurs of excitement and
anticipation. The Most Beautiful Day Feast
was really happening, and people could
hardly wait.

Lamont wasn't even sure what Gismonde
was planning. And until he did, he wouldn't
know how to stop it. Or at least try. All he
knew for certain was that tents like this were
going up all over the city. And in just two
and a half days, the tents would be filled
with people—men, women, and children.
And they were all in danger.

Lamont spotted a group of guards leaning
against a truck lift at the far end of the park.
As his squad-mates watched, one of the
guards casually lifted his rifle and sighted in
Lamont's direction. Lamont's feline muscles
tensed. His fur stood straight up. He heard
the pop from the firing chamber. Lamont
leapt into the air, propelled by his powerful

hind legs, just as the bullet punched a hole in the rim of the trash can lid.

As he spun through the air in what felt like slow motion, Lamont heard the guards laughing, like bullies in a schoolyard. He saw the pavement rushing up at him and twisted his body to land lightly on his feet— all four of them.

CHAPTER 81

THE NEXT EVENING, at the World President's Residence, just forty-four hours before the promised feast, the richest citizens of the city gathered for the annual Most Beautiful Night Gala. Decorated with strands of tiny lights, the Presidential Residence had a beautiful glow. In the circular driveway, luxury cars and official vehicles paused as excited guests stepped out. The walkway was flanked by guards in white uniforms standing at attention, their rifles held tight to their chests.

One couple held back, watching from the shelter of a hedge at the edge of the property.

"It's been a while since we crashed a party," said Lamont.

"Are you sure we're dressed for it?" asked Margo.

Lamont had caught wind of the costume gala on his way back from watching the banquet being set up early that morning. He heard the police complaining about being assigned to patrol the streets during the event. And as dangerous as it was, Lamont couldn't resist attending. It felt like a perfect scouting opportunity.

The guests arrived two by two, all clearly wealthy, poised, and elegantly dressed. The costumes were impressive—a dizzying mix of queens and magicians, painters and pirates, explorers and high priests. One man was dressed as a medieval jester, another as a knight, complete with lance. One young woman wore a daringly brief leather bustier and carried a whip.

In many ways, the whole scene resembled the parties that Lamont and Margo had thrown in this very house. Except that tonight, everybody was wearing masks. These privileged guests had nothing to fear from FR cameras. The masks were part of the costumes that had been required in the invitation. Unlike the crude plastic designs worn by the poor and desperate around the city, these masks were stylish and sophisticated. Most of the men opted for simple black satin, but the women had masks that melded into full headdresses—jeweled, feathered, and dazzling.

Lamont adjusted his own outfit—a black trench coat, leather hat, and red scarf. Once again, Jessica had surprised him with her resourcefulness. When he and Maddy described the Shadow's costume, she'd rummaged through a secondhand market after dark and put together an excellent replica.

Lamont looked as if he'd stepped right off the cover of one of those dime-store novels. Margo was wearing her classic white evening dress, and in Lamont's opinion, she had never looked lovelier. From a few feet away, the costume jewelry Jessica had scavenged for her could pass for real.

"You know we're taking a crazy risk," said Margo.

"It could be our last chance to figure out exactly what they're planning," said Lamont. "Besides, it's a way to mingle in high society. Just like old times."

Lamont lowered his simple black mask over his eyes. Margo straightened her pink embroidered version. Arm in arm, they walked past the gauntlet of guards, up the steps, and into the wide foyer. For a brief moment, they stood under the shimmering light of the crystal chandelier, the one Lamont had imported from Paris long ago. Margo took a deep breath.

"Lamont," she whispered. "The house is still beautiful!"

"Yes, it is," he said. "Except for the tenant."

The parlor to the left of the entrance had been transformed into a cocktail lounge, where white-jacketed servers circulated with trays of canapés and champagne. To the right, in the oak-paneled library, a string quartet played Bach. Guests circulated through the marble-floored lobby on their way from one room to the other. From the balcony over-looking the main hall, a man in a somber dark suit looked down. He wore a color-ful mask that mimicked a long, graceful bird beak.

Suddenly a pair of presidential guards ap-peared at the head of the staircase. A few guests tapped their champagne glasses for attention and the happy buzz of the crowd quieted down.

"It's him," somebody whispered. "He's coming."

Even for citizens of means, an invitation to the World President's Residence was clearly a very big deal. The tingle of anticipation was electric.

Gismonde emerged from the upstairs hall-way and stood at the top of the wide main staircase, pausing for effect. He was wear-ing a perfectly fitted pinstripe suit, with a mask in matching fabric. But the kicker was the robe—gold satin with an ermine collar. Breathtaking. Lamont recognized it right away. Margo grabbed Lamont's arm.

"You were right," she whispered. "It's him."

"Our humble host," said Lamont.

Gismonde descended the staircase slowly to applause and glass-tapping from the guests. The hem of the robe trailed behind him on the carpet. He stopped on the second-to-last step, which left him at least a foot higher than everybody below.

"Welcome!" he said, turning left and right to take in as many faces as possible. "So many friends I don't recognize! But of course, that's the *fun* of it!"

Champagne-fueled laughter echoed through the foyer.

"Please," said Gismonde with a gracious sweep of his arm. "Enjoy the evening— *whoever* you are!" More laughter.

"I'd like to slip him a mickey," said Margo, straining against Lamont's arm.

"You mean like he did to us?" said Lamont.

At the bottom of the steps, Gismonde mingled politely with a few guests bold enough to approach him. In the library, the quartet began to play again, a lively gavotte. As the music swelled, the foyer became an impromptu dance floor, with costumed partners gliding and twirling elegantly over the checked marble.

"Shall we?" asked Lamont.

"Do we really have time to dance?" said Margo.

"We *always* have time to dance," said Lamont.

He took Margo by the hand and led her to the center of the floor. From the railing above, the long beak looked down. Margo rested her hand gently on Lamont's shoulder and leaned in close so that her lips were just an inch from his ear.

"By the way," she asked, "do you have a plan?"

"I think I might have some leftover dynamite in the basement," said Lamont.

"So crude," said Margo.

"You're right," said Lamont. "Too many casualties." He glanced around at the guests. "Not that this crowd would be missed."

Lamont leaned in to press his cheek against hers. He could smell her neck, her hair. He could feel her moving with him, gliding, bending, turning. For a few minutes,

Lamont forgot everything except being with her. Margo was an excellent dancer, lithe and smooth. Sometimes it was hard to tell who was leading whom.

As they circled under the gleaming chandelier, Lamont felt a soft tap on his shoulder. He and Margo paused in midstep. Lamont turned. World President Gismonde's face was just inches from his mask.

"May I cut in?" he asked.

CHAPTER 82

LAMONT GLANCED AT Margo. She didn't even blink. Behind her mask, her eyes were as cool as ice.

Lamont stepped aside, lowering the brim of his hat. He moved quickly toward the other end of the room. Gismonde clasped Margo's hand lightly in his at shoulder level. His other hand came to rest gently against the center of her back. Gismonde bent his knees, lifted onto his toes, and wheeled Margo expertly across the floor as other couples moved to the perimeter.

Lamont worked his way behind the circle of guests, trying his best to blend in. He was sweating a little under his mask and the wool scarf began to itch his neck. As the string music soared, Gismonde led Margo in a series of slow, sweeping turns.

"Have we met?" he asked.

"I'm just another face in the crowd," said Margo.

"Your dress is lovely," said Gismonde, pulling away slightly to let his gaze run from Margo's neck to her ankles and back again.

"But my jewels are fake," she said.

"Don't worry," said Gismonde softly. "I'll never tell. Besides, everybody here is pretending, are they not?"

"And what are *you* pretending, Mr. World President?" asked Margo.

Gismonde smiled and leaned in close to her.

"I'm pretending that I'm still young," he whispered.

Margo felt someone beside her. A mask in the shape of a beak was almost brushing her arm.

"Mr. World President," came a deep voice from beneath the mask. "My apologies."

Gismonde pulled away and gave Margo a small bow.

"To be continued?" he said.

"Of course," said Margo.

Gismonde looked directly into her eyes, as if the mask weren't even there.

"Until we meet again," he said. "Miss Lane."

A shiver shot through her. Gismonde turned on his heel and followed the man with the beak to the far corner of the room. The man with the beak beckoned a guard. That guard beckoned two others.

Suddenly Margo felt Lamont over her shoulder, his lips close to her ear.

"Do you remember the powder room wall?" he whispered.

"I do," she said.

"I'll meet you outside."

Margo slipped quickly through the crowd and into an alcove off the main hall. She opened the door to an elegant powder room with two marble sinks and an enclosed toilet stall. A velvet settee sat against one wall.

Back in the foyer, the guards advanced. Lamont backed into the crowd.

He needed to buy some time. Just a little.

Margo darted to the right-hand sink. She

reached below the marble bowl and found a hidden metal lever, just as she remembered. She yanked the lever up, hard. There was a loud snap as the handle broke off in her hand. Margo moved quickly to a section of tile wall at the far side of the powder room. She pressed on it, then pounded. But the wall did not move.

Margo heard a knock on the powder room door. The door opened. A woman in a red satin dress and an elaborate mask slipped in.

"Do you mind?" the woman said, pointing toward the stall. "Too much champagne!" Margo quickly assessed the woman's height and size. Perfect.

"My goodness," said Margo softly. "I *love* your dress."

CHAPTER 83

THE GUARDS STEPPED slowly toward Lamont, trapping him in a corner of the vestibule. Finding the girl could wait. The man was their main target. And they were obviously trying to prevent panic. In a crowded room like this, it would be too easy to shoot somebody rich and important by mistake.

Gismonde stood on the staircase, his hand clenched tight on the railing.

"Everyone please step away slowly," said one of the guards. Lamont circled as if looking for a gap in the crowd. He twirled the long scarf off his neck and dropped it. He shrugged the heavy trench coat off his shoulders. He flipped his wide-brimmed hat toward the side, where the woman in the bustier caught it.

The guards took another step forward, their rifles trained on Lamont's chest.

"Don't move!" they said.

"Don't blink!" said Lamont.

Then he disappeared.

Some guests gasped. Others applauded.

"Excellent!" shouted the man in the jester costume. "Well done!" He thought it was the best party trick he'd seen in a long time.

The guards rushed toward the spot where Lamont had been standing, their boots trampling over his empty coat. Gismonde stepped angrily across the room and pushed through the crowd, his gold robe swirling behind him.

"You *had* him," he said to the guards. "Now *find* him."

On the front portico, Lamont stepped aside while the guards charged past him. In seconds, the front lawn and driveway were alive with armed men. Lamont slipped through a hedge and moved behind the mansion—to a corner of the garden where the powder room tunnel exited. But where was Margo? She should be here already. He saw movement at the far side of the garden. A woman in red was walking toward him on the flagstone path. Lamont squinted into the darkness.

"Lamont," the woman whispered. "Where are you?"

Lamont rustled a tree branch. Margo quickly walked over.

"They were looking for a white dress," she said. "So I borrowed a red one."

"What about the tunnel?" said Lamont.

Margo held up the broken handle.

"Faulty materials," she said.

They could hear the pounding of boots coming from the front of the mansion. Lamont grabbed Margo's hand and pulled her through the hedge that led to the rear gate. A minute later, they were on a dark side street, heading back downtown. Margo had ditched her elaborate headdress and Lamont was visible again, exhausted from the effort.

"I *told* you it was too dangerous," said Margo. "We could have been killed—again."

"I promise," said Lamont, "next year I'll turn down the invitation."

Margo was clearly in no mood for Lamont's little jokes and evasions. She stopped and grabbed him by the arm.

"Lamont," she said. "You said it yourself— whatever is going to happen will happen tomorrow. What are we going to *do*?"

"We'll be ready," said Lamont. "So will Maddy."

Lamont headed back down the street. Margo caught up with him.

"Maddy?" she said. "She's too young. She's been through enough. Leave her out of it."

"I know," said Lamont. "I should keep her out of it. But she's as stubborn as you are."

As they made their way down the dark streets, Lamont and Margo passed huge tents on almost every block, empty and waiting. Lamont stopped at a construction wall. He tapped the Most Beautiful Day poster that was tacked to it.

"See that?" he said. The type on the poster read "3:00 p.m." "We have until then."

"You always leave things to the last minute," said Margo.

After a few blocks, the straps of Margo's high heels started to dig into her flesh. They were a size too small. Not bad for dancing, but useless for hiking.

"Lamont, wait," said Margo. He stopped. She leaned on his arm, reached down, and yanked her shoes off one at a time. She rubbed the sore red stripes on her feet and ankles, then tossed the shoes into a trash can.

"What are you doing?" said Lamont. "We've got miles to go!"

"Believe me," said Margo. "I'm better off barefoot."

For the first time in her life, she wondered how it would feel to ride a scooter.

CHAPTER 84

BY TEN THE next morning, the World President's Residence had mostly returned to normal. Ministers bustled through the halls with papers and portfolios as kitchen workers carried glassware, trays, and unopened champagne bottles back into storage.

In the basement security room, a team of analysts played and replayed the scene from the previous evening's disturbance. The man's mask thwarted the facial recognition software, but in one viewer's mind, at least, there was no doubt about the identity. Sonor Breece leaned over the monitor.

"It's Lamont Cranston," he said. "There's nobody else it could be."

Breece noted the current time on the monitor display. This was a big day. The Most Beautiful Day. And he was already late for his next appointment. No matter. Last one into the room is the most powerful, no matter what the size of the meeting.

"Tweak the algorithm," said Breece to the analysts. "Keep trying. And the woman with him. The one in white. Find her, too. Nothing can interfere with today's event. *Nothing!*"

Breece walked down the stairs to the first floor and moved briskly down the long corridor. Across the hall from the dining room was a small study with a view of the rear garden. It was Breece's favorite room for morning meetings because it got such beautiful sun. Breece pushed the door open.

As Breece entered, both visitors jumped to their feet.

"Sonor Breece," the chief of staff said, shaking hands with the men in turn as they introduced themselves.

"Creighton Poole, attorney at law," said the first.

"Julian Fletcher. *Doctor* Julian Fletcher," said the other.

"Ah, a man of medicine," said Breece. He gestured to both men. "Please sit."

"Chemist, actually," said Fletcher.

"Noble profession," said Breece with a smile. "I'm a bit of a chemist myself."

The door opened again. An attendant entered, holding a tray with three flutes of champagne.

"We had some festivities here last night," said Breece. "I thought we might enjoy some of the leftovers."

The attendant set the tray down on the glass table in front of the sofa and quickly left the room.

"But first," said Breece, looking at Poole. "About your message. Very intriguing."

"Yes, Mr. Breece," started Poole. "If you'll allow me to lay out the parameters…"

Breece knew the start of a lawyer's speech when he heard it. He held up his hand.

"You have information on Lamont Cranston—is that correct?"

Poole recalibrated. Less was more.

"Yes," he said. "We do." He shifted his eyes toward Fletcher. Fletcher cleared his throat.

"Mr. Cranston," said Fletcher, "was the subject of an experiment in my family's laboratory."

"In the 1930s," added Poole.

Breece kept his eyes on Fletcher. "Experiment?"

"Mr. Cranston was...ill at the time," Fletcher continued. "My ancestor had devised a process that allowed for preservation of the human body in a form of suspended animation."

"Cryogenics?" said Breece.

"A modification of that theory, yes," said Fletcher. "But one that permits the body to function and survive over a long period of time without significant cellular deterioration."

"Fascinating," said Breece. "And Mr. Cranston was the beneficiary of that process?"

"He was," said Fletcher. "I performed the revivification myself."

"And may I assume your laboratory is the only one of its kind?"

"The only one that works, that's for sure!" said Poole, looking for a way back into the conversation.

"And Mr. Cranston?" asked Breece. "Where is he now? Alive and well, I presume?"

"I saw him three days ago," said Fletcher.

"Doctor," said Breece. "I salute your achievement. Let's drink to science!"

Breece handed a flute of champagne to Fletcher and lifted one of his own.

Fletcher took an eager sip. Instantly, his eyes widened and a stream of white foam began to spill from his mouth. He collapsed forward onto the glass table, cracking it with his skull. Poole jumped to his feet. In a corner, a pair of finches fluttered in their cage. Breece shifted slightly in his chair.

"I'm sorry that was so unpleasant, Mr. Poole, but I don't wish to give Mr. Cranston another chance at . . . What was the term?"

Poole's lips trembled with the word. "Revivification."

"Exactly. And now, Mr. Poole, about the other matter you mentioned?"

Poole's hand shook as he reached into his pocket. He pulled out a folded document wrapped in blue legal paper. On the top fold in legal script was the title "Last Will & Testament of Lamont Cranston."

"What have we here?" asked Breece.

Poole cleared his throat and wiped the sheen from his upper lip.

"In 1937," he began, "my great-ancestor was Lamont Cranston's attorney. He advised Mr. Cranston to write a will. But Mr. Cranston didn't want to bother. He had no wife. No children. Thought it was a waste of time. So on the night when Mr. Cranston met his ... unfortunate fate, my ancestor wrote a will *for* him and forged his signature."

"An ethical breach," said Breece, pursing his lips.

"No question," said Poole, "but one designed for Mr. Cranston's ultimate benefit. And I believe that what I know about certain provisions of this will would be of value to you. Provisions that Mr. Cranston, of course, is totally unaware of."

Breece took the document and unfolded it.

"The final page," said Poole helpfully, "the inheritance clause."

Breece glanced at the legal text. He folded the document.

"This could be useful indeed," said Breece. "And nobody else knows about this forgery?"

"I'm the last of my line," said Poole. "The secret dies with me."

"In that case," said Breece, "why don't we discuss your retainer?"

Breece tucked the document into his pocket and put a hand on Poole's shoulder.

"But first, I'll need the location of that laboratory."

CHAPTER 85

THE MOST BEAUTIFUL Day is here. I'm at the warehouse, tossing a twine ball for Bando to fetch. Over and over again. I have to do *something* to keep from jumping out of my skin. I don't think I've ever been this nervous. But I don't want to show it. If I seem too twitchy, Lamont and Margo might leave me behind. And I can't let that happen. Whatever they're doing today, I need to be part of it.

Lamont and Margo walk out of their nook.

"You ready?" asks Lamont.

"I'm ready," I say.

All three of us are wearing the same outfit. Black pants and black shirts with no loose fabric—more secondhand finds, with a little extra tailoring by Grandma. For me and Lamont, she even replaced the zippers with plastic buttons, so we're one hundred percent metal-free. If you ask me, we all look like old-time burglars, especially with the black masks. But I'm not complaining. Anything is better than those bike shorts.

"Watch Bando while we're gone, Grandma," I say.

"Don't worry about us," she says. Then she looks at Lamont.

"Do you know what you're doing, Lamont?" Grandma asks.

"Not entirely," he says. At least he's honest.

"Lamont likes to make things up as he goes along," says Margo.

"It's called being in the moment," says Lamont. "Acting on instinct. Finding the spontaneous solution."

"It's called winging it," says Margo.

Grandma grabs Lamont by the arm. She looks at Margo.

"Don't you two *dare* let anything happen to my Maddy," she says. "Remember, without her, none of us would be here."

"You have my word," says Lamont.

I give Bando a bye-bye belly rub and then wrap my arms around Grandma.

"Do not answer the door, no matter what," I tell her.

"I promise," she says. "And anyway, I have the world's bravest guard dog." She leans over to hold Bando so he won't follow us out the door.

"Good luck," she says, scratching Bando's head. "Be careful."

I feel like going back to hug her one more time, but Lamont and Margo are in a big rush. So I just blow her a kiss. She blows one back.

I follow Margo and Lamont down the stairs and out the front entrance. The neighborhood is empty. I guess everybody is uptown, where the big tents are. People in this neighborhood are always hungry, and free food is the best possible lure.

We move out along the riverfront, heading north. The sky is bright blue and the air is warm. It *is* a beautiful day—weather-wise, anyway.

All of a sudden, there's a loud crack behind us, like a huge tree branch snapping. We all duck. I turn around and look back at the warehouse just as a huge lightning bolt shoots out of the sky and hits the top floor! In one second, the whole warehouse is blasted to pieces. The shock wave knocks me onto my back.

I hear Lamont yell to Margo.

"It's Khan!"

"Grandma!" I scream at the top of my lungs. *"Grandma!"* I get to my feet and start to run back. Bricks and pieces of wood are still falling from the sky all around me. The warehouse isn't even there anymore. There's nothing left but clouds of thick gray smoke.

Before I get ten feet, Lamont grabs me and pulls me down. I'm still screaming. I try to fight him, try to break free, even though I know there's nothing I can do. I'm on my knees now, grinding my fists against my head. When I try to look up again, Lamont is in front of me, covering my head so I can't see.

"Maddy! Maddy! Listen to me!" It's Margo. She's kneeling next to me, her arm around

my shoulders. "We have to get out of here! There's no going back. There's nothing we can do but go forward. *Forward!* Do you understand?" She says it again, louder, closer to my ear. "Do you *understand*?"

I twist my shoulders and shove her arm away. I stand up. My eyes are stinging from the smoke, and my throat burns from screaming. Lamont and Margo let me go. They stand for a few seconds, looking back at the warehouse. Then they start walking north again.

I still can't move. My whole body is numb. I'm confused. I'm in shock. And I'm madder than I've ever been in my life. Lamont and Margo are widening the distance. They're about twenty yards ahead—almost ready to turn through the alley toward the street. They stop and look back at me. They wait. I brush the dirt off my knees. I start walking toward them. One foot in front of the other. What else can I do? Two weeks ago, I didn't know Lamont Cranston and Margo Lane really existed.

Now they're all I've got.

CHAPTER 86

AS WE MAKE our way up First Avenue, a squad of TinGrins races past us toward the river. Maybe they heard the explosion. Maybe they think it's some kind of uprising or sabotage. Nobody would believe the truth. When I turn around, I can still see the column of thick dark gray smoke against the blue sky. Nobody's talking. Not Lamont. Not Margo. Not me. There's nothing to say.

We see another patrol heading our way, just ahead. Too close. Before they can spot us, Lamont shoves open a door to an old office building. We follow him in. The stench in the lobby is terrible. There are dirty blankets and clothes all over the floor. It looks like about a hundred people slept here last night. The lobby is fancy, or at least it used to be. Lots of marble columns and carved wood-work. An old insurance building maybe, or a bank.

At the far corner of the lobby, I see a group of women kneeling in a circle on the floor. They turn to look at us, scared. Maybe because we're all in black. Lamont holds his hands up.

"We're not government," he says. "We just need to get off the street for a minute."

From the center of the circle, I hear a woman scream. Margo heads right over, stepping her way through all the abandoned stuff on the floor. I follow with Lamont.

In the center of the circle is a girl. A teenager. Probably younger than me. She's lying on her back on a pile of old blankets and papers. Her knees are bent up and her middle is covered with a thin sheet. Her belly is huge. She screams again.

"How long has she been in labor?" asks Margo.

One of the women in the circle looks up. "Since last night."

"She's worn out," says another woman.

The girl lets out another scream. It echoes around the lobby. The girl looks exhausted and terrified. So do all the women around her.

"She needs a doctor," says Lamont.

"Can't move her now," says a woman in a red scarf who is kneeling at the girl's feet. She lifts the sheet draped over the girl's legs and peeks her head under. "She's crowning."

"I can't do it!" the girl yells. Her face is all contorted and red. Her hair is matted down with sweat. Margo leans down right next to her and wipes her hair back from her face.

"Yes, you can," she says.

The girl bites her lip and shakes her head. She doesn't believe it. Then she leans back and screams again.

Margo turns to me and Lamont.

"Kneel behind her," she says. "Support her shoulders."

Lamont takes the girl's left side. I take the right. Her shirt is drenched in sweat. I can feel her bony arm and shoulder blade through the wet cloth.

"What's your name?" asks Margo.

"Ava," says the girl.

"Hi, Ava. I'm Margo. And you're about to have your baby."

Margo squats near Ava's heels. She looks at the woman with the red scarf. The woman's eyes are red and her face is almost gray.

"How long since you've slept?" Margo asks.

"A while," says the woman. "She came in from the street yesterday afternoon. Didn't know anybody. Her water broke last night about eight. Been with her the whole time."

"Sit back for a minute," Margo tells the woman. "Rest."

The scarf woman nods. She slides over against the wall a few feet away and leans her head back against the marble. Ava screams again. Margo moves between her knees and lifts the sheet. Ava bends forward at the waist, trying a new position to relieve the pain. Her shirt is so slick she almost slips out of my grip. She leans her head back toward the ceiling and screams again—so loudly it echoes around the lobby.

"*Push*, Ava!" says Margo. "You have to push. You have to push *now*!"

"I can't," says Ava. She's sobbing and trembling. Her eyes are shut tight and tears are squeezing out. "I can't anymore." The last word trails off like she's passing out, or dying. Some of the other women are starting to panic. I can see it in their faces. My heart is pounding and my mouth is really dry. I look down at Margo. She's totally calm. She leans forward across Ava's belly and looks into her face. She claps her hands together once, real loud. Ava's eyes pop open wide again.

"Ava," she says. "The next time you feel a contraction, don't scream. *Push*."

Ava is panting hard now, her mouth open, her chest heaving up and down. Lamont and I tighten our grips. Ava's eyes roll back. She grits her teeth and lets out a noise that's part moan, part growl. It goes on for a long time. Margo puts her hands back under the sheet.

"Good, Ava," she says. "Once more. Just like that."

Ava leans back. More panting. Margo wedges herself even tighter between Ava's spread knees. Another grimace. Another howl. And then...

Another cry. A small one. From under the sheet.

Ava's head drops back. Her neck is resting on my arm. I can feel her warm, wet hair through my sleeve. Margo lifts the baby up. It's covered with blood and white gunk and there's a thick purplish cord attached to its belly. And between the legs, a tiny bud— like a miniature acorn.

"It's a boy," I whisper into Ava's ear. "You have a little boy."

Ava's crying full out now, tears streaming down her cheeks.

"He's alive?" Ava asks, bending her head forward.

"He's perfect," says Margo.

Margo lifts the baby, cord and all, and lays him on Ava's stomach, very gently. Now the other women are gathered around close, leaning in, making soft whispery sounds. One woman wipes the baby's head. Another woman reaches into his mouth and pulls out a gross little wad of mucus. Ava reaches down to feel the baby's wet scalp with her hand.

Lamont and I move aside as the woman in the red scarf moves back over. She lets Ava's head rest in her lap and wipes the sweat off her forehead. Margo gets up slowly. Someone gives her an old shirt. She wipes the blood and goo off her hands. Lamont puts his arms around her and kisses the top of her head.

"What just happened?" asked Lamont.

"Well," says Margo. "I think we just helped to birth a baby."

"You were amazing," he says. "Have you done that before?"

Margo leans in to Lamont, holding him close, shaking.

"No," she says. "Not that I can remember."

CHAPTER 87

I SHOVE OPEN the doors from the lobby and burst out onto the sidewalk, gasping for air. My head is buzzing and my stomach is doing flip-flops. I didn't realize that having a baby was such a noisy, bloody mess.

On the sidewalks and in the middle of the street, people are moving uptown for the feast. They've got a little more lift in their step, a little more hope on their faces.

I step into the street and merge into the crowd. Two blocks up, I see a huge tent—so big that it takes up the whole block. We saw tents all the way up from the river this morning, but this is the biggest one yet.

People are already milling around underneath. The feast isn't scheduled to start for another hour, but I guess nobody wants to take a chance on being late. Kids are already running around the tables, and people are gathering in big groups, happy and smiling. Even the TinGrins at the entrance seem more cheerful than usual. "Have a *most* beautiful day," they say to everybody.

"And you as well," everybody says back.

I duck inside the tent. On the street side, huge kitchen trucks are backed up with their generators humming. Giant fans are sending out some pretty amazing aromas. Roast meat. Baking pies. There are huge screens mounted to the tentpoles. They're showing scenes of wheat fields and orchards and streams full of fish. There's music, too—sweet and happy-sounding—coming out of huge black speakers.

One corner of the tent is separated from the seating area by thick black drapes hanging from a metal pipe. A huge guard stands at the barrier. I step right in front of him, face-to-face.

"You can't go back there," says the guard.

"Sure I can. Watch how it's done."

The guard stiffens up and grips his rifle tighter.

"Let me through. Right now."

The guard steps aside.

"See how easy that was?" I say.

Behind the draping, I see worktables and stainless-steel carts loaded with food. *Mountains* of it. Trays with whole turkeys and thick slabs of beef, platters of mashed potatoes and green beans, bowls filled with fruit. Now that I'm back here, nobody's paying any attention to me. There's too much going on. No reason to waste my invisibility energy right now.

I spot some movement under one of the prep tables. I lean down for a look. There's a scrawny kid, maybe six or seven years old, crawling like a worm, keeping out of sight of the guards and the workers. Every few seconds, he stretches his hand up and grabs anything in reach. He's taking small bites and stuffing the extra food in his pockets. His mouth is already full of bread and now he's reaching for a bunch of red grapes dangling down from the edge of the table. He stuffs a few grapes into his mouth.

All of a sudden, his eyes bulge out and foam starts to spill out of his mouth. I get down on my knees and slip under the table. The draping hides us. He's on his back now. And he's not breathing. I shake him by the leg. I touch his neck. Nothing. It was over that fast.

I look up at the mounds of food. Now it clicks. I know exactly what's about to happen. It's going to happen all over the city.

And I don't know how to stop it.

CHAPTER 88

LAMONT AND MARGO were waiting in the lobby when Maddy burst back into the building. She was panting hard, her cheeks puffed out and red.

"Poison!" Maddy wheezed. "It's poison!"

"What's poison?" asked Lamont.

"The food! The feast!" said Maddy, getting the words out in small bursts. "They're going to poison them. They're going to kill everybody!"

Back in the corner, the women clustered around Ava and her baby looked up. Lamont took a step toward them.

"Stay here!" he said. "Do not move from this spot!"

Margo walked to the corner and gave Ava a kiss on the top of her head.

"Take care of that baby," she said.

"I will," said Ava. She reached out and grabbed Margo's hand. She held on tight for a few seconds and squeezed.

"Thank you," she said.

Margo smiled. Then she turned and followed Lamont and Maddy out the door. The crowd on the street was thicker now. Excitement was high. The screens along the route were now beaming the images of delicious food, with string symphony accompaniment.

Suddenly, all the screens went black and the speakers crackled with static. After a second, a live picture appeared. It was Gismonde. His smooth face almost filled the screen. At the sight of the world president, the crowd paused. Conversation stopped. Parents shushed their children. Mothers jostled infants in their arms to keep them from fussing. Up and down the street, people turned to the nearest screen.

Gismonde smiled warmly. He looked

directly into the camera, his eyes clear and bright. His delivery was expertly paced, almost hypnotic.

"Today," he began, *"we celebrate our fertile fields and farms, our rich seas, and the bounty from around the world..."*

Lamont moved closer to one of the screens. For this special event, Gismonde had picked his setting carefully. He spoke from an elegant desk. Behind him was a low stone arch of pink-veined marble. The world president was captivating and telegenic, but it was the background that caught Lamont's attention. In a split second, he recognized the room. It was a place he hadn't seen in more than a hundred years.

Lamont turned back to Margo and Maddy and tugged at their sleeves.

"Let's go!" he said. "The bastard is in my wine cellar!"

CHAPTER 89

WE START ELBOWING our way through the crowd, but we can't move fast enough. We're dodging and weaving, going two steps sideways for every one step forward. People are crammed tight all around us, excited and happy. They have no idea.

"Go back!" Lamont is yelling. "Stay away from the tents! It's a trap!"

Nobody believes him. They think he's just another anti-government crackpot. They all keep moving forward, like robots.

"Have a *Most* Beautiful Day!" somebody shouts back, and a bunch of other people pick it up like a chant.

"Most Beautiful Day! Most Beautiful Day! Most Beautiful Day!"

I feel like screaming back at them, but I know it won't do any good.

"We have to get to the mansion!" Lamont shouts back over his shoulder to me and Margo. "We have to move faster!"

"Look!" yells Margo. "Over there!"

Across the street, a big black cargo truck is sitting with its engine running.

I've never driven a truck before, but so what? This week has been filled with firsts. I squeeze through the crowd and hop onto the running board. The driver is leaning back in his seat, half asleep. I pull open the door. The driver looks up and starts to shoo me away.

"Scram!" he says.

"Get out," I say.

He slides out of his seat with a big fat grunt. As soon as his feet hit the sidewalk, I jump up into the cab.

"Stand there and stay quiet," I tell him.

Lamont and Margo slide in on the passenger's side. I hit the horn and press the gas pedal. The crowd clears a path ahead of me—but not fast enough. We were better off walking.

"Too crowded!" says Margo. "Take Park!"

I hook a hard right and feel a rear tire bounce over the curb. The whole truck rattles and creaks. On Park Avenue, there's a wide center meridian for people to walk on, so the street is mostly clear. I hit the gas.

"Goddamn him!" Lamont is muttering to himself. "We have to stop him!" I've never heard Lamont like this. Even in bad situations, he mostly keeps his thoughts inside. But now he's mad, pumping himself up for a fight—the biggest fight of his life. I can feel it.

By Fifty-Second Street, the speedometer is touching fifty. Buildings and people are flying by. I'm dodging other vehicles left and right. Just as I start to make the turn onto Fifty-Seventh, a TinGrin steps out into the middle of the crosswalk ahead of me, waving his hands over his head. Could be a security stop, or maybe he just wants me to quit driving like a maniac. I know I could talk my way out of an ID check, but the hell with it. No time. I don't slow down. I speed up.

"Hold on!" I shout.

Margo and Lamont brace themselves against the dashboard. I swerve around the TinGrin at the last second. Miss him by an inch. Lucky him. Lamont's shoulder rocks against me as I crank the wheel, but his eyes stare straight ahead. He's still muttering.

"Ten thousand years," he's saying. "That's how long he's been planning this. A hundred goddamned *centuries*!"

Lamont sounds possessed, and I don't blame him. But if he's scared, he's not showing it. That's okay. I'm scared enough for both of us. All *three* of us.

I pull over about a block from the mansion. As soon as I kill the engine, Lamont stops muttering and takes charge. He looks me in the eye.

"Stay focused. Stay calm. Don't stretch it," he says.

I feel the vibration that tells me he's turning invisible—to everybody but me. I close my eyes and focus. I feel the warm wave wash through me. A second later, I'm invisible too.

We all step out of the truck and look up

the street at the mansion. It's hard to explain, but when I'm invisible, I can feel stuff I don't usually feel. Energy. Vibrations. Sixth sense. I don't know what to call it, but I feel it now from the mansion, even from a block away. Something dark. Something twisted. Then, out of nowhere, a voice comes into my head. It's the voice from the radio show. It always sounded kind of silly to me before.

"Who knows what evil lurks in the hearts of men?"

It doesn't feel so silly right now.

CHAPTER

I HAVE TO say, getting onto the mansion grounds is almost too easy. Margo tells a guard to open the rear gate, and he does. She walks straight through. Lamont and I are right behind her.

Talking her way past the guard in the loading area is no trouble either.

A minute later, Lamont leads us into the dark basement. "Over here," he says, moving into a dark corner. He reaches up and pulls down a thin metal ladder, like the fire escapes at school. He climbs up the ladder and opens a hatch in a metal duct that runs along the ceiling. Margo follows him up. I follow Margo. We're in a metal rectangle so tight, we can only fit by lying on our bellies.

"Lamont!" Margo whispers. "Where the hell are we?"

"My air conditioning system," says Lamont. "First of its kind. Runs through the whole basement." He points off into the darkness. "That way." He crawls off and we follow. Three ants in a tunnel.

As we crawl along, we pass over grates that look down into different rooms in the basement, one after the other. Storage area. Workshop. Boiler room. When I move toward the next grate a few yards ahead, I get a weird tingle in my gut. Something tells me not to look down into the room, but I do anyway.

It's a room full of bodies.

They're all lying face-up on metal tables. Their skin is pale and bluish and their eyes are open and dull. Two of the bodies are right below me, staring up through the grate. It takes me a second to recognize their faces. Julian Fletcher and Creighton Poole. Two people I never wanted to see naked. I get a bitter taste in my mouth and my heart starts thumping like crazy. I start crawling faster.

A few yards ahead, Lamont stops and raises his hand. I crawl up next to Margo, so close our hip bones are touching. We're looking down through a thick grated hatch into the room below, bigger and brighter than any of the others. The walls are lined with shelves, and the shelves are filled with bottles. I hear a voice coming from the room, and that dark, twisted energy blows right off the charts.

Gismonde's voice.

CHAPTER 91

AS THE THREE intruders huddled above, Lamont and Maddy visible again, they could hear that the world president was in fine form.

"Dear friends," he began. "The most beautiful moment of the Most Beautiful Day has arrived. The time has come to share the earth's plenty with those we love." To the audience of millions around the city, his delivery radiated warmth and goodwill.

"And now," Gismonde intoned. "The bounty is yours. Enjoy . . . and thrive!"

"Fire in the hole," whispered Lamont.

Maddy and Margo wrapped their arms around their heads. Lamont blasted a fireball against the grate. A huge section of ductwork and plaster dropped down into the cellar. Lamont hit the floor first, with Margo and Maddy right behind him. The air was filled with plaster dust, and sparks were shooting from ripped-out light fixtures. Lamont turned toward the elegant desk in front of the arched stone background.

But the desk was empty. There was nobody there.

"Congratulations, Mr. Cranston!"

Lamont spun around at the sound of the voice. On the other side of the room a cluster of video monitors hung above a control console. A dozen of them. The screens showed a variety of views of Gismonde's face, some framed so close that they showed only his mouth or his eyes, like a bizarre puzzle.

"Very resourceful," said the world president. "You've reached your destination. But as you can see, you're a bit too late!"

The images on the screens switched to views of the food sites in tents around the city. Margo and Maddy moved up next to Lamont. As they watched, white-jacketed

attendants appeared from behind the draping near the food trucks, wheeling serving
carts loaded with food. At the sight of the
overflowing platters, the crowds under the
tents exploded with gasps and cheers.

"No!" Lamont shouted. "You can't do this!"

On screen after screen, attendants set huge
platters of food in front of wide-eyed guests.
Impatient children reached out for their first
taste.

"I'm glad you're there to see it, Mr. Cranston," said Gismonde, his face blinking back
onto the center screen. "It's a pity I can't be
there with you."

Suddenly, a lightning bolt knifed through
the cellar wall, turning stone into gray vapor.
Video screens exploded and thousands of
wine bottles shattered, spraying the room
with glass shards and purple foam. The foundation rocked. Lamont shielded Margo and
Maddy with his body as the blast knocked
them to the floor. The room was filled with
smoke and fire. On the one remaining monitor, Gismonde's face reappeared, distorted
and pixilated. Lamont punched hard at the

screen with Gismonde's face, putting his fist right through the plasma membrane. As he pulled his hand back, he spotted a microphone lying on the console. He grabbed it. He didn't know if his words would be enough. But he had to try.

At the tent sites, the speaker columns blasted a burst of static—then Lamont's voice came through, loud and clear.

"Stop! Do not eat the food! Not a single bite! It's all been *poisoned*!"

For a second, there was silence across the city. People around the tables seemed frozen in place. Was it possible? It couldn't be! Then, one by one, people started to stand up.

"Bastards!" an elderly man cried out.

"Murderers!" a woman shouted.

The angry shouts spread from table to table, tent to tent, block to block. Mothers yanked food out of their children's hands and citizens rose up with fury in their eyes. Men started flipping the heavy tables over, spilling huge platters of food onto the ground. As soon as they saw the uprising, the attendants fled out of the tents, tearing off their white jackets as they went. Police raised their rifles and shouted for order, but they were overpowered in seconds by the surging crowd.

A few shots were fired, but most went harmlessly into the air. The tables had turned, in more ways than one.

"That was a huge mistake!" roared Gismonde from the broken screen.

"Goddammit, where are you?" Lamont yelled at Gismonde's crazed image.

Maddy struggled to her feet, aching and bruised. She stared at the distorted image on the screen and felt the evil energy radiate through her like a homing beacon. She wiped blood from a cut on her cheek and turned to Lamont.

"I know exactly where he is," she said.

CHAPTER 92

THE BUILDINGS THAT surrounded Times Square were still covered with billboards and displays from the last century, but the lights had been out for a long time. With its boarded up windows and empty sky-scrapers, the former Crossroads of the World looked more like the old slums of Detroit or Johannesburg.

Lamont, Maddy, and Margo emerged from the subway tunnel near the building where a ball made of Waterford crystal once dropped to announce the new year. Now angry crowds surged through the streets, wrecking whatever was left to wreck. Huge bins of burning trash spilled into the street, filling

the air with acrid black smoke. Fleeing
TinGrins ducked behind buildings and fired
into the crowd, but it was like trying to stop
an ocean wave. Lamont pulled Margo and
Maddy behind a row of cement barriers as
ragged citizens rushed past.

"Where the hell is he?" asked Margo.

"Khan!" shouted Lamont. His voice was
lost in the crowded canyon.

"Trust me," said Maddy, "he's here." She
could feel it.

"Show yourself!" Lamont yelled, turning
in a slow circle. "I'm not waiting another
hundred and fifty years!"

The roar of a powerful engine echoed
off the buildings. Suddenly a red double-
decker tourist bus careened into the square,
its engine whining. It jumped a divider and
bulldozed a statue of some long-forgotten
actor, sending chunks of bronze and granite
flying into the air.

"Lamont!" Margo shouted.

Lamont spun around in time to see the bus
heading straight for them, less than twenty
yards away, accelerating fast. Lamont stared

through the broad Plexiglas windshield. There was no driver. Margo wrapped her arms around Maddy and pulled her behind a wooden kiosk. Fifteen tons of steel hurtled through the intersection. Lamont stood his ground.

"Lamont!" Margo screamed. "For God's sake, run!" She pulled Maddy close and braced herself against the back of the flimsy shelter.

Lamont didn't move. He focused. The bus was just yards away, roaring like a locomotive. A split second later, a solid brick wall appeared across the width of the street. The bus rammed into the barrier with the force of an exploding bomb. The front end crumpled into a smoking heap. A second later, a blast of light illuminated the square.

The wrecked bus was gone. It had transformed—into Shiwan Khan. He floated in a swirl of vapor, black hair waving, eyes blazing. He was dressed in a blue tunic and jeweled breastplate. His gold robe fanned out behind him. His body radiated heat and light, generating its own field of energy.

"The Shadow lives!" said Khan. "With new talents!"

The wall of bricks evaporated, transformed back into Lamont Cranston.

"Invisibility is so last century," said Lamont.

"I couldn't agree more," said Khan. "All this changing and disappearing and pretending to be things that we're not—*exhausting!*"

"From here on," said Lamont, "let's just be ourselves!"

"Indeed," Khan replied.

He unleashed a flurry of lightning bolts, shattering the pavement at Lamont's feet. Warning shots meant to intimidate, not to kill. Not yet. Lamont knew that Khan was toying with him.

Lamont thrust out his hand and unleashed a fireball. It stuck Khan in the chest, knocking him back. But it didn't leave a mark on him. Didn't even singe his tunic. He stepped forward again, eyes wide.

Lamont and Khan circled in the center of the street, gathering their strength, biding their time. All around the crossroads, clusters of ragged citizens huddled in doorways, like spectators at the Colosseum.

"Do you remember our days with the monks, Cranston?" said Khan. "Our boyhood competitions? Do you remember why I was always the stronger one? It's because I came from *pain*. Because I knew what it was like to *lose*." He looked around at the crowd. "At the hands of rabble like this, I lost *everything*!"

Khan swept his arms out to his sides. On walls and rooftops all around Times Square, huge signs blinked to life for the first time in over a century, filling the space with a riot of iridescent colors.

Khan flicked his fingers. All at once, the massive displays blasted away from their supports and tumbled to the streets in a shower of sparks and twisted metal. Screams rose from the crowd as people ran for cover. Lamont looked up just as a massive light tower came down on him, pinning his leg under a rusted metal strut. Maddy and Margo fell to the ground as a blinking display crushed the top of the kiosk. When Margo rolled to the side, she was directly in Khan's line of sight. Khan's mouth curled into a thin smile.

"Miss Lane!" he called out. "I knew we'd meet again!" He turned his wrist in her direction. "Shall we finish our dance?"

Margo rose off the ground, kicking and flailing, as if pulled by a rope.

She felt tight pressure around her throat, and jolts of pain shot through her body.

Her head rolled back. Lamont grimaced as he strained to pull his leg free.

"Margo!" he shouted.

"She's strong, Cranston," said Khan, as Margo dangled helplessly above the street. "Stronger than I thought! Maybe stronger than *you*!"

Behind the crumpled kiosk, Maddy took a deep breath. She rose to her feet and spun out into the open. She was trembling with a mixture of fear and fury. She was not invisible now. She wanted to be seen.

"Khan!" she screamed.

As Khan turned toward Maddy, Margo dropped to the ground, gasping for breath. Maddy thrust her arm forward toward

Khan. She did it without thinking—a reflex, buried deep. A loud crack echoed through the square. A blast of light shot out from her palm.

A lightning bolt. Her first.

The powerful charge hit Khan in the shoulder, sending him into a backward spin. Margo stared at Maddy, not believing what she was seeing. With a final heave, Lamont wrenched himself free of the metal beam. He looked up, stunned. Maddy looked down at her hand, as if it were part of another person.

Khan recovered and rose above the debris, robe swirling, his fierce gaze turned on Maddy, the glow around his body intensifying. Lamont stepped between them.

"Leave her alone!" he shouted. "She's just a kid. She's nothing to you!"

"Nothing to me? *Nothing* to me?" roared Khan. "Cranston, I'm insulted. Did you think I wouldn't recognize my own flesh and blood?"

CHAPTER 93

"HE'S LYING!" YELLS Lamont. "This is the kind of game he plays!"

What the hell is happening? My palms are burning, but I'm not burned. My muscles are pulsing, but I'm not in pain. I feel strong and terrified at the same time. Out of nowhere, I have the power to fire lightning bolts from my hands. And now Shiwan Khan thinks I'm a long-lost relative? This is insane!

"You chose the wrong side!" says Khan, looking right at me. Right *through* me.

What's he talking about? I feel pressure in my brain, like he's trying to explode my skull from the inside. I can't think. I can't move. All I can see right now is Lamont in front of me, trying to protect me.

"Don't touch her!" Lamont screams at Khan. "This is between you and me. Like always!"

I'm gasping, trying to catch my breath. Ten thousand years! That's how long this battle has been boiling up. I'm just a little speck in that story.

Khan is totally focused on Lamont now. I can feel the hate. I can almost *smell* it.

"This is the last time you get in my way!" Khan roars back. His voice isn't human. It sounds like it's coming from a dark canyon, louder and deeper than any voice I've ever heard.

Khan unleashes a lightning bolt at Lamont's head. Lamont puts his arm out and deflects it with a fireball. Am I really seeing this? It's right out of a Shadow novel—except it's real. Nonfiction. Happening right in front of my eyes. And I'm in the middle of it. My heart is racing and I can't get enough air. I'm scared for Lamont—scared that this could be the end for him.

Khan raises both arms above his head and brings them down hard. This time lightning bolts shoot out of *both* hands. Lamont dodges one bolt but the second one hits him, knocking him to the ground. It stuns him for a second, but he gets back on his feet. Then he rushes at Khan, no fireballs now. Just his fists. He punches Khan with all he's got. But his punch just bounces off. So Lamont tackles him, takes him to the ground. I can hear them grunting and struggling, like two bears in a cage. I hear the sound of bones cracking—but whose bones? Khan throws Lamont back like he's tossing a doll.

"Lamont!" I shout. I reach for his arm. But he waves me off.

"Get away!" he yells. "Let me handle him."

There is no way that's going to happen. I've come this far, and I need to finish it, one way or the other.

"My fight too, remember?" I yell back at him.

Then I turn toward Khan. It may be stupid, but I don't care.

"Do you hear me, you son of a bitch? I'm not going anywhere!"

Lamont stands up next to me so we're shoulder to shoulder. I feel my energy flowing into him, like we're one unit. One mind. One purpose. At the same instant, we push our hands out, palms forward. A ball of fire and lightning spins out in front of us, getting bigger and bigger. Khan throws a massive bolt at us.

"Now!" Lamont shouts.

We both whip our arms forward at the same time. The ball shoots forward like a rocket and hits Khan's lightning bolt in mid-air, splitting it in two. It hits Khan right in the chest and he explodes in a huge ball of flame! The heat sears my skin. For a second, I'm totally blinded.

Then—it's over.

When I open my eyes again, Khan is gone.

All that's left is a pile of gray ash on the pavement.

It's finished. Destroyed. Ashes to ashes.

All around Times Square, I can see TinGrins creeping out of their hiding spots. One by one, they drop their rifles and start running for their lives. They're on their own now. Good luck.

Lamont reaches out and wraps his arms

around me. He squeezes me tight and rocks me from side to side.

"It's finished," I say. "It's finally done. We did it. We did it together!"

Then, suddenly, I feel sick.

Lamont tenses up and pulls back. We both look up. In the center of the square, the pile of ash starts to spin. It gets thicker and thicker and starts to rise up off the ground. In two seconds, it's an actual tornado. Flashing lights and scraps of metal are whipping all around us. The funnel rises up until it's ten stories tall. The sky goes black.

"Get down!" Margo is screaming from behind us. "Get down!" The wind is so loud, I can barely hear her.

Lamont shoves me down behind a cement barrier and I wrap my arms around it.

The twister lifts into the sky until there's only a snaky coil touching the ground. At the top of the funnel, I can see blasts of lightning getting bigger and bigger, brighter and brighter. Suddenly, the whole sky explodes. The shock wave hits me—and everything goes black.

CHAPTER 94

FOR A FEW seconds after the blast, Times Square was totally silent. The wind died down and every bulb and LED fizzled out. From all sides, people started creeping out of broken buildings, stunned and shaken, not sure if they had just witnessed a nightmare or a miracle or both.

Near the epicenter of the blast, Lamont lay on his back against a pile of wreckage, barely conscious. Margo crawled to him over the rubble. She wrapped her arms around him. He winced with pain.

"He's gone," Margo said gently. "You won."

Lamont shook his head. Even that hurt.

"That wasn't Khan dying," he said. "That was Khan escaping."

Lamont leaned forward. His brain was throbbing and it felt like hot knives were stabbing him through the chest from the inside.

"Maddy," he said, his voice raw from dust and smoke. "Where's Maddy?"

Margo turned with him to scan the area. All around them, pavement heaved up at odd angles and small flames flared up from the crevices. A few yards away, a curled hand was poking out from under a jagged metal plate.

Maddy's hand.

Margo and Lamont crawled over piles of broken asphalt and twisted beams to get to her. For Lamont, every move was agony, but he pushed through it. With Margo's help, Lamont braced one shoulder against the huge section of metal and heaved it aside. Maddy was on her back underneath. Blood and soot covered her face. She was pale. Still. Not breathing.

Lamont slid his hand under Maddy's neck. Her head tipped back, limp.

He pressed two fingers against the side of her throat. No pulse. Not even a quiver.

"No!" Lamont shouted, leaning over her. The pain in his chest erupted again. His face twisted with pain and his vision blurred.

"Move back." Margo's voice. Now steady and determined.

Lamont rocked slowly back onto his heels, his knees still touching Maddy's body. Margo leaned in close from the other side. She rubbed the dust from Maddy's lips. Then she placed her mouth over Maddy's mouth and began to breathe into her. She didn't know how. She didn't know why. It was as if Maddy were telling her to do it.

She exhaled in quick, hard puffs. Again and again. She paused and turned her head to see if Maddy's chest would rise on its own. It didn't. Margo leaned in again, her tears falling onto Maddy's face. She pinched her nostrils. More breaths. Then more. It felt like hours, but it was only minutes. After that, it was no use. Margo stopped. She looked up at Lamont and shook her head. Lamont pressed his fists against his temples as if he were trying to crush his own skull. He gritted his teeth and squeezed out two words.

"I'm sorry," he said.

It would be hard to list all the things he was sorry for. Sorry for putting the people he loved in danger. Sorry for believing he could protect them. Sorry that he was alive instead of Maddy and Jessica. Sorry that the Shadow's mighty powers had failed them both.

Margo rocked gently, eyes closed, tears streaming down her cheeks. She rested her hand on Maddy's head. She'd known this girl for such a short time, but she loved her in a way that went very deep. And now she felt hollowed out and helpless.

Suddenly, Maddy's whole body shuddered. Her neck arched back. Then her mouth opened wide in a loud, rattling gasp.

CHAPTER 95

I CAN FEEL myself being carried somewhere. And feeling is about all I can manage
at the moment. That and breathing. There's a
jumble of crazy images tumbling through my
mind, like pieces of a puzzle. Weird. Bizarre.
Surreal. Grandma in her prison jumpsuit.
TinGrins in animal masks carrying platters
of food. A classroom full of kids with white
foam running out of their mouths. A man in
a wide-brimmed hat and red scarf running
across a desert with mountains in the background. A baby wailing but making no sound.
Then a burst of light that erases all of it.

Now I'm resting against a doorway with
something soft behind my head.

I'm not sure if I'm dead or alive or some-where in the middle. Khan is not here. I know that much. I can sense it. The absence of him. I also know that my arms hurt, my back hurts, my legs hurt—*everything* hurts. I guess that's a good sign.

There's smoke in the air and people all around me, crowds of them, moving past in every direction. Then two faces come into focus. Lamont and Margo. I can see them leaning over me. They're scared. Maybe I'm alive, but dying. Kind of feels that way.

Margo is holding my hand and whispering something in my ear. But my head is ring-ing so much that it sounds like she's talking underwater. All I can hear are muffled sylla-bles. Then, all of a sudden, the ringing stops and I can hear her perfectly. She's saying my name.

"Maddy!"

I nod my head and open my eyes wider. Margo and Lamont lean in closer. Margo is half smiling and half crying.

"You're a fighter," she's saying. "You're such a fighter."

I don't know what she means, exactly. Does she mean I'm good at fighting evil? Or good at fighting my way back from the dead? I'm still pretty groggy and it hurts to talk, but I manage to get out one sentence.

"I come from a long line of fighters."

It might be the truest thing I've ever said.

CHAPTER 96

WHEN SONOR BREECE emerged from the culvert pipe, he wasn't exactly sure of his location. It had been a frantic scramble from the mansion after the mob broke through the perimeter. He'd made his way across town through the old E-train tunnel and found the enormous cement duct running along the east side of the city. But now the pipe had run out—another unfinished infrastructure project. He was standing on the lip of the final section with nothing ahead of him but an empty ditch.

Above him at street level, he could see a crowd of citizens filling the roadway. He heard the pop of gunfire and hoped that the government forces in this sector had restored control. But as soon as he climbed up the embankment, he could see that the guns were in the hands of citizens instead. The shots were celebratory, fired into the air— or into video screens.

Breece hung briefly on the margins of the crowd. He pulled his hood forward to shield his face, then filtered into the flow, moving uptown alongside the East River. In his salvaged clothes, he blended in with the masses. If he kept heading north, he would soon be out of Manhattan and into the safety of the upstate wilderness. *Just keep moving,* he told himself. *Don't stop for anything.*

Ahead of him on the right, he saw the bridge that led to Rikers Island. For a moment, he thought that the prison compound might be a final holdout, a stronghold for loyalists. But he quickly saw that it was just the opposite. As he watched, squads of TinGrins were being herded over the bridge toward the prison, hands bound behind them with plastic ties. Spilling across the bridge from the other direction were hundreds of newly

freed prisoners, still in their yellow jump-
suits, jumping and shouting and embracing
everybody along the route to the mainland.

Breece tried to wind his way through the
congestion at the city side of the bridge, but
he found himself engulfed in the crowd. The
more he tried to force a path forward, the more
he kept getting jostled backward. A chunky
young man in a yellow jumpsuit bumped hard
against Breece's shoulder, knocking the hood
back from his face, just for a second. But long
enough. The man started to say "Sorry," then
stopped short.

"Hey!" he said to Breece. "I know you!"
He said it with snappy emphasis—a comic's
timing. Sonor Breece had a photographic
memory for names and faces. He remembered this one from an arrest order. Danny
Bartoni. Illegal comedy performance. Inciting
insurrection.

"I don't think so," Breece muttered. He tried
to move away through the crowd, but his
path was blocked by a cluster of citizens and
prisoners. *Former* prisoners. Bartoni grabbed
his arm and leaned in for a closer look.

"Yes!" he shouted. "You're *him*! You're Sonor Breece! You're the Beak!"

Breece felt a chill run through him. He reflexively reached into his pockets for the stack of bills he had stashed for bribes and safe passage. When his hand came out, a legal document fell onto the ground. It was crushed and torn by crowding feet. The bills were knocked from his hands and fluttered through the crowd like confetti.

"Hey, everybody!" shouted Bartoni. "Look who it is!" He stood on tiptoes and pointed emphatically at Breece, as if introducing the next act at the comedy club. "Let's hear it for the Beak!"

Bartoni knew how to command an audience. Even in the noisy intersection, his voice carried. People in the scrum around him quieted and turned his way. They had only seen Sonor Breece in pictures or in rare public appearances, always in Gismonde's shadow. He looked smaller in person, but the profile was unmistakable—the kind that would look good on a coin. No doubt about it. It was him.

"Where ya headed, Beak?" a man taunted, pulling Breece's hood all the way back, exposing his bald skull and wrinkled neck.

"Time to fly the coop?" said another, speaking right into his face.

Slow, rhythmic clapping started to rise from the crowd, and then the mantra began...

"Beak! Beak! Beak!"

The sound grew louder and more insistent. Breece twisted one way and then the other. But it was no use. There was nowhere to go. The circle started to tighten. Breece tried to raise his arms to push back, buy himself some space, but he was now compressed so tightly that he couldn't move at all. He could barely breathe. Within seconds, he only had room to swivel his head from side to side, like a terrified bird.

"Help me!" he screamed. "Somebody help me!"

"What a comedian!" said Bartoni.

The circle closed in.

CHAPTER 97

LAMONT, MARGO, AND Maddy climbed the steep stairs to Jessica's apartment. Their clothes were ripped and their faces were streaked with blood and soot. For Lamont, every step was agony.

When they got to the top of the stairs, Maddy reached up and ran her hand along the ceiling molding over the door. The spare key was stuck in the notch where her grandma always kept it. Maddy pushed the door open.

As they walked in, Lamont grabbed a gallon container of water from the kitchen counter. They passed the jug around, taking deep gulps until the water spilled down their chins and necks. Maddy realized that Margo was seeing the apartment for the first time.

"So this is it," said Maddy. "This is where I live."

Margo looked around, taking in the tiny kitchen, the battered tile floor, the chipped walls.

"Not quite your style, I know," said Maddy.

"It's a home," said Margo softly. "That's all that matters."

"I can give you the tour," said Maddy. "Won't take long."

"Sure," said Margo. "I'd like that."

Maddy led the way from the kitchen into the living room, where the sofa took up most of the floor space. A worn blanket hung over the armrest. Bando's scruffy bed was pushed up against one wall. Maddy's eyes started to sting, but she blinked back the tears. She took a deep breath, in and out.

"This is me," she said, leading the way through the curtain into her tiny alcove. Discarded clothes covered the rumpled bed and half-melted candles lined the windowsill.

"Suits you," said Margo.

They walked back into the hall and hooked around the partition into Jessica's room. The bed was neatly made and three pairs of shoes were lined up against the wall. A hairbrush and a jar of lotion sat on the polished nightstand.

"And this is...this was Grandma's," said Maddy.

Margo ran her fingers along the blanket on the bed and picked up the jar from the nightstand. She lifted it to her nose, closed her eyes, and sniffed.

"Lilac," she said, with a soft smile.

"That was her," said Maddy. "That's how she always smelled. Like lilacs."

Margo pushed aside the pale blue curtains and paused for a moment to look out on the street below. She turned to follow Maddy back into the living room. Then suddenly, she froze. On the dresser near the door sat a photograph of a young woman. A blonde. Margo was staring at a black-and-white image of herself.

"Maddy," she called out. "Why is this here? *How* is this here?"

Maddy turned back into the room. Lamont stepped into the doorway. He let Maddy do the talking. And Maddy could only say what she knew.

"It was Grandma's," she said. "She got it from her parents."

"I don't understand," said Margo softly.

She took the photograph in her hands. She passed her fingers lightly over the image of her own face. She remembered the day it was taken and the name of the studio. And she remembered how much she was looking forward to seeing Lamont at the restaurant that night. That's when she would tell him . . .

Suddenly, Margo's knees gave way. Lamont jumped forward to catch her as she fell. He helped her onto the bed. Margo felt a rush in her head and saw a flash of images, like a movie playing in fast motion. A restaurant with toys hanging from the ceiling. Glittering lights. People laughing. Lamont smiling. And then—her hand on her belly over a smooth white dress.

Margo bent forward, silent. Tears started pouring down her face.

"What is it?" said Lamont. "What's wrong?"

Margo's throat was burning. She could hardly speak.

"Lamont," she said softly. "I was going to tell you—that night. I was planning to tell you..."

Lamont wrapped his arms around Margo's shoulders. She was trembling, struggling to find the words.

"Lamont," she said, "I was...I was *pregnant.*"

Lamont's face went white as Margo shuddered in his arms. And then a jumble of feelings rushed into his mind at the same time—sadness, pain, regret, guilt. *That* was her secret! He should have guessed that night. He should have *known*! Margo was sobbing so hard now that her words came in short, unfinished bursts.

"We lost everything..." she said softly. "We lost..." She couldn't finish her thought. It hurt too much.

CHAPTER 98

MADDY SILENTLY STEPPED out into the hall and walked quietly to her room. She knelt down and reached under her bed. From inside the box of *Shadow* magazines she pulled the medical record—the page she'd saved from the warehouse file. The one she didn't truly understand until this very moment.

She walked back into Jessica's room. Margo looked up, her eyes red.

"My God, Maddy," she said. "All those years ago. Lamont and I. We lost ... we lost our baby."

Maddy sat down on the bed with the yellowed paper folded in her hand.

There was nothing to do but to just say it, plain and simple.

"No," said Maddy softly. "You didn't."

She unfolded the paper and handed it to Margo.

Margo held the paper up. Lamont looked over her shoulder. It took a few seconds for them to realize what they were looking at, and a few more to comprehend the scribbled notes at the top:

Year. Date. Time of birth.

Margo stiffened. She inhaled and exhaled slowly. Her heart was racing. She looked at Lamont.

"No," she said. "No. It's not possible."

Maddy understood. She'd thought it was impossible too. But now she realized that it was true. And she finally knew how it all fit together. She sat down on the bed.

"I know you don't remember," she said, "but it happened. It did. You delivered a daughter. While you were sleeping. They never wanted you to know. Your daughter grew and got married and had children. And those children had children—all the way down to me. I didn't come out of nowhere. I'm not some random freak. I'm part of you. I come from you. From *both* of you."

Lamont and Margo looked at each other, stunned and silent. In their mental fog, they were both doing the same calculations, trying to add up the decades and generations that had led to this place, this time, this girl.

Their living, breathing descendant.

CHAPTER 99

I DON'T KNOW what I was expecting. Cheers. Shouts of joy. A group hug. Instead, Margo and Lamont just keep staring at me like I'm some alien creature. Margo won't let go of the paper. She's holding on to it for dear life.

"You *must* have wondered," I say. "Why was I the one? Of all the people in the world, why was I picked to find you? Did you think it was some crazy coincidence? And my powers—mind control, invisibility. Did you think those were just learned skills? Something I picked up from a *Shadow* novel?"

Margo looks around the room. She's still wobbly, but I can see her mind turning.

"Jessica..." she says to herself, like she's trying to solve a riddle. "She was...?"

"Your great-great-granddaughter," I say. "Making me your great-great-great-great-granddaughter." I count out the "greats" on my fingers.

It's hard for me to wrap my head around it. But for Margo, it's too much. She stands up. She's a little shaky on her feet, but her voice is clear.

"I need some air," she says. "I need to think."

She walks out through the living room. I hear the front door close behind her.

Lamont looks at me.

"Why didn't you tell us?" he asks. "Why didn't you say something as soon as you found that file? Why did you keep it to yourself?"

"Because it didn't seem real," I tell him. "I didn't really believe it, until..."

"Until when?" asks Lamont.

"Until today," I say. "Until just now. I had to hear Margo say it. About the beginning. About her secret. So did you."

Lamont reaches over and hugs me. He knows I'm right.

We walk downstairs and find Margo sitting on the front steps of the building. The sun is getting low in the sky. This is the time of day when people usually start to take cover from TinGrin patrols. But today there aren't any patrols. Now the TinGrins are the ones on the run. Up the street, a couple of kids are throwing stones at a video screen on a light pole.

I sit down next to Margo. She doesn't say anything. She just slips her arm through mine and squeezes it tight.

"Somehow," she says, "I never pictured myself as a great-great-great-great-grandmother."

"I know," I say. "They probably don't even have cards for that."

Lamont sits down on the other side of Margo. He puts his arm around both of us. This seems like the time to say something momentous about our family tree, but for some reason I feel more comfortable changing the subject. Moving things forward. Focusing on the future.

"We need someplace else to live," I say. "This place is way too cramped for three grown humans." What I don't say is how much it depresses me to be here. There's too much of my grandmother in those rooms.

"I hear there's a mansion uptown that's available," says Margo. "The basement needs a little work."

"Worst possible idea," says Lamont. "That's the first place he'll look."

Margo's face tightens. "You think he'll be back?" she asks.

"He always comes back," says Lamont. "It's just a matter of time."

"How can you be so sure?" says Margo.

Lamont looks at me.

"Oh, go ahead," I tell him. "Say it."

So he does. With the whole deep voice and everything.

"The Shadow knows."

CHAPTER 100

SUDDENLY, I HEAR barking from around the corner. Then I see a flash of brown fur in front of the steps. I get a twinge in my gut. That dog could be Bando's twin. He's even got...

"Bando! Wait up!" Grandma's voice.

Grandma's voice?

I jump up just in time to see her coming around the corner. We both freeze for a second. It can't be. Is this a *dream*? I run into her arms, crying and shouting like crazy. As soon as she grabs me, I know it's her. It's really her. She smells like lilacs.

"Grandma! You're *alive*?"

"Don't say it like it's a question," she says. "Of *course* I'm alive."

"Jessica?" shouts Margo. She can't believe it either.

"Nice to see you all breathing," says Grandma.

"The warehouse!" says Lamont. "How did you...?"

Grandma reaches out to hug Lamont and Margo while Bando runs happy circles around everybody.

"As soon as you all left this morning," says Grandma, "Bando started to get antsy. So I took him out for a walk. Which, as it turned out, was excellent timing. When I looked back, there was nothing but a cloud of smoke."

I *still* can't believe it. I can't believe she's here. My heart feels like it's about to pop right out of my chest. I go right back to hugging her. I can't get enough.

"And what happened to *you*?" she asks. She's looking at the scratches on my face and the bruises on my arms. "Did you get into another fight?"

"I did," I say. "But I came out on top."

"That's my girl," says Grandma. Always my biggest fan.

"Have you heard?" she says. "Gismonde's gone. Everybody's celebrating. They're shooting holes in his video screens all over town." She looks at Lamont.

"Did the Shadow have anything to do with this?"

Lamont puts his arm around her shoulders and leads her up the steps to the building. Margo follows right behind.

"Jessica," says Lamont. "We have a lot to catch up on."

I'd say that's putting it mildly.

Bando is jumping all over me, begging for some attention. I pick him up in my arms as we head up the stairs. He licks my face, and I kiss him right back. Now we *definitely* need a new place to live.

Big enough for a family of five.

CHAPTER 101

AT DAWN THE next morning, Lamont and Margo walked slowly toward the place where they had spent more than a century of their lives.

"Lamont," said Margo. "In case you've forgotten, I really hate this neighborhood."

"We won't stay long, I promise," said Lamont.

The warehouse foundation was still smoldering. The blast had collapsed the south wall of the building next door and reached all the way to the river. The wooden docks were shattered and the ghost ships had been blown apart. The ruins of Khan's power.

Lamont knew Khan wasn't really defeated. Somehow, he'd find a different realm where he could gather his strength and return in a new form—more dangerous than before. The difference in Lamont's world was that he now had a family to protect. And a great-great-great-great-granddaughter to teach. That thought alone made his head spin. He also had a life partner whom he didn't intend to lose ever again.

"This place gives me the creeps," said Margo. "Why are we here?"

"I'm looking for something," said Lamont. "It's a long shot. But it might still be here."

"Please," said Margo. "There's nothing left. Let's go."

It was high tide and the water was almost lapping at what was left of the entry steps to the lab. In the explosion, the second floor of the warehouse had pancaked down onto the ground floor. Pieces of the massive stove were scattered among tangles of wire and lab equipment. At the center of the wreckage, part of the vault was still standing, its walls twisted from the heat.

Lamont stepped onto the smoking pile, but Margo refused to go any farther.

"Lamont," she said. "Stop! You'll step on a nail and get lockjaw!"

Lamont scanned the splintered flooring, the collapsed walls, the bent pipes. Lying near the center was a cluster of charred blankets. Their bed. Lamont stood in debris up to his ankles as he pawed through the scraps of cloth and wood nearby. His hands were scratched and covered in soot.

Then suddenly, against all odds, there it was—an object so small that only a trained detective would have spotted it. Lamont reached carefully into the debris to pull it out, then closed his hand around it.

"Lamont!" Margo called out. "This is no time for souvenirs!"

Lamont moved carefully through the wreckage on his way back toward her. For a moment, he thought about walking her to a different location. But in a way, this place felt completely right. It was where his life— and hers—had started again.

"Believe it or not," he said, "I found what I came for."

"What are you talking about?" said Margo.

Lamont got down on one knee on the cement step. He opened his hand and held up a diamond ring.

Margo gasped. Her eyes opened wide.

"Margo Lane," said Lamont, "will you...?"

She didn't even let him finish the question.

"Yes!" she said. "Absolutely! Yes!"

Lamont smiled. "You don't want to wait and think it over?"

Margo shook her head as the tears began to come.

"Lamont," she said. "I think we've waited long enough."

She held out her left hand. Lamont slipped the ring onto her finger. Then he stood up and wrapped his arms around her. When she tipped her face up to kiss him, he couldn't believe how beautiful she was, and how much he loved her.

It was the happiest he'd been in, well, over a hundred years.

ABOUT THE AUTHORS

JAMES PATTERSON is the world's best-selling author and most trusted storyteller. He has created many enduring fictional characters and series, including Alex Cross, the Women's Murder Club, Michael Bennett, Maximum Ride, Middle School, and I Funny. Among his notable literary collaborations are *The President Is Missing*, with President Bill Clinton, and the Max Einstein series, produced in partnership with the Albert Einstein Estate. Patterson's writing career is characterized by a single mission: to prove that there is no such thing as a person who "doesn't like to read," only people who haven't found the right book. He's given over three million books to schoolkids and the military, donated more than seventy million dollars to support education, and endowed over five thousand college scholarships for teachers. For his prodigious imagination and championship of literacy in America, Patterson was awarded the 2019 National Humanities Medal. The National Book Foundation presented him with the Literarian Award for Outstanding Service to the American Literary Community, and he is also the recipient of an Edgar Award and nine Emmy Awards. He lives in Florida with his family.

Brian Sitts is an award-winning advertising creative director and television writer. He has collaborated with James Patterson on books for adults and children. He and his wife, Jody, live in Peekskill, New York.

JAMES
PATTERSON
RECOMMENDS

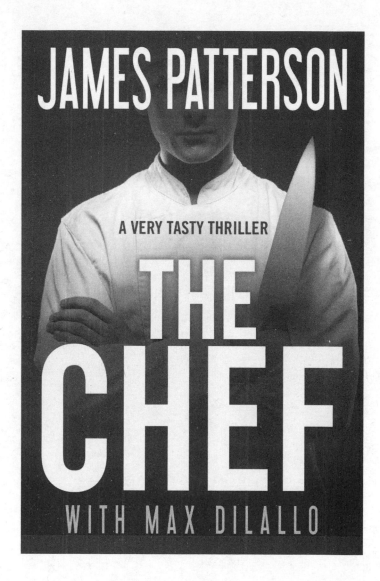

JAMES PATTERSON

A VERY TASTY THRILLER

THE CHEF

WITH MAX DILALLO

THE CHEF

In the Carnival days leading up to Mardi Gras, Detective Caleb Rooney is accused of murder—committed in the line of duty as a Major Crimes investigator for the New Orleans Police Department. I know what it's like to love your home, so Rooney is in anguish as his beloved city is under attack. And the would-be terrorists may be local.

Amid crowds of revelers, Rooney follows a fearsome trail of clues, racing from outlying districts into the city center. He has no idea what—or who—he'll face in defense of his hometown, only that innocent lives are at stake. This might be my most delicious thriller yet.

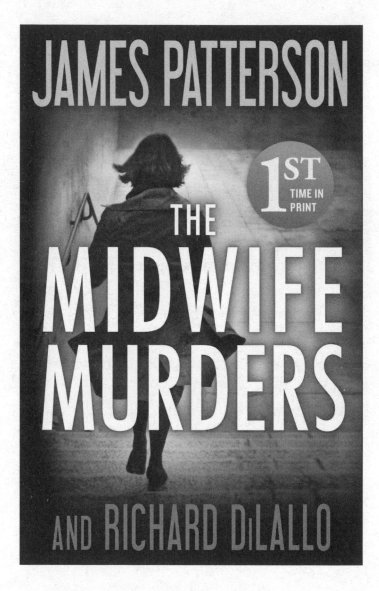

THE MIDWIFE MURDERS

I can't imagine a worse crime than one done against a child. But when two kidnappings and a vicious stabbing happen on her watch in a university hospital in Manhattan, her focus abruptly changes. Something has to be done, and senior midwife Lucy is fearless enough to try.

Rumors begin to swirl, with blame falling on everyone from the Russian mafia to an underground adoption network. Fierce single mom Lucy teams up with a skeptical NYPD detective, but I've given her a case where the truth is far more twisted than Lucy could ever have imagined.

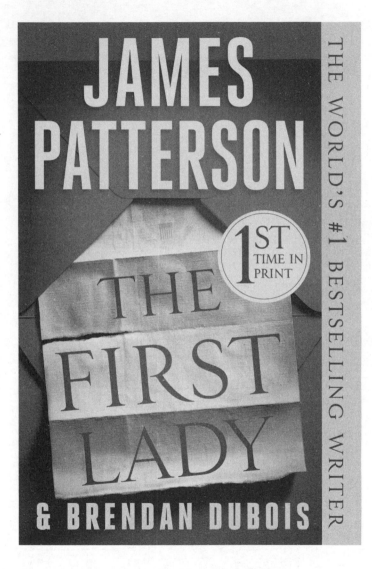

JAMES
PATTERSON

1ST
TIME IN
PRINT

THE
FIRST
LADY

& BRENDAN DUBOIS

THE FIRST LADY

The US government is at the forefront of everyone's mind these days and I've become incredibly fascinated by the idea that one secret can bring it all down. What if that secret is a US president's affair that results in a nightmarish outcome?

Sally Grissom, leader of the Presidential Protection Division, is summoned to a private meeting with the president and his chief of staff to discuss the disappearance of the First Lady. What at first seemed an escape to a safe haven turns into a kidnapping when a ransom note arrives along with what could be the First Lady's finger.

It's a race against the clock to collect the evidence that all leads to one troubling question: Could the kidnappers be from inside the White House?

TEXAS RANGER

So many of my detectives are dark and gritty and deal with crimes in some of our grimmest cities. That's why I'm thrilled to bring you Detective Rory Yates, my most honorable detective yet.

As a Texas Ranger, he has a code that he lives and works by. But when he comes home for a much-needed break, he walks into a crime scene where the victim is none other than his ex-wife—and he's the prime suspect. Yates has to risk everything in order to clear his name, and he dives into the inferno of the most twisted mind I've ever created. Can his code bring him back out alive?

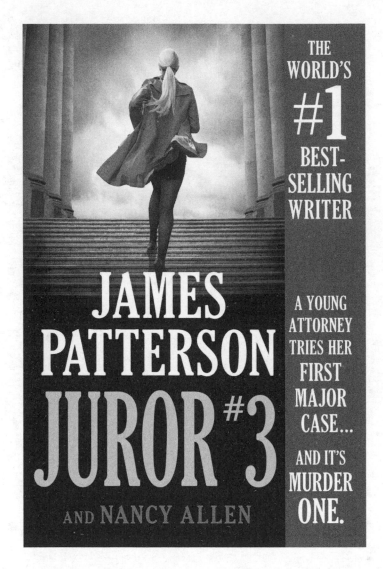

THE
WORLD'S
1
BEST-
SELLING
WRITER

A YOUNG
ATTORNEY
TRIES HER
FIRST
MAJOR
CASE...
AND IT'S
MURDER
ONE.

JAMES
PATTERSON
JUROR #3

AND NANCY ALLEN

JUROR #3

In the deep south of Mississippi, Ruby Bozarth is a newcomer, both to Rosedale, and to the Bar. And now she's tapped as a defense counsel in a racially charged felony. The murder of a woman from an old family has Rosedale's upper crust howling for blood, and the prosecutor is counting on Ruby's inexperience to help him deliver a swift conviction.

Ruby is determined to build a defense that sticks for her college football star client. Looking for help in unexpected quarters, her case is rattled as news of a second murder breaks. As intertwining investigations unfold, no one can be trusted, especially the twelve men and women on the jury. They may be hiding the most incendiary secret of all.

For a complete list of books by

JAMES PATTERSON

VISIT
JamesPatterson.com

 Follow James Patterson on Facebook
@JamesPatterson

 Follow James Patterson on Twitter
@JP_Books

 Follow James Patterson on Instagram
@jamespattersonbooks